Driftwood Lane

A NANTUCKET LOVE STORY

DENISE HUNTER

THOMAS NELSON
Since 1798

NASHVILLE   DALLAS   MEXICO CITY   RIO DE JANEIRO

Published in Nashville, Tennessee, by Thomas Nelson. Thomas Nelson is a registered trademark of Thomas Nelson, Inc.

Thomas Nelson, Inc., titles may be purchased in bulk for educational, business, fund-raising, or sales promotional use. For information, please e-mail SpecialMarkets@ThomasNelson.com.

Publisher's note: This novel is a work of fiction. Names, characters, places, and incidents are either products of the author's imagination or used fictitiously. All characters are fictional, and any similarity to people, living or dead, is purely coincidental.

Library of Congress Cataloging-in-Publication Data

Hunter, Denise, 1968–
    Driftwood lane : a Nantucket love story / Denise Hunter.
        p. cm.
    ISBN 978-1-59554-800-9 (softcover)
    1. Nantucket Island (Mass.)—Fiction. I. Title.
PS3608.U5925D75 2010
813'.6—dc22   2010010408

Printed in the United States of America

10 11 12 13 14 RRD 5 4 3 2

Driftwood Lane

One

Meridith Ward surveyed the mess cluttering Delmonico's kitchen and shuddered. The staff scurried in quick, jerky movements, but then, it was lunch hour, and a hundred St. Louis business people had to get fed and back to their jobs.

The owner, Angelo Bellini, burst through the swinging door, nearly slamming into Meridith's back. "Please . . . we were not expecting you," he said over the din of clattering pans and voices shouting orders.

"That's kind of the point, Mr. Bellini." Meridith opened her notebook and continued the inspection.

The owner discreetly removed raw chicken breasts from the sink, setting them in a nearby skillet. He did not wash his hands.

Meridith made another note on the list of infringements.

"Meridith . . ." His accent caressed her name. He flashed his dimple.

She shot him a look.

"Ms. Ward," he continued, "we have had an unusually difficult morning. My cook, he called in sick, my prep boy did not even show up, and I have our host cutting vegetables." He gestured wildly. "He does not even know what he is doing. Such a day!"

Meridith strolled through the kitchen, still writing. The cook staff wove around her as though their moves had been choreographed. Despite the disorder, the savory smells of garlic and roasted chicken filled the air.

"I cannot even tell you!" Mr. Bellini continued. "Please, we can do this another day. I would be happy to show you around myself tomorrow."

Meridith's phone vibrated in her pocket. "Excuse me," she shouted over the whir of a machine roaring to life.

She retreated to a quieter corner of the kitchen and opened her phone, so eager to escape Mr. Bellini she didn't check the caller ID. "Meridith Ward."

A moment's silence made her wonder if she'd missed the reply. "Hello? This is Meridith."

"Meridith Ward?" A male voice, unfamiliar.

"Yes, may I help you?"

"Do you know T. J. Ward? Terrance James Ward of Nantucket?"

It was a name she hadn't heard spoken in years. A name she tried not to think about, usually with success. The name sucked the moisture from her mouth, set her heart racing, stole the reply from her tongue.

"Hello?"

It was just a phone call. She cleared her throat. "Yes, you have the right Meridith. How may I help you?"

"My name is Edward Thomas. I need a moment of your time, but it sounds like I've caught you in the middle of something."

Her excuse to avoid this altogether. She could hang up and never accept another call from Edward Thomas. But problems didn't resolve when you ignored them; they got worse. She scanned the kitchen. Case in point.

She drew a shaky breath and pulled herself to her full five-foot-three inches. "Now is fine, Mr. Thomas. Go ahead."

"I'm an attorney on the island of Nantucket. First of all—and I'm so sorry to relay this over the phone—we've been trying to locate you for two weeks. I'm afraid that your—that T. J. Ward and his wife, Eva, were involved in a boating accident. They didn't, that is . . . I'm afraid neither survived, Meridith."

Her racing heart skipped a beat, like the wheels of a tire hitting a speed bump, then continued on its frantic way. They were gone? Both of them, just like that?

She waited for the numbness to dissipate and the wave of pain to wash over her. But it didn't come.

She should feel something. Something other than this cold void. Was there something wrong with her? Maybe she needed time to process. Two weeks ago, he'd said. The funerals were over by now. It was all over, and there was nothing for her to do.

"Meridith?"

She watched Mr. Bellini continuing his belated cleanup. She remembered her relief at the call and realized now that she'd chosen the worse of two evils.

"Thank you for notifying me, Mr. Thomas. I appreciate your taking the time to locate me, but I really must return to work."

"Wait, Meridith, I–I'm afraid there's more. I handled T. J. and Eva's legal matters."

Of course, there was the matter of his estate. This was a lot to digest.

"I'm sure you're aware that T. J. and Eva ran a bed-and-breakfast—I'm not certain how long it's been since you've seen them."

"Quite awhile." *Years, actually.*

Mr. Bellini was yelling at the prep guy, making imaginary chops with the side of his hand.

"I surmised as much. Nonetheless, T. J. and Eva were very clear in their provisions, should the unthinkable happen. They wanted Summer Place to go to you. Furthermore, they've named you as guardian of the children."

Summer Place . . . the *children?*

An inappropriate bubble of laughter caught in her throat.

"I know this must come as a shock. I'm not unaware that—"

"There must be some mistake." Her hand worked its way to her throat. The children? Three of them. How old were they now?

What did it matter? This was a mistake. A clerical error.

"I spoke with T. J. and Eva myself. The will was drawn up several years ago, but I've spoken with them regularly since then. We were friends as well."

Then they should've left the children to you! Meridith pressed her fingertips to her forehead. Impossible. What did she know about children? Especially these children?

"I don't know what to say, Mr. Thomas." A gross understatement.

"This is a lot to take in all at once, I understand. But we're in a bit of a pickle here. An elderly neighbor has been staying at Summer Place, caring for the children. As I said, it's taken two weeks to locate your number. Mrs. Hubbard is in poor health, and there's no one else. Your presence is needed rather immediately."

"My job . . ."

"Might I suggest a short leave of absence?"

There had to be somebody. Somebody *else.* Eva had a brother, didn't she?

As if reading her mind, Mr. Thomas continued. "We've been unable to reach Eva's brother. He's traveling, and last the children heard, he was in Georgia, but that's all we know. You should know that he was named as a possible guardian in the event that you declined the task. But again, the need for help is immediate."

She played with her engagement ring. She couldn't leave Stephen, couldn't leave her job, could she? The thought of leaving St. Louis, leaving all that was familiar, even for a short time, brought a tidal wave of anxiety she hadn't felt since college. She drew a deep breath, then another.

"The fact is, the children are in dire need of your assistance, Meridith. Since Mrs. Hubbard fell ill, members of the church have been taking shifts. Very kind of them, of course, but it can't go on. If you don't come quickly, I'm afraid I'll have no choice but to alert Child Protective Services. I'd hate to see the children go to foster care, even temporarily. And there's no assurance they'd be placed together."

Foster care! Meridith imagined suited men coming into their home, carrying them off. She imagined the littlest, a boy, screaming for his mommy.

From somewhere deep inside compassion swelled, followed quickly by a surge of protectiveness she didn't know she was capable of. She had no doubt there were decent foster homes. But the thought of the children being separated seemed cruel when they'd just lost their parents. Besides that, they were orphans. And didn't the Good Book admonish them to look after the orphans?

She had to do something. It was her responsibility, even if she'd never met them, because T. J. and Eva had named her the children's guardian. And because, like it or not, she was their sister.

Two

"Summer Place Bed-and-Breakfast, please." Meridith buckled her belt, settling into the cab's cracked vinyl seat.

As the driver accelerated, Meridith eyed the pedestrians strolling the brick sidewalks. So this was it. The place where her dad had started a new family with his young wife. It was a far cry from the St. Louis neighborhood that had been her childhood home. No window-barred stores here. No sign of potholed pavement or littered curbs. Nantucket boasted shingled storefronts and pristine tree-lined streets made of cobblestone. How quaint.

She folded her hands in her lap. She didn't want to think about her father today. As it was, her stomach churned, not from the waves that had rolled under the ferry, but from the stress of being away. She hadn't traveled since college, and now she remembered why. She longed for her tidy lawn, her garden window over the porcelain sink, even her nappy rug that welcomed her home.

Soon enough, she comforted herself. After receiving Mr. Thomas's call, she'd decided she'd stay with the children until their uncle returned from his vacation. They had a relationship with him. He was the obvious person for the job, and as soon as he returned, she'd be on the first plane back to St. Louis. Surely that was as far as her Christian duty extended.

A bed-and-breakfast. What did she know about running a business?

Meridith stuffed the fear down. How hard could it be? She knew how to cook and clean and be professional. She'd probably only be there a week or two. Her boss hadn't been happy about the leave of absence, but he'd reluctantly granted her two weeks.

When the driver turned down a pebbled lane parallel to the shore, Meridith read the street sign. Driftwood Lane. She was nearly there. The houses were parted by generous lawns that sprouted barren trees. Skeletal flower beds lined the walks and drives leading to the shake-shingled homes. Come spring, the lawns would probably blossom into a virtual fairy tale, but winter hadn't yet released its cold grip on the island.

"Here we are." The driver pulled into a hedge-lined drive. Gravel popped under the tires as he drove down the lane and stopped by the walk.

Meridith got out, removed a few bills from her bag, then surveyed the house while the driver retrieved her luggage. Like most of the island homes, Summer Place was clothed in weathered gray shingles and trimmed in white. A widow's walk perched on top and no doubt provided a stunning view of the harbor. A shaded porch stretched along the house's front, wide and welcoming. Between the porch's columns, a handmade shingle proclaiming "Summer Place" swung in the breeze. Wasn't this cozy.

Meridith paid the driver and started down the flagstone path, pulling her suitcase. The house looked older as she neared. The white paint was peeling in spots, and the thick vines that crawled up the house hadn't appeared overnight. The porch was not quite level, as if time and gravity had weighed it down.

A plethora of wind chimes stretched the length of the porch, bits of shells, glass, and bamboo tinkling and rattling together. She wondered if Eva had collected them. If her dad had gifted her with the chimes on her birthday, on their anniversary.

The detail made everything too real. Her dad had lived here. His kids were inside right now. Her brothers and sister.

Something thudded hard inside her, and she told herself it was only the echo of the suitcase bumping along the walk. She steadied her breathing as she approached the steps.

A woman's voice leaked through the screen door. "She's here . . . Come on, Max. Noelle! Hurry up, honey!"

Meridith lowered the suitcase's pull bar and carried it up the wooden steps. The porch spindles were poorly spaced, she noted. Just wide enough for a child's head.

The screen door opened, and through it came a plump brunette. Her dark hair was cut in a long bob so glossy it looked like a bottle of sunshine had been poured over it. A cluster of faint freckles covered her nose, and a twinkle lit her eyes.

A small body was latched on to her right leg.

"Welcome! You must be Meridith."

A large dog darted out the door and sniffed Meridith's hand.

"Yes, hello." Meridith pulled her hand from the dog's slimy nose and extended it to the woman, but found herself enveloped in a fleshy hug. She stiffened. Her fingers tightened on the luggage handle until her nails bit into her palm.

"I'm Rita Lawson from the church," the woman said, drawing away. "And this is . . . Ben, honey, you have to let go just for a second. Give your sister a hug."

Your sister.

The sandy-haired child turned his face toward Rita's waist.

I understand just how you feel, buddy. "That's okay," she said to Rita, then addressed Ben. "Hello there, Ben." Meridith extended her hand, but the little boy only buried himself more deeply into Rita. She saw little of her father in his face. *He must favor his mom.*

Rita ruffled his short hair. "He's feeling a little shy, I guess," she said, then mouthed *Later.* "Ben is seven and a little sweetheart, aren't you, honey?" Rita rubbed the dog behind the ears. "And this is Piper. Such a good girl!"

The golden retriever wagged her tail.

"Well, come in, Meridith, you must be tired after a long day of travel." Rita let Piper inside, and Meridith imagined the dog hairs flying around on the loose, getting in guests' food.

She followed Rita, stepping over a high threshold. Tripping hazard.

She noted the wide staircase that undoubtedly led to the room where she'd be sleeping and left her bag at the base. The house smelled of something savory, a hint of lemons, and a faint essence of Old House. The wood floors creaked under her feet as she followed Rita and her extra appendage across a living room that was dominated by a massive cobblestone fireplace. Original, Meridith guessed. Antique furniture circled an oval rug, driftwood sculptures posed on every table, and paintings of beach scenes on the walls reminded guests they were on vacation.

She had a sudden mental image of the apartment where she'd grown up. Sticky carpet and Goodwill furniture, tiny rooms with dirty walls. This was a far cry from Warren Street.

Clomping footsteps on the stairs drew her attention to a dark-haired boy. He had a stout build that probably had him shopping in the husky department and chubby cheeks that dimpled when he smiled shyly.

"Max, come here." Rita encouraged him, but the boy willingly extended his hand.

"Hi." He ducked his head, but not before Meridith saw her dad's brown eyes.

"I'm Meridith. It's nice to meet you."

Rita gestured to one of the vintage mahogany-framed sofas that flanked the fireplace. "Have a seat."

Ben settled into Rita's side on the other sofa, Max beside him. Piper plopped down on Max's scruffy tennis shoes.

"Max is ten," Rita said, looking toward the stairs. "Noelle, honey, come downstairs, please!" She addressed Meridith. "You must have a million questions, and I'll try to answer as many as I can, but I have to leave in about"—she checked her watch—"ten minutes to pick up my daughter from cheerleading practice and my son from wrestling. Then there's homework and dinner, but you don't need to hear all that!"

"Do we have guests at the moment?"

"Not until the weekend, and even then, it's only one couple. This is a slow time for tourism, as you can imagine. Mrs. Hubbard probably knows more about running the place, but bless her heart, she's recovering from pneumonia just now."

"She goes to our church too," Max said.

"Well, I'm certain I'll figure things out. I appreciate all you've done for the children, Rita."

"Oh, it's my pleasure. Max, will you go tell your sister to come along?"

"I already did."

"Well, go get her, please. Ben, you go with him."

After the two boys were up the stairs, Rita leaned closer to

Meridith. "I wanted a few minutes to chat with you in private. The kids have had a terrible blow, of course. You saw how clingy Ben is, and Noelle . . . well, she's thirteen, and you know how that is even under happier conditions."

Meridith nodded.

"Max is probably the most stable of the group. He likes to talk, build models, and I think that helps him cope. But of course their loss is devastating and their world is suddenly unstable."

Meridith knew all about unstable. "Do the children know I've been granted guardianship?"

Rita nodded. "You might as well know Noelle isn't happy about that—no offense, she just doesn't know you. The boys have been less vocal about their opinions. I left their schedule on the island in the kitchen and wrote down everything I could think of that might be helpful."

"Thank you. That'll make this easier on everyone."

Rita folded her plump fingers in her lap. "I wasn't sure if you'd ever visited."

The truth embarrassed her, though she had no reason to feel that way. It wasn't as if her dad had invited her into their lives. Well, he had now.

"No, I haven't," Meridith said.

"Well then, that makes your sacrifice all the more admirable. You must have a very big heart, and I'm sure God will bless you for it."

Well . . . I'm only doing my Christian duty after all." An awkward pause prompted her to continue. "Has there been any word from their uncle?"

"Unfortunately, no. You may know he's traveling at the moment, and I guess he doesn't carry a cell phone. Noelle says he checks e-mail sporadically, but I really wanted to tell you—"

A clomping on the stairs alerted them to Max's appearance.

"She's coming."

Close behind him, Ben two-footed each step, hand on the railing, then ran to the couch and curled into Rita's side.

"Here she comes," Rita said.

At the top of the stairs, fuzzy purple socks appeared, then jean-clad knees, followed by the rest of Noelle. She was short and slight, with straight blonde hair.

When she reached the bottom of the steps she stopped, her thin arm curled around the thick balustrade.

"Well, come on over and meet your big sister, honey."

Noelle approached, stopping just shy of the area rug. She favored her little brother in coloring and body frame, but her small triangular chin was a duplicate of Meridith's.

"Hi, Noelle. I'm Meridith."

Noelle pressed her lips together, crossed her arms. "Hi."

Rita scooted to the edge of the couch, checking her watch. "Noelle's into the computer, chatting, e-mailing, all that."

"She chats with her *boooyfriieeend*," Max said.

"I don't have a boyfriend, runt."

"Come sit down, Noelle," Rita said.

Meridith thought the girl might defy the woman, but she walked around the armchair and plopped into it.

Ben loosened himself from Rita's side, then squeezed into the chair with Noelle. She curled her arm around him.

Rita stood. "I hate to take off like this, but . . ."

"I understand." Meridith walked her to the door.

"The kids can show you to your room. If you have any questions, anything at all, I left my cell and home numbers on the schedule. Oh, and dinner's in the Crock-Pot."

She was a godsend. "Thank you for everything."

"Bye, kids." Rita gave one last wave, snagged her purse and jacket, and then she was gone.

Meridith closed the door and turned toward the three faces of her siblings: Max wore a casual grin, Ben peeked from his sister's armpit, and Noelle stared back defiantly.

Meridith looked at them, the silence opening a wide chasm between them, and wondered if she'd bitten off way more than she could chew.

Three

A rattle of some kind sounded from behind the wall, breaking the silence. Maybe the dishwasher was running.

The children seemed to be waiting for Meridith to make the next move. She crossed the room and set her hand on the sofa back. "Does anyone have homework?"

"We do it after school," Max said.

Ben peeked out. "I don't have none," he said softly.

"Don't have any." Noelle tossed her hair over her shoulder.

Her brown eyes seemed older than her thirteen years and contrasted with the youthful smattering of freckles on her nose.

Ben was tucked into her side, though he was at least peeking at Meridith now. He had greenish eyes and small features that made him seem fragile. Who was she kidding? They'd just lost their parents. They were all fragile, including Noelle.

Meridith sat beside Max. "I'm really sorry, guys. I can only imagine what it's been like for you, losing your mom and dad."

"He was your dad too," Noelle said. "How old are you anyway, like, nineteen?"

Not much younger than your mother, Meridith wanted to say. Instead she tried for a smile. "Twenty-five. I know there've been a lot of people coming and going, but I'd like to keep things as normal as possible. Routines are important at times like this."

"Uncle Jay will be calling soon," Noelle said. "And when he finds out what happened, he'll come back."

Meridith read the unspoken message. She and Noelle wanted the same thing, but Meridith had learned long ago to hold her cards close to her chest.

"I'm sure he will, Noelle."

Max shifted, his eyes trained on his stubby fingernails.

"We want him to be our guardian, don't we, boys?" Noelle said.

Max moved his head in a motion that may have been a nod or a shrug. Ben's face disappeared into Noelle's side.

"Why don't we talk about this later," Meridith said firmly. "How about you show me around so I don't get lost."

Reluctantly, Noelle stood, and the kids showed her through the downstairs, Piper tagging behind, her toenails clicking on the floor. The large dining room had a braided rug anchored by a long oak table. Above it hung an ornate chandelier that had three unlit bulbs. A buffet lined one wall, but the focal point of the room was the picture window that overlooked the harbor. A pier jutted out into the water, and beyond that there was nothing but ocean.

"The kitchen's through here," Max said, leading the way.

Meridith entered the sunny yellow room. The countertops were durable Corian, and the linoleum was clean but worn. She saw a trickle of water and followed it to a puddle at the base of the dishwasher, which hummed loudly. She turned off the machine and grabbed a towel from the stove handle.

"It does that sometimes." Noelle tipped her chin up.

"It does that *all* the time," Max said.

"How would you know?"

"'Cause Mom was always complaining about it," Max said.

"Shut up."

"All right, that's enough," Meridith said. "I'll look at it tomorrow."

If it had been leaking for long, the floorboards were probably rotted. If the water had gotten back to the wall, they might be looking at mold.

After soaking up the water, she followed the kids up the back staircase to the second story. The stairwell was narrow and the wooden stairs were covered with a non-skid runner, but there was no banister. She started a mental to-do list.

"Our rooms are on this side of the house," Max said.

The upstairs opened to a loft with five doorways and a hall. Another chandelier hung from the center, shedding golden light over seafoam green walls. The wide chair rail and baseboard looked to be on its tenth coat of white paint.

"This is my room," said Max.

"And mine." Ben scrambled up the bed's ladder and dived onto the top bunk, making the whole unit shake.

"Careful," Meridith said belatedly.

A few clothes littered the floor. The room smelled like dirty socks. Boat models lined a shelf, and a decorative oar hung above the top bunk.

"Somebody likes boats," Meridith said.

"Me." Max grinned. "Noelle's room is next to ours, and here's our bathroom." Max nudged open a five-panel door and flipped the switch. Nothing happened.

"Sometimes it don't work," Max said.

"Doesn't." Noelle disappeared into her room.

Meridith flipped the bathroom switch off, then back on. Still dark. She'd have to check into that.

When Meridith peeked into the room, Noelle was leaning over a computer desk, her hand on the mouse. Her walls were cotton candy pink, and her drapes and bedspread were a delicate eyelet white fabric. The shaggy green rug between her bed and desk was the only item that said *teenager*.

"I like your rug."

Noelle barely looked away from the screen.

"Anything from Uncle Jay?" Max asked Noelle, who shook her head no.

So that's what she was checking. Can't wait to get big sis out of the house.

That wasn't fair. The children needed familiarity, and their uncle was the closest family they had.

"When's he due back from his vacation?" Meridith asked.

"We don't know," Max said. "He runs around during the winter on his cool Harley."

Noelle glared at her brother. "He *travels* through the south during slow season."

Max shrugged. "That's what I said. He e-mails when he finds a computer."

"How often is that?" Meridith asked.

"As often as he can," Noelle said.

"I miss him." It was Ben's soft voice coming from the top bunk. He was lying on his side, his knees drawn into his stomach. Meridith was sure the little boy missed more than his uncle.

"This was Mom and Dad's room." Across the hall, Max touched the doorknob reverently.

"Don't, Max," Noelle said.

Meridith wondered if the girl had eyes in the back of her head. She wandered into the only other bedroom. "Is this my room?" It was noticeably cooler inside. Maybe the vent was closed when the room wasn't in use.

"Yeah. Rita put on fresh sheets and stuff," Max said.

She had a view of the front yard from an old wooden window. A quilt hugged the full-size bed. A matching dresser stood across from it, bare except for a dainty ivory runner. A nightstand and chest rounded out the room. Rita had cleaned, if the lemony pine scent was any indication.

"It's lovely."

"Wanna see the guest wing?" Max asked.

"Sure."

She followed him down a short wide hall, leaving Ben and Noelle. Pictures of the children dotted the walls, then the hall opened into a loft identical to the family wing.

"These two rooms are suites. They have their own bathrooms and everything. These two don't."

There was nothing but a short corridor dividing the family wing from the guest wing, which meant strangers frequently slept just down the hall. Unacceptable. It seemed negligent that their parents hadn't secured the family wing. They needed a solid keyed entry at the hallway and another at the back stairway.

Meridith peeked into the rooms. Honey-stained floors stretched under quaint rugs. Each room had its own beachy color scheme, each bed covered by coordinating quilts and puffy pillows. Homey. Attractive.

A loud rumble made her jump. "What in the world is that?"

Max shrugged. "The furnace."

It sounded like a rumble of thunder. She wondered how old the heating system was. Oh well. Not her problem. She was only here until Uncle Jay returned. Max's description of him nagged at her, but she pushed the thought from her mind.

She had to do something about dividing the guest quarters from the family's, though. She added it to her growing mental list.

"Want me to get your suitcase?" Max asked.

Meridith smiled. "That's very sweet. Thank you."

While he clomped down the stairs beside Piper, Meridith wandered back to the family wing to check on the others. Ben was sprawled across his top bunk, eyes closed, mouth gaping. Poor little guy. He probably wasn't sleeping well.

It was close to dinnertime. Maybe Noelle would like to help her in the kitchen. She walked toward Noelle's closed door and raised her hand. The furnace kicked off, and in the sudden silence, another sound caught Meridith's ear. She leaned closer to the door and heard the unmistakable sound of stifled sobs.

Four

Jake Walker straddled his Harley and popped the kickstand, settling into the worn leather seat. He needed a good meal, shower, and sleep, not necessarily in that order. He was tired of the greasy diner down the road, though the service was friendly enough, but his stomach was rumbling too loud to be picky.

"Hey, Jake, hang on a minute."

Jake released the handlebars and leaned back while Levi ambled down the new porch steps of the Habitat for Humanity home they'd been building for two weeks.

"How about a real bed tonight? Mary said not to take no for an answer."

Jake drove his thumbs into his jeans pockets. "I don't mind sleeping on the ground." A pup tent, sleeping bag, and a Harley—all a man needed.

"Mary's fixing pork roast. Haven't you had about all you can stand of Clyde's Diner? Or is it the flirtin' that's bringing you back?"

Jake grinned. "Man's got to eat."

Levi laughed. "So he does. But Mary's roast will make up for any flirting you miss, and she's already fluffed up the pillows in the spare room. Plus, you can check in with your family. Use our phone, or we have a computer now. Don't know how to use it, but there it sets."

A home-cooked meal and soft bed did sound appealing. And it had been a few weeks since he'd checked in with Eva. "Don't mind if I do. Mighty kind of you."

"You're doing me a favor. Mary woulda had my neck if I came home without you. Follow me."

Levi climbed into his pickup and started the old thing. Minutes later they were on a two-lane highway, headed east. The air rushed over Jake's skin, billowed his shirt. Ahead of him, Lookout Mountain rose into the cloudless sky. Maybe he'd explore it over the weekend. A change of scenery would be nice, though March in the Alabama mountains might get chilly.

Levi turned onto a gravel road, and Jake followed him a couple miles until he turned into the drive of a white farmhouse, set back off the road in a pine grove.

When they entered the house, Levi introduced him to Mary, who fussed over him, then showed him to his room.

Supper was a treat. Roasted pork, mashed potatoes, corn, and homemade bread. Made him miss his sister's good cooking. They lingered, talking about the Habitat house, Mary's garden plans, and his own family back on Nantucket. After the meal he took a long hot shower, and by the time he was done, he realized it was too late to call Eva. An hour later on the island. Eva would wring his neck if he woke the kids on a school night.

It would have to be e-mail. He wandered past the living room, where Levi and Mary watched TV, into the office where they'd told him to help himself to the computer.

The machine was a monstrosity, and Jake wondered if it even worked. But five slow minutes later he was online and opening his e-mail account.

There was probably a long newsy letter from Eva awaiting him, to which he'd hunt and peck his way to a four-sentence reply that would take him until midnight.

He typed in his password and waited for his inbox to appear, drumming his fingers on the scarred oak desk that hogged the tiny room. The chair squeaked as he settled back.

His inbox appeared, and he frowned as he scanned the messages. None from Eva. There were a bunch from Noelle and a couple from addresses he didn't recognize.

He opened his niece's oldest one first, dated three weeks ago.

Uncle J, please call as soon as you get this!!!

A smile tugged his lips. No doubt a teenage tragedy involving a boy. No one could say his niece was short on dramatics. It was Noelle who had started his nickname when she was no more than a baby. Unable to pronounce the *k* in Jake, she'd shortened his name to J. The name had caught and stuck.

He opened the next message from Noelle dated the following day.

Please call Uncle J!!! Something bad has happened!!

He frowned. What was going on? He was suddenly sure the urgency was more than teen angst.

Her next e-mail was sent later on the same day.

Uncle J, I didn't want to tell you this in an e-mail but I can't stand it anymore. Mom and Dad died! There was a boat accident and they're never coming home again! I'm so sad I haven't stopped crying. The funeral is in two days and we need you here!!!

Jake stopped reading. Eva and T. J. gone? His big sister, gone just like that? How could he not have known the instant she left this world? How did it happen? Why? His eyes burned, and he rubbed them hard.

The kids.

He opened Noelle's next e-mail.

The funeral was this morning. It doesn't seem real that Mom and Dad aren't coming back. I keep waiting for Dad to come home from work then I realize he's not going to. Mom's friend Mrs. Hubbard is staying with us. Where are you, Uncle J?

A heavy weight sat hard on his chest. *I'm right here!* he wanted to shout through the computer. But he hadn't been there when they needed him. The weight nearly suffocated him.

Eva. He pictured her swingy blonde hair caught up in a messy ponytail, her small oval face, her sparkling green eyes so full of life.

Only they weren't full of life now. They were still and cold. Lifeless. He couldn't stand the thought of not seeing her again. Of not getting to say good-bye. He pounded the desk with his fist. Why had he left? If only he'd stayed home this winter. If only he'd called sooner.

The kids. He had to think about the kids. Who was taking care of them? He opened Noelle's next message.

I can't believe it!!! Dad's attorney said that his other daughter is supposed to be our guardian!!! We don't even know her!!

The next e-mail from Noelle was dated almost a week later.

Dad's other daughter came today. I so hoped she wouldn't come but now she's here and obviously planning to stay. She doesn't even care about us!!

The last one was sent just the day before.

Meridith is crazy!! You wouldn't believe what she's doing! She's changing everything and is so strict I want to scream!!! I don't care if she is my sister, I hate her!!! She isn't fit to take care of us!! Come home, Uncle J! I know they'll change their minds when they see how much we love you!!

Jake stood abruptly, and the office chair rolled away at the force. He paced the room with long, quick strides. He had to talk to Noelle, make sure they were okay. He stopped at the desk and picked up the phone, then slammed it back down. What good would it do to wake her?

He had to get back to the island. What the heck was this Meridith woman doing? And why had Eva and T. J. left the kids to her?

Well, who were they going to leave them to? You? He wasn't the most settled man alive, and sure, maybe he had a wild streak or two . . . but he loved the munchkins.

Noelle's anguish had come through loud and clear. He pictured Benny's little face, so like Eva's, and Max's sad brown eyes. They must be lost without their parents. He knew what that was like.

Knew what it was like to be unwanted, to feel like you didn't belong anywhere.

Something in Noelle's e-mail jarred his memory. He went back to the computer and opened the last e-mail. *Meridith is crazy!! You wouldn't believe what she's doing!*

He remembered something Eva had told him back when she and T. J. first married. T. J.'s ex-wife had bipolar disorder, a mental illness. Was it hereditary? What if Meridith had it too? What if the kids were in the hands of a mentally ill woman?

He put his hands over the keyboard and pecked his way to a search engine to look up the disorder. It took an eternity for the list to appear.

When it did, he clicked on a link and skimmed the information. *Psychiatric disorder . . . mania . . . hallucinations . . . depression . . .* and then the nugget of information he'd feared.

"Genetics are a substantial contributing factor to the likelihood of developing bipolar disorder. Symptoms often appear in late adolescence or young adulthood."

Jake clicked back to Noelle's e-mails and reread them, his breath catching again at the news of his sister's death. *Why Eva, God?* He was going to miss her so much.

But he had to focus on the kids now. There would be time for grieving later.

His niece definitely thought there was something wrong with Meridith, had even called her crazy. If this woman had inherited her mother's disorder, there was no way she was fit to care for his niece and nephews. No way Eva would've wanted her to.

He had to get back there. Now.

He returned to his room and stuffed the few items he'd unpacked into his bag. It would take too long to drive back. He'd take the first flight he could and send for his cycle later. He'd already missed the funeral, missed being there for the kids. He kicked his duffel bag across the wood floor, and it *thunked* against the closed door.

He felt like punching someone. Himself. For not being there when they needed him. For not even knowing his sister was dead and cold in the grave.

A knock sounded on the door. "Jake, everything okay?"

Jake slowed his breathing before he opened the door.

Levi stood on the threshold, his gray brows drawn together.

"There's been an emergency back home. I need to go." He explained what happened.

Mary had appeared at Levi's side. "What can we do?"

Jake ran his hand through his damp hair. "I need to get a flight. What city is closest? Atlanta? Birmingham?"

"I'll handle the arrangements," Mary said. "You go to the campsite and pack up your gear. When you get back I'll have your reservations set."

"And I'll drive you to the airport," Levi added. "We can ship your cycle to you."

"Thanks." Jake fished his credit card from his wallet and handed it to Mary. "Get the quickest flight you can. I don't care what it costs."

Jake exited the taxi and shouldered his duffel bag. Nantucket was still in the throes of winter, and he was glad for his leather jacket. Summer Place loomed ahead, big and sprawling under the clouded sky.

It had been a long night of travel, and he still hadn't arrived before the kids left for school. He checked his watch as he walked up the drive.

Just as well. He needed to get a feel for this Meridith woman. He'd had a lot of time to think on the flight—God knew he hadn't slept—and he didn't like what he was thinking.

Why would a woman who'd never bothered to meet her siblings suddenly have an interest in becoming their new mommy? Why would she leave her life in whatever city she lived in to come care for the kids?

Was he supposed to think it was her big heart and tender spirit? They were talking about the guardianship of three kids, for crying out loud. Three kids she didn't even know, much less love.

He was no fool. Summer Place might be old, but it was over three acres of oceanside property and worth a mint. Did she think she could come here and take so easily what Eva and T. J. had worked so hard for?

Not on his life.

And yet, his sister and T. J. had granted her guardianship. He knew for a fact T. J. hadn't seen his daughter since she was in school. Why would they leave the kids to her? But Jake knew how important family was to Eva. Having only had each other so much of their lives, blood was key to her. And the kids only had two blood relatives left. Him and Meridith.

But he was the logical choice, wasn't he? As he turned up the familiar flagstone path, he recalled Eva's merciless teasing about his being a confirmed bachelor. And he was. He'd told his sister more than once that he wasn't even sure he wanted kids. But these children were his blood relatives, the only ones he had left. He wished he'd never said those things to Eva.

But none of that mattered now because T. J.'s daughter had legal rights to the kids, according to Noelle. And if he knew anything, he knew how complicated bureaucracy could be. It had stolen too much from him. There was nothing he could do about those years, but no way would he let them bungle his niece's and nephews' lives.

When he neared the porch, Piper raced around the corner.

"Hey, girl." He rubbed behind her ears, then took the porch steps, steeling himself for the fact that Eva wouldn't be waiting with a gentle hug. Steeling himself for the stranger inside. The one who surely had ulterior motives.

If she'd taken the kids to get the property, she wasn't going to come out and say so. He had to be smart. Careful. He needed to get a read on her. _Wise as a serpent, harmless as a dove,_ like the Bible said.

He started to turn the doorknob, then his eyes caught on the white paper taped firmly to the door. He read the neatly typed words. PLEASE KNOCK AND WE'LL BE RIGHT WITH YOU. THANK YOU.

What the . . . ? It was a bed-and-breakfast. People came and went all the time.

He guessed the note applied to uncles too. Shaking his head, he dropped his duffel bag on the bench beside the door and knocked. He wondered what other rules she'd implemented. Eva and T. J. had been pretty relaxed.

He rubbed his jaw, feeling the whiskers he hadn't shaved in a couple days. He was wearing his old _Comfort Heating and Plumbing_ T-shirt and a faded pair of jeans. Maybe he should've gone to his loft first, been more presentable. But then, who was he trying to impress?

The door opened, and his eyes lowered to the face of an attractive brunette with wide brown eyes and a guarded smile. She was small with curves in all the right places. She didn't _look_ crazy, but after researching the illness, he knew the phases of depression and mania could be separated by periods of normality.

"May I help you?"

Before he could respond, her eyes dropped to his T-shirt. "Oh, you're with Comfort." She checked a clipboard, and a tiny frown puckered her eyebrows. "I didn't expect you until tomorrow, but no matter. Come in."

Jake offered a stilted smile, then stepped over the threshold. He should explain. He didn't work for Comfort during the winter, though he was sure his buddy Wyatt would be glad to have him back early. Still, he should correct her.

But then he glanced to the left, where the kids' school photos stair-stepped up the wall. Noelle's cute freckles, Max's dimpled smile, Benny's missing tooth. Then he glanced back at the woman, possibly a mentally unstable woman, who held their futures in her greedy little palms.

Wise as a serpent, gentle as a dove . . .

Five

Raw manpower. Those were the first words that entered Meridith's mind as the man from Comfort Heating and Plumbing stepped over the threshold and shrank the room in half. She held Piper outside with her knee, then shut the door and pulled the clipboard to her chest, sizing the man up. He had a certain restrained energy. Confident. No, cocky. There was a definite cockiness to his square jawline and direct stare.

And he was staring.

So was she. She cleared her throat. "I'm Meridith Ward."

He held out his hand. "Jake."

He had brown eyes. Caramel, really.

His hand swallowed hers in a firm, warm grip, then released it just as quickly. She swiped it down her leg as if she could erase the touch.

"I have an extensive list of repairs and projects, and I'm in the process of getting bids." She perused her list. "You're licensed for heating and plumbing?"

"Right." He had a nice voice. Smooth, deep. Like good espresso.

"Let's start with the boiler then. It's in the basement." She wound her way through the dining room and down the wooden stairs, conscious of Jake's presence behind her. These bids were eating up her days, between the heating, plumbing, carpentry, and electrical problems.

"Well, there she is." Meridith gestured to the boiler and explained the problem they were having keeping the house warm.

While Jake looked it over, Meridith paced. She'd come to a couple crucial decisions in the past week. Number one: Uncle Jay was not getting his hands on her siblings. She'd heard enough from Ben and Max to realize why she'd been her father's first choice. The uncle was little more than a vagabond, irresponsible and lacking in good reasoning skills.

Number two: She would accept guardianship of the children. What other choice did she have? She couldn't let them go to foster care, and according to Mr. Thomas there was no one else. Her fiancé was a reasonable and loving man. He'd understand once she got up the nerve to tell him.

Number three: She couldn't uproot the children in the middle of the school year. She'd let them finish the year, then they'd move back to St. Louis. She lived in a nice neighborhood in a great school district, and while her house wasn't huge, there were three bedrooms and a cozy fenced-in yard. Meanwhile, she'd get Summer Place up to snuff so it would sell quickly and painlessly.

She'd finalized the financial matters with Mr. Thomas and signed the guardianship paperwork. T. J. and Eva had a small life insurance policy, but after funeral costs, there wasn't much left. When she did get the check, she wanted to put it back for the children's college fund anyway.

Thank goodness there were enough funds in the business bank account to make the repairs on the house. At least, she thought there would be. She was only beginning to receive bids. Unfortunately, there wasn't much equity in the place, apparently due to a second mortgage Eva and T. J. had taken out a couple years before.

She didn't know why her father and Eva hadn't made the repairs already. Some of the problems were potential health risks; others were lawsuits waiting to happen.

Unfortunately, when she'd requested an extension on her leave of absence, her boss denied it. It was the children or her job. She'd chosen the children.

So when she returned to St. Louis, she'd be looking for another job, but with her connections and experience, she was confident she could find one. In the meantime, paying her mortgage back home would eat into her savings, but it couldn't be helped.

"All right, got what I need," Jake said.

Meridith led him back upstairs to inspect the dishwasher. Did he have to walk so close behind her? She jogged up the remaining few steps and turned toward the kitchen.

"Nice place," he said as they entered the kitchen. "Had it long?"

"Uh, no." She crossed the room, her heels clicking on the tile. "The dishwasher's been leaking." She moved in front of the sink.

"Let's have a look."

Meridith turned on the faucet and washed her hands, then dried them on a nearby towel. When she turned, Jake was inches away. She hadn't realized he was so . . . broad. There was something about him. He was like a cougar ready to spring. Contained passion. She pressed her spine to the sink ledge.

His jaw sported at least two days' stubble. His upper lip dipped in the middle, just the right size for a fingertip.

"Need in there," he said.

Under the sink. Of course. Heat flared up her neck, into her cheeks. She bolted across the room while he opened the cupboard and sank down to his knees, straining his Levis.

He was *so* not getting this job.

He looked under the sink, fiddled with the pipes and hose. Meridith turned and stared out the window. The sun sparkled off the water, blinding. The ocean continued for miles, disappearing into a hazy sky.

She was so far from home. So far from all that was familiar. No wonder she was jumpy. Her life was on hold, her job gone. Then again, what did she expect when she'd requested three months' leave. Still, she'd never taken so much as a vacation.

"Looks like a crimp in the hose. New one, and you'll be leak-free."

Well, that was good news. The last guy made it sound worse. Maybe they wouldn't need a new dishwasher after all.

Jake pressed on the cabinet base. "Looks like you've got water damage, though." He sat back on his haunches.

"I have some carpenters coming to bid on it and a few other projects."

She pretended to jot a note on her clipboard as he sprang to his feet, surprisingly agile for his height.

"I do carpentry."

"Are you licensed?"

"In pretty much everything—can build a house from the ground up and then some."

Oh. Working with one contractor would be more convenient than five or six. But there was still the matter of cost. And the matter of—

Her eyes darted toward him, then back to the clipboard. She found herself hoping for a high bid.

"Well, let me show you the other projects. The first thing I want completed is a divider between the main house and the family wing." She led him to the staircase. "I'd like a door here with a double cylinder dead bolt. Something heavy-duty like metal and—do you have a notebook or something?"

"Good memory."

Strike two. Detail-oriented people got the job done right, in her experience. He'd be lucky if he remembered every project. The thought comforted her as she took him upstairs, pointing out the missing banister, the switch in the bathroom, and the corridor that needed a doorway.

"I'd like to keep the business going while repairs are being made." She didn't know why she said that. He was not getting the job.

"I'll work around your schedule," he said when they were descending the main staircase. "What are your plans for the place?"

That information was given on a need-to-know basis, and he didn't need to know. "Just getting the place up to code."

She went to the front door and pulled it, eager to see the back of him. When she turned, she found herself wishing she'd worn higher heels. It didn't help that the man didn't seem to have a regard for personal space.

Meridith cleared her throat. "Well, get back with me and let me know how much we're looking at."

He nodded. "Will do."

She closed the door and loosened the clipboard from the clutches of her cramped arms. Removing the pen from the clamp, she followed the list of contractors down to the words *Comfort Heating and Plumbing* and scratched through it with a dark, deep line.

Six

Jake set the flowers on the mound of dirt beside a collection of clusters in varying stages of decay. A breeze ruffled the cellophane and carried the tang of salt and the earthy smell of freshly turned dirt.

It hadn't seemed real until two minutes ago when he'd found T. J.'s and Eva's fresh gravesites at the foot of a barren tree. She really was gone. His beautiful, sweet, funny sister. He would never again walk into one of her warm hugs or pester her until she smacked him on the arm. She would never serve him up a platter of eggs and bacon and tease him about his bottomless stomach. His eyes burned and he clenched his jaw, fighting the emotion.

They were in a better place now. He could be thankful for that. Eva had never been shy about her faith. He stared at the clusters of browning flowers, a tangible reminder of the time that had passed since their deaths, and a hollow spot formed inside.

"I'm sorry I wasn't here," he said.

The kids had been Eva's world. If she were watching from heaven these past weeks, he was sure she was screaming for him to get his roaming butt back to Nantucket and see to the kids.

But she and T. J. had left Meridith in charge. The realization was a sucker punch. They'd thought he wouldn't want to be saddled with three kids, that he wouldn't rearrange his life for them, that he was too unsettled.

Maybe it was true. It wasn't something he could've seen himself doing before. But now . . . now he was the kids' only lifeline. He couldn't turn his back on them.

He was certain Eva never dreamed it would come to this. How often were kids orphaned these days? He felt a sense of déjà vu.

But the unthinkable had happened. And now that woman had legal guardianship of his niece and nephews. His chest expanded and deflated rapidly.

He reviewed the time he'd spent with Meridith that morning. Why was she having all the work done on Summer Place? Was she going to sell it and move the kids away? Away from their home, their school, their friends? The poor kids wouldn't know what hit them. Was she even capable of making rational decisions?

He stared at the freshly turned earth. Those kids weren't going to suffer more than they already had. Not on his watch. And he sure wasn't going to stand by while this stranger stripped them of everything familiar and subjected them to God knows what.

"I'll take care of them, Eva. I promise." He swallowed over the lump in his throat, backing away.

When he turned toward the road, he checked his watch. He had just enough time to shower and call Wyatt at Comfort Heating and Plumbing before the kids' school dismissed.

Jake leaned his elbow out his truck window, watching the front doors of the school as if he could will them to open and produce his niece and nephews. Now that his plan was in motion he was impatient to proceed.

A line of yellow buses snaked along the drive waiting for kids. Would he have time to explain? Was it too much to expect from them, especially young Benny?

But he had to do it. The opportunity couldn't be coincidental. It was almost as if Eva were orchestrating it from heaven. He wasn't going to blow it.

He hopped from the truck and went to stand behind the nearest tree. He was grateful he had the pickup, but he missed his cycle. He'd called Levi from his loft, and the man had already arranged shipment.

A faint bell trilled, and Jake took two automatic strides closer to the front door. He had to be careful. It wouldn't do to be recognized by anyone but the kids. He shoved his hands into the pockets of his leather jacket and waited, praying they wouldn't be the last stragglers.

Finally he saw Noelle in a pack of giggling girls. He put his fingers between his lips and blew. The piercing whistle all but disappeared on the wind, but Noelle stopped, scanning the yard, the pack of girls leaving her behind.

He knew the instant she saw him. She went still, her face broke into a smile. And then she was running.

She was in his arms ten heartbeats later, squeezing, crying, "Uncle J!" Her sobs caught him in the gut.

He wrapped his arms around her little blonde head. "I'm here, baby. I'm here."

When she finished crying, she leaned back, and he wiped her tears with the tail of his T-shirt. "We don't have much time. Where're Ben and Max?"

She scanned the mob of students rushing from the building.

"Max, Ben!" she called, waving.

Jake stepped behind the tree to wait.

Noelle walked into his embrace again. "Why didn't you answer my e-mails? I waited and waited, and now *Meridith* has taken over."

"Uncle J!" Max threw himself into Jake's arms, followed closely by Ben. They clung to him like he was their life preserver on an open sea.

He clenched his jaw. Maybe that's what he was.

"I'm sorry I wasn't here, guys. It's gonna be okay. I promise."

"You have to come home with us and make Meridith leave," Noelle said.

"Yeah!" said Max. "Come live with us!"

"It doesn't work that way, guys. Meridith has legal custody."

"We don't want her!" Noelle said.

"I know, I know." The mob of kids had thinned. The buses wouldn't stay much longer, and the kids had to arrive home like normal.

Jake crouched down. "We don't have much time, and I have a lot to say, so listen, okay?"

They nodded.

"I'm going to try and get custody, but it'll be tricky. You're not old enough to decide for yourselves. I don't want Meridith to know I'm back, understand? You can't tell her."

"But how can—"

Jake held up a finger. "You know Meridith's getting bids on projects around the house, right?"

"Right . . ." Noelle said.

"I'm bidding on the job. I need time there to see what I'm dealing with." He wouldn't tell the kids about the mental illness. Didn't want to scare them. "If she's doing things that are . . . inappropriate, I'll see firsthand, and we'll have evidence against her. That's the only way I'll be able to get custody of you munchkins. We have to show that Meridith's not suitable, get it?"

"But that'll take too long!" Noelle said.

"Maybe not. And in the meantime, I'll be there with you guys a lot."

"Cool!" Max said.

"*But*—you all have to listen close here. You *cannot* call me Uncle J. You have to pretend you don't know me—like I'm just some guy there working on the house, understand?"

"That'll be hard," Ben said.

"Very hard," Jake said.

"What if we slip up?" Max hitched his book bag higher.

"You won't if you're careful. When Meridith's not around, you don't have to pretend. And don't tell anyone else I'm back either, understand? It might get back to her." Jake felt a prick of guilt. Was he doing the right thing, asking the kids to take part in deception? It went against everything he stood for. But what other option did he have? Surrender the kids to a crazy woman? He had to play by the system's rules whether he liked it or not.

Ben tugged on Jake's sleeve.

"Yeah, Benny?"

"Are Mom and Dad really in heaven now?"

Jake swore he felt a crack splinter through the middle of his heart. They needed him now more than ever. He gripped the boy's shoulder. "Yes, they are. God promised, and you can always believe God's promises, 'kay?"

Ben nodded.

There were only a few stragglers walking toward the buses now.

"You guys have to run, you're going to miss your bus. Noelle, review this with them on the way home, okay? Make sure they understand."

"But Meridith's getting tons of bids. She, like, overdoes *everything*!" Noelle rolled her eyes. "What if you don't even get the job?"

Jake straightened from his crouch. "Oh, I'll get the job, don't you worry. Now, go on. Scoot!"

They gave him one last hug before scurrying toward their bus, their heavy book bags bouncing on their shoulders.

Seven

"Summer Place, may I help you?" Meridith shouldered the phone, nudging Benny to her other side.

"Hello, I'd like to make a reservation, please."

"Certainly." The brown leather reservation tablet was on the counter where she'd placed it. "What dates are you looking for?"

"We're coming for the Daffodil Festival, April twenty-third through the twenty-fifth. I hope you still have openings. I'm a little late calling this year. Is this Eva?"

"Uh, no, it's not." This wasn't the first caller who'd asked, but Meridith found it best to move the conversation along, especially when Ben was nearby. He was stamping a stack of brochures. "It does look like we have a room available that weekend."

"Wonderful. You can put us down for those two nights. We're the Goldmans." She gave her contact information and a credit card number. "We're looking forward to it. We so enjoy Eva and T. J. and the children when we visit."

Meridith marked them in the book. Mrs. Goldman seemed to know her father and Eva pretty well. An explanation was in order. She stepped away from the desk, walking toward the dining room, away from Ben's ears, hoping he wouldn't follow this once.

She lowered her voice. "I went ahead and booked the nights for you, Mrs. Goldman, but I'm afraid I have some sad news. Eva and T. J. were in an accident a few weeks ago. I'm afraid they didn't make it."

Meridith stared through the wavy glass window and saw Noelle slouched in one of the Adirondack chairs, facing the ocean. The cord of her iPod was like a constant spaghetti noodle dangling from her ear.

"Oh dear," Mrs. Goldman was saying. "Oh my, those poor children. Are they all right?"

"They're doing as well as can be expected. I'm their new guardian, their big sister from Missouri." It always felt so strange, that word. Sister.

"Oh. I didn't realize they had an older sister. I'm so glad they have you."

Noelle changed positions, slumping sideways over the chair, laying her head back onto the arm. If only Noelle were glad. She seemed to make a hobby of avoiding Meridith. But maybe that was for the best. The encounters they had weren't pleasant.

She felt Ben before she saw him. He wrapped his arms around her waist, leaning into her hip.

"Yes, things are going fine. I have you down for the Daffodil Festival weekend. We're looking forward to your visit."

"That was Mrs. Goldman," she told Ben after she hung up. "Do you remember her?"

He nodded against her hip. Meridith patted his head awkwardly. His blond cropped hair was baby fine and soft.

"She's looking forward to seeing you."

"She decorates the galaxy," Ben said.

Decorates the galaxy? Was he into Star Wars and space? He'd

never talked about science fiction before. She squatted down. "What do you mean, Ben?"

His green eyes were earnest, sad. "Dad's old car in the garage. She helps us decorate it for the festival."

Meridith breathed a laugh. "Oh, the *Galaxie*. I thought you meant—" She shook her head. "Never mind."

Max tromped down the stairs, grabbed his jacket from the hook. "Done with my homework! Going outside."

"Dinner will be ready in ten minutes," she said as he blew past. The back door opened and slammed shut.

Meridith straightened. The casserole was in the oven, the vegetables steaming. "Would you like to set the table?"

Ben shrugged and headed toward the kitchen for the plates.

Now what had she been doing before the phone call? The mail. She set the phone in the cradle and sorted through the pile. Bills, credit card offer, mailers. Ah! Three more bids. She'd received the first one yesterday and still had sticker shock. Hopefully these were more reasonable.

She ripped open the first and gasped. And that was only the furnace and plumbing work. *In your dreams.* The other bid was for the carpentry. She sighed. It was like these people knew her account balance and conspired to take every last dime.

Well, there was still one bid coming. Two, if you counted Comfort, but she didn't.

She opened the remaining mail, trashing the credit offers.

The phone rang, and she pulled the reservation book closer as she greeted the caller.

"This is Jake from Comfort Heating and Plumbing. I was out yesterday to bid on your projects."

She recognized his voice before he identified himself. "Did you have questions?" *That's why you take notes, Mr. Comfort.*

"Put some numbers together for you and have your bid." He named a dollar figure that left Meridith skeptical. Clearly he'd forgotten something. Some*things*, judging by the quote.

"I prefer a written bid, if you don't mind." Not that she was signing anything with this Jake guy.

"You were in a hurry, so I thought I'd call. Be glad to drop off the papers."

Then she could see everything that was missing. Whatever. "Sure, drop them by. There's a slot on the front door."

"Will do."

Meridith ended the call and wiped her palms down her legs. What was it about that man? She could only imagine hiring him, having him here all day. Alone with him all day. The thought made her palms sweat. No. Not happening.

The kitchen timer dinged, and she went to remove the casserole from the oven. After setting the food on the table, she called Max and Noelle—Noelle three times, compliments of the iPod.

"Didn't Ben do a great job setting the table?" Meridith broke the silence five minutes later. After she'd made Noelle turn off her music, the only sounds were the scraping of forks on plates and the sound of Ben chewing with his mouth open.

The phone rang.

"Aren't you going to get it?" Max asked two rings later.

"Not during dinner. That's what voice mail is for."

"Mom always answers," Max said.

"Answer*ed*," Noelle said.

"Shut up, Noelle."

Meridith's nerves rattled. "All right, you two, that's enough. Did everyone finish their homework?"

"You already asked that."

Why did everything out of Noelle's mouth have to sound snide? *Patience, Meridith.* Maybe a happier topic. "What would you like to do this weekend? I saw there's a whaling museum on the island. How about that?"

Noelle took a bite of broccoli and rolled her eyes.

"We've already been there," Ben said.

"Field trips." Max pushed his food around his plate. "We could go ice skating on Hummock Pond . . ."

"Yeah!" Ben said.

"Oh," Meridith said. "I don't know. That sounds a little danger-ous. The temperatures haven't been below freezing. And while we're on the topic of safety, Ben, I got something for you today." The injected enthusiasm sounded as fake as it was.

"What?"

"A booster seat for the van. Isn't that great? You'll be able to see up over the seat and have a great view."

"A *booster* seat . . ." Noelle lowered her fork. "That's retarded."

"It will boost him higher." She gave Noelle a pointed look.

"I don't want a booster seat," Ben said quietly, and Meridith wanted to wring Noelle's neck for putting a nasty spin on the whole thing.

Meridith laid her hand on Ben's arm. "The safety recommenda-tions are to use a booster seat until you're four foot nine. You still have several inches to go. I got a really cool one."

"Yeah, his friends are going to think it's really cool." Noelle again.

Meridith pursed her lips.

"She's right." Max set his fork down. "It's not cool."

"Well, it may not be cool, but it's safe."

"It's cruel, is what it is," Noelle said. "They'll make fun of him."

"No one has to know."

Noelle huffed. "May I be excused?"

Sarcasm was not pretty on a young girl. "You may. Max, you've hardly eaten a bite."

"I'm not hungry. Can I be excused too?" His sad brown eyes melted her.

"Of course."

The chairs scraped as they exited, and Meridith sighed as the two disappeared into the kitchen, then clomped up the back staircase.

After she and Ben finished, she washed dishes while the boy dried. He seemed happier when he was doing something. Maybe not happier, just . . . busier.

She knew about grief, but what did she know about children? Music blared from upstairs. Meridith sighed again. Apparently nothing.

She didn't like Noelle shutting herself in her room. It didn't seem healthy, though she understood the desire. More than once she'd wanted to close herself in her own room and pull the covers over her head. She hadn't felt that way since she lived with her mom.

When the last dish was shelved, she turned to Ben. "Why don't you ask Max and Noelle if they want to watch a movie. I saw your DVD collection in the library—surely we can agree on something."

While Ben scampered up the stairs, Meridith went to check the voice mail. Before she reached the guest desk, a white envelope by the front door caught her eye.

The bid.

Well, he didn't waste any time. *This should be good.* Comic relief, if nothing else. She slid her finger under the flap, pulled out the papers, and unfolded them. Her eyes found the back page, bottom figure. Just what he'd quoted on the phone.

Now to see what he'd forgotten to price.

She scanned the list of jobs and materials. It was detailed, the make and size of the furnace, the brand name of the door, even the brand name of the lock sets. She double-checked the list.

He hadn't forgotten a thing. It was even more detailed than the other bids. How could he do it for so little? She read the fine print on the contract and warranty. All standard.

She flipped to the back page and stared at the project bid, her stomach sinking like a lead weight in a tub full of water as she realized the offer on this paper was too good to turn down.

Eight

"Come in," Meridith said.

Jake nodded as she opened the door.

It was a struggle to keep Piper outside. Meridith put her body in front of the door. "She likes you."

Jake shrugged from a weathered leather jacket and took off his shoes, the movement sending a whiff of man her way. Woodsy, spicy. Masculine.

"Know you wanted to get those partitions up," he said. "But thought I'd get your dishwasher running first. Have it done in thirty minutes."

"You know the way." She gave him a wide berth, glad to see he'd brought tools this time.

She followed him through the living room and dining room to the kitchen, noticing how quickly his long legs ate up the distance. This house was going to feel a lot smaller. She hoped he was fast. She could hardly turn down the bid, and his references had checked out too. Naturally.

He was already pulling the dishwasher from its home. It creaked and groaned, protesting the relocation.

"Thing's pretty old."

While Jake lowered himself to the floor, Meridith grabbed the sanitizer and sprayed down the counters, scrubbing at the dried blob of jelly Max left by the toaster. Next she filled the coffeemaker with grinds and water, plugged it in, then pushed the On button.

While the coffee brewed, she tidied up. Noelle had left out the cereal box, Ben's crumb-filled plate remained on the table beside a half-empty glass of milk, and Max's boat model mess was strewn across the end of the table. She wasn't used to clutter, and clearly the children weren't used to picking up after themselves.

When the coffeemaker beeped, she poured a steaming mug, inhaling the rich brew. For all the outdated appliances, Eva had understood the importance of a good cup of java.

The deep-roasted smell filled the kitchen. It would be rude not to offer the man a cup. His legs sprawled across the kitchen floor, extending from the dishwasher's side. She followed the length of them down to the white sock where his second toe peeked through a hole. Somehow that little detail made him very real.

She shook her head. Silly.

"Coffee?"

"Maybe later, thanks."

He was making noises under there with his tools. She hoped he knew what he was doing. While he worked, Meridith retrieved Eva's tattered cookbook. They had guests arriving that night for the weekend. Max had said Eva's cinnamon rolls were always a hit, and the repeat guests expected them.

In preparation for the guests, she'd had a talk with the children about Piper. No amount of explaining about food and dog hair or dander was enough to satisfy them, so she'd finally just stated the rule: Piper was now an outdoor dog. She made a nice comfy bed of old quilts in the garage, but even that wasn't enough to soothe the children, especially Noelle.

Now Meridith opened the cookbook to the cinnamon roll recipe. She needed a reason to stick around and make sure Jake wasn't cutting corners.

She set the ingredients on the counter, including the packet of yeast. "Is it okay to run the water?"

"Sure."

She filled a bowl with warm water, then moved away.

"You the new owner then?" Jake's voice carried from the cabinet's cavity.

"How'd you know there was a new owner?"

He strained, grunting, his legs shifting for better hold. "Small island."

Just because it was a tourist destination in the summer didn't make it immune to small-town gossip, she supposed.

She wondered if Jake had known Eva and T. J., then decided she didn't want to know. Didn't want to know anything about him. Best to keep it—

"Where you from?"

She ripped open the yeast packet and dumped it into the water, then added a teaspoon of sugar. "St. Louis."

"The 'show-me state.' Where'd that phrase come from anyway?"

"There are several theories." None of which she wanted to discuss. She read the directions again. "Let the yeast sit until it dissolved." No mention of how long.

"How are the kids coping?"

She sighed. It really was a small island. "As well as can be expected. How's that leak coming?"

He slid from under the sink and stood, a hose dangling from his hand. "There's a crimp. Looks like—someone—tried to tighten it."

His hands were large and dark-skinned. Long fingers, tapering down to squared-off tips. Nice hands.

Back to the hose. "Oh."

Two seconds later he was under the sink again. She turned back to the yeast. It looked the same, so she started on the dough.

"What did you do in St. Louis?"

Well, wasn't he Mr. Chatty today. "Safety inspector."

"Aaaahh."

There was something more to that *aaahh*, but she didn't care to know what.

"Commercial, residential . . . ?"

"Restaurants and hotels mainly." Maybe she should hand him her résumé and be done with it. She poured in the flour and dumped in the yeast mixture.

"That's handy."

She set the beaters into the mixture and turned it on. She smiled as a nice loud buzz filled the room. She worked the beaters around the dough, adding flour as she thought necessary. When it was well blended and stiff, she turned off the mixer. Now for the kneading. She removed her engagement ring and placed it on the counter.

"Nice rock."

She jumped at the voice, nearer than she expected.

Jake wore a crooked grin. "All fixed." He had a cleft camouflaged by the stubble on his chin.

She stepped around him. The dishwasher was back in place, the cabinet closed.

"Should I run it through a cycle to make sure?"

"It's fixed. I'll take a look under the cabinet later to see if there's rotting. You wanted those partitions up first, right?"

"Right."

He made some measurements at the base of the stairs, then exited the room, taking his woodsy scent with him. It was a relief to have him gone. Meridith reheated her coffee, added a dash of cream and sugar, and took a deep sip.

Jake might be convinced the leak was fixed, but she wanted to be certain. She punched the button, starting the wash cycle.

She was up to her wrists in dough when he returned with lumber. He set down the wood, and a few moments later he began hammering, the loud, sharp *thwack*s echoing off the walls. She cast occasional glances at the dishwasher base.

"Leave your fiancé back home?" *Thwack, thwack, thwack.*

"Yes."

He grabbed another nail. One side of his mouth twitched as he lined up the nail. *Thwack, thwack, thwack.* "What's he do?"

"He's an accountant."

"Aaaahh."

That same tone. She didn't know what it meant, but it was annoying. She shook the thought and checked the dishwasher. Satisfied it was fixed, she began loading the breakfast dishes.

"Must be hard to be apart." *Thwack, thwack, thwack.*

She gave a tight smile, then returned to scrubbing the plates. How she felt about being apart from Stephen was none of his business. The fact was, it hadn't been too hard. He called every couple days, and it wasn't as though they saw each other daily at home. His schedule this time of year didn't allow for that. It was tax season, after all.

"I bought the doors already, but if you don't like them, you can pick out different ones."

"They're steel? With dead bolts?"

"Yes, ma'am."

She was sure there was sarcasm in the drawled word. Or maybe it was that twitch of his lips again.

"Then they'll be just fine." She loaded the forks and started the machine. It whirred loudly into motion.

She decided to start the laundry, as much to put some space between them as anything. Between the kids' clothes and the bedding, it seemed she was always running a load. She started the washer, then vacuumed the guest suite and fluffed the pillows. Satisfied the room was perfection, she returned to the kitchen to check the dough.

She lifted the cloth and frowned. It was the same smooth ball it had been before. Maybe it needed more time.

She re-covered it and forced herself to check on Jake, stifling the inner voice that was coaxing her to hide in her bedroom the rest of the day.

The new door unit leaned against the wall, so big and heavy-looking it was hard to believe he'd managed it by himself. Her eyes scanned the length of his arms, the width of his shoulders. Okay, maybe not so hard.

She forced an image of Stephen into her mind, the one from the photo on her nightstand upstairs. Wearing a jacket and tie, hair nicely clipped, jaw freshly shaven. The picture of an ideal man.

Feeling reassured, she turned her attention to the doorway. The framing looked sturdy, but the opening seemed wider than the door unit. Or maybe it was the angle.

He held a nail in place and gave three hard taps, driving it home.

"Are you sure it'll fit?" she asked.

He pulled a nail from between his teeth and set it in place. "I'm sure." *Thwack, thwack, thwack.*

"How do you know?"

"I measured."

She pursed her lips. Well, of course he measured, she just hoped he'd measured right. "I didn't know the door would come with the frame thing already attached."

"It's pre-hung."

Meridith stepped closer to the new unit and ran her hand over the smooth surface; then she knocked, getting a feel for the door's sturdiness. It seemed solid.

When she turned, Jake was standing over her. His nearness startled her. "Oh!"

"Need my level."

Did the man not understand personal space? She stepped back.

His lips twitched as he retrieved the tool. Not just the corner, but his whole lips. Not that she was looking.

"Is something funny?"

He reached toward her, his caramel eyes holding her captive.

Her breath caught in her throat as his hand brushed the side of her face. The touch was nothing but a whisper, but it left a trail of fire. She couldn't move if she tried. And she wasn't sure she wanted to.

He held up his finger, and she pulled her eyes from his. "Flour," he said.

Her scrambled brain took two full seconds, then she turned, wiping her cheek, hating the blush she knew was flooding her face as she exited the room.

Nine

Jake checked his watch, then set down the hammer and took a deep drink of Coke. The kids would be there soon. His ears were tuned for the screeching bus brakes. If he were smart, he'd have told Meridith he had to leave at three o'clock each day so he wouldn't run the risk of them giving him away.

But then he wouldn't get to see them, make sure they were safe. Besides, how was he supposed to gather evidence if he didn't see Meridith with them? So far she seemed relatively normal, but time would tell.

The downstairs partition was complete except for drywall and paint touch-up, but this upstairs doorway was wider, required more framing. He thought the whole concept was ridiculous anyway. What did Meridith think, a serial murderer was coming to stay at a B-and-B on Nantucket? But maybe paranoia was a part of the illness.

He couldn't help but wonder, though, why she was having the other work done. Was she fixing up the place so she could stay, or fixing it up so she could sell? He couldn't imagine her fiancé leaving his job and home to come care for someone else's kids.

The phone rang, and he heard Meridith answer at the base of the stairs. She'd been busy all day, though she made time to stand over his shoulder plenty.

However, he'd discovered the key to getting rid of her. Just a few personal questions, and she ran for cover. He smothered a grin. Might be kind of entertaining.

The screeching bus brakes drew his attention. He hoped Noelle had reminded Ben and Max to be careful. They'd see his truck. At least, he hoped they would. Meridith was still on the phone—good that she was distracted.

The door clicked open, followed by the shuffles of three kids and the rustling of jackets. Had they seen his truck?

They clomped up the stairs, arguing about something someone said on the bus. He heard a smack.

"Stop it! I'm telling!" Ben said.

"Who you going to tell?" Max said.

"Meridith!"

"Shhhhh!" Meridith called. "Children, I'm on the phone with a guest."

"She's on the phone with a guest," Noelle mimicked quietly.

They were nearly to the top now. They hadn't seen his truck. He had to warn them.

They rounded the corner and he drew his finger to his lips. But not soon enough.

"Uncle J!"

Noelle slapped her hand over Ben's mouth.

The boy's eyes rounded. He stopped on the spot.

Noelle froze. So did Max, his eyes widening. Silence filled the loft.

Not a sound came from downstairs. Only the muted pings of the wind chimes stirring on the porch.

Was Meridith still on the phone? Why was she so quiet? Was she on her way upstairs?

Noelle pulled her hand from Ben's mouth.

"Moron!" Max whispered.

Ben looked ready to cry. Jake set a hand on his shoulder.

Then the muffled sound of Meridith's voice drifted up the stairs. "I understand. Let me check those dates." Pages rustled.

Jake released a breath he didn't realize he'd held.

The kids sagged. Then they threw themselves at him, making Jake stagger backward.

"I'm so glad you're here," Noelle whispered.

"Shhh." He pulled them down the hall toward their own cluster of rooms, farther from Meridith's ears.

"I'm sorry," Ben said.

"No damage done. But you're all going to have to watch it."

"I won't do it again."

"Did you find out anything?" Max asked.

"He's only been here a day," Noelle said.

"Your sister's right, this is going to take time." Though he'd been here long enough to see Meridith was a control freak. Clearly caution was her default.

He could still hear her on the phone, but couldn't make out the words.

"She's making Benny ride in a car seat!" Noelle said.

"What?" Ben might be a little guy, but he was too big for that.

"For *safety*." Max rolled his eyes.

"Anything else?"

"She took away my iPod."

"Only during dinner," Ben said.

"Well, she took your ropes away," Noelle said.

"Yeah, she did." Ben frowned.

"You know how he loves his ropes."

Benny loved practicing knots and rigging up hauling devices for his bike.

"Why'd she take them?"

"Because they're too *dangerous*, of course. He might hang himself, you know."

"Shhhh." The woman obviously had issues, if not mental illness. Still there was nothing that seemed cruel or dangerous. Nothing helpful. He'd have to—

"Children," Meridith called.

The kids scrambled for the stairs. "What?"

That's not obvious. Jake sighed.

"Homework time."

"Great," Noelle whispered.

Max cast one last persecuted look before they trampled down to meet their fate.

Their guests arrived just after dinner. Mr. and Mrs. Brown were a lovely couple from Maine taking a trip down the coastline to celebrate his retirement. Mrs. Brown had vacationed on the island as a child and couldn't resist the chance to reminisce.

By the time the children and the Browns were tucked away for the night, Meridith was ready for bed herself. She closed her bedroom door and changed into her nightshirt. It wasn't until she slipped under the covers that the full weight of her exhaustion hit. The clock only read twenty-five past ten, but her body said it was much later. She flipped off the lamp and let her body sink into the mattress.

Between readying the rooms, dealing with her failed cinnamon roll recipe, getting the kids through homework and dinner just in time to plaster on a fake smile for the Browns, she was ready to pull the covers over her head and greet oblivion.

Only to do it all again tomorrow.

But it was the weekend, so at least she wouldn't have to deal with Mr. Fix-it. She could be thankful for that.

The first strains of Vivaldi's "Spring" filled the room. She felt for her cell phone on the nightstand, then read the screen. She fell back against the pillows and tried to conjure some enthusiasm as she flipped it open.

"Stephen. Hi." He didn't usually call so late, but it was an hour earlier there.

"I didn't wake you, did I?"

"No, no, I was just settling in for the night." Meridith pulled the covers to her chin and closed her eyes.

"Sorry I haven't called in a few days."

"That's okay. I know you're busy."

"How are things there? Are the kids behaving any better?"

She felt a strange urge to defend them but pushed it aside. "They're as good as can be expected. The repairs are underway, and we have guests for the weekend, a nice couple."

"I drove by your house today and checked on things after I grabbed a quick lunch. Your neighbor has been watering your plants and collecting your mail as she promised."

She'd told him Mrs. Winters was taking care of everything; why couldn't he just leave it at that? Meridith sighed. She must be tired to be so irritable. "Thanks for checking."

"You're welcome. You say you've hired the contractors? I hope you got reasonable bids."

"I did. I ended up hiring one contractor to do all the work." Jake's dark eyes and cocky grin sprang to mind. She shook the image away. "He seems competent."

"Is he licensed for all that work? You have to be careful about contractors. They're not the most ethical creatures."

"I checked him out. He had glowing references and a very reasonable bid."

"Well, it sounds like you've got it under control. I expected no less from my little go-getter."

He began talking about one of his client's sloppy records and the debacle it had caused for him that day. Meridith wanted to tell him about her ruined cinnamon rolls and a story Max had shared over dinner, but by the time he finished his detailed story, her energy had evaporated and she was eager to be off the phone.

She needed to tell him about her decision to keep the children, but it was late, too late to introduce a heavy topic, and besides, she was losing energy by the second.

Ten minutes later she flipped her phone closed and drifted off to the muted sound of the wind chimes.

A voice screamed. Meridith bolted upright. *What was that?* Had she been dreaming? She checked the clock. It was after midnight. Her heart beat so hard, the bed shook with the pounding. Her ears perked, listening for whatever had woken her.

"No!"

Max! She leapt from the bed and raced toward the boys' room. What if someone was hurting him? What if the nice-seeming Mr. Brown really wasn't nice at all? If only Jake had finished the upstairs partition.

It seemed to take an hour to reach the room. She flipped on the light. Max thrashed in the bed, his face screwed up as if he were in torment. He whimpered. In the top bunk, Ben somehow slept peacefully.

Meridith perched on the bed's edge and shook his shoulders. "Max!"

He moaned and jerked his head.

She shook harder. "Max! Wake up."

His eyes opened. They were glassy, staring sightlessly into the corner.

"Max, you were having a nightmare."

The poor kid. It might've been kinder to let the nightmare continue. At least then he wouldn't wake to the reality that his parents were indeed gone.

Max blinked, looked around the room, trying to find his bearings. His gaze lost the foggy look, then settled on Meridith.

"You were having a nightmare," she said again, not knowing what else to say. His eyes teared up, then overflowed.

Meridith swallowed against the lump in her own throat. "It's okay." She wished she had words that would erase the pain on his face.

He drew in a shuddery breath and closed his eyes. A fat tear clung to his long eyelashes.

"Do you want to talk about it?"

He shook his head. Poor dear. She wished she knew what to do. Wished she were more like Rita and could just envelop him in a tight hug, but her hands lay in her lap, uncertain.

"Okay. Well. Try to get some sleep." She eased off the mattress.

"Don't go!" His fear-filled eyes popped open. His chubby fists clenched the quilt, then loosened, opening and closing compulsively.

"It's okay. I'm right across the hall."

He bolted upright, his head narrowly missing the top bunk. "Please!"

Meridith looked at the tiny twin bed. No room there, but there was a large rug beside the bed. If she grabbed her covers, she could make a pallet.

"Okay. I'll be right back." She went to her room, dragged the covers from the bed, and grabbed her pillow and clock. When she returned, Max was still upright, waiting.

She spread the blanket on the rug, lay down, then folded it over. Only when she was settled did Max lie back.

She listened to Ben's soft breathing and wondered how long it would take poor Max to fall back asleep.

"Meridith?" he whispered.

"Yeah?"

"What's heaven like?"

His quiet question echoed through her mind, searching for an answer that would put his mind at ease. "There are golden streets. And gates of pearl. It's beautiful there."

"And God's there."

"Yes. God's there."

He was quiet so long she thought he might have drifted off. But then he spoke. "They loved God a lot, so they're happy to be with him, right?"

Meridith couldn't imagine any parent being happy absent their children. Still. "Heaven is a happy place. No tears or anything . . . only joy."

The words seemed to soothe his worries, and he fell quiet, his breaths gradually growing deeper.

She wondered about Max's nightmare. Did he have them often? Was it normal for a child who suffered a trauma?

What did she know about kids? Normal kids, much less those who'd recently suffered a tragedy? How was she equipped to handle this? What if she did everything wrong and they ended up with a childhood as warped as her own? The anxiety knotted her insides, tensing her muscles.

She started her progressive relaxation technique, beginning with her facial muscles and working down into her torso, legs, then feet. Five minutes later her muscles were more relaxed, but her mind still fretted.

She hated this. Hated the lack of peace she'd had since coming here. She wanted life back the way it was, back to orderliness and structure. Back to her quiet world.

Beside her a deep snore erupted from Max. At least he was sleeping. Now if only she could quiet her own nightmare. After taking a few calming breaths, she began counting backward from one thousand in multiples of twenty-three.

Ten

Meridith tugged the sheet and tucked it tightly under the mattress. In the doorway, Ben ran his fingers up the painted doorframe, humming. He'd hardly left her side since he'd rolled out of bed.

The Browns' room was tidy, the bed hardly slept in. The room still bore the lingering remnants of old lady perfume. Meridith pulled up the quilt and fluffed the pillows.

After gathering the dirty towels, she went to the laundry room to retrieve a fresh stack, Ben following. The leftover smells of cinnamon and bacon filled the house, and Meridith felt a swell of pride that breakfast had turned out so well. The Browns had raved over the cinnamon rolls and quiche Lorraine, making her efforts worthwhile. Of course, Noelle had taken one bite of her roll and pronounced it subpar to her mother's. Meridith wasn't about to admit it had taken her two tries to get them right.

Still, she was glad it was Saturday and she could spend the day bonding with the kids. And best of all—no Jake.

"When are we leaving?" Max stuck his head into the laundry room. He seemed to have recovered from the nightmare, especially when she'd mentioned the idea of golf lessons after breakfast.

"As soon as I'm finished with the Browns' room. Give me fifteen minutes, and would you tell Noelle to be ready?"

The girl had been in the shower half an hour, and their lessons were in thirty minutes.

None of the children had golfed before, but they seemed eager to learn. Or maybe they were eager for a distraction. Staying busy was a wonderful coping strategy.

Meridith was delivering the towels when a knock sounded at the front door. It was too early for the Browns' return. Besides, they had a key.

Ben followed her down the steps. Max was nearly to the door.

"I'll get it," Meridith said. Didn't the children have any sense of safety? He couldn't even reach the peephole.

She leaned into the door and peeked through the hole. Jake smiled at her with that cocky grin of his.

She huffed, pulling the door. "What are you doing here?" And with tools, she thought, her gaze running over his leather tool belt.

"I work here."

"It's Saturday."

"I work Saturdays." His eyes went over her shoulder, and she heard Max shuffling his feet behind her.

"I'm sorry, I should've clarified the hours. Monday through Friday will do."

"Thought you'd want that partition finished at least."

Her mind raced back to the scare the night before when she'd heard Max scream. She did want that thing finished, but she couldn't leave the man here without supervision. What if he robbed them blind? Robbed the Browns blind?

And staying was out of the question. The children were excited about the golf lessons, and they had to come first. Besides, she was sure the Browns were harmless.

"I'm sorry, but the children and I have plans today, so I'm afraid—"

"That's okay!" Max said in a peculiar rush. "I mean, we can have lessons another time, right, Ben?"

"Uh, right." Ben nodded thoughtfully, looking more grown-up than his seven years.

Strange, she'd thought they'd be disappointed.

"It's settled then." Jake stepped in, nudging her aside.

"Now wait a minute, I made reservations," she said, and then addressed Ben and Max. "And boys, I think Noelle was looking forward to this."

"I'd rather stay," Noelle said from the stairs. Her hair had been carefully styled into a fashionable ponytail. "I mean, lessons are cool, but I'd rather just hang around here today anyway."

Meridith eyed the kids one by one. Maybe there was a strange virus going around. Or maybe they were secretly eager to get that partition up too. Maybe after losing their parents they needed security.

Jake tossed her a smug grin and started up the stairs. So much for a peaceful day.

Meridith spent the morning doing laundry and prep work for the next day's breakfast. She checked on Jake a few times, but couldn't bring herself to hover as she had the day before. Even so, just having him in the house ruined her sense of serenity. She needed to make sure he wasn't coming the next day. Surely he didn't work Sundays.

She made the children a simple lunch, then they disappeared upstairs again, even her tagalong. At least they were together. Their muffled laughter seeped through the ceiling as she stuffed the towels in the dryer and started the cycle.

That done, she went out back to enjoy the unseasonably warm day for a few minutes.

The grass had greened up after the rain a couple days before, and the sun shone brightly in a sky so blue it hurt her eyes. She sank into one of the Adirondack chairs on the beach and closed her eyes.

A breeze ruffled her hair and pebbled the skin on her arms. She should coax the children outside to enjoy the fresh sunshine and soak up some vitamin D. She was surprised they weren't outside enjoying the reprieve from winter.

The waves lapped onto the shore in quiet, relentless ripples. A seagull screeched from somewhere down the shoreline, and another bird replied. She missed home, the comfort of her padded swing, her tall shade trees and scented lilac bushes. If she closed her eyes and blocked out the sound of the waves, she could almost imagine that she was back home in her garden, dozing on her swing under the tall oak—

"Hey, Meri!"

Jake's voice shattered the illusion. She craned her head around, following the sound of his voice to an upstairs window. His elbows perched lazily on the ledge.

She glared up at him. "*Meridith.*"

"Wanna come take a look?"

She'd rather beat the smug grin off his face. "Be right there."

Her bones ached as she climbed the main stairway, a repercussion of her night on the hard floor.

Just beyond the guest loft, Jake stood in front of the doorway, making some final adjustment to the latch. It looked different with the area closed off from the hall. The smell of wood and some kind of chemical hung in the air.

"What do you think?"

He'd already hung the drywall, and the patching was drying, which explained the smell.

He swung the door open, showing her the thumb-turn on the other side, then closed the door and demonstrated the lock with the key.

Thank you, Vanna. "Are both doors keyed the same?"

"Yep." He threw her the new set of keys, and she caught it clumsily. She'd keep one set in her room and find a hiding spot in the kitchen for the other.

He gathered his tools and supplies.

Now that he was finished, maybe she could take the kids to the driving range. She could teach them how to tee off.

Jake capped the drywall compound, then walked through the new doorway toward the family suite.

"Where are you going?" Meridith followed him down the hall.

"Patching up the other partition."

"I thought you were done."

"If I get them both patched, they'll be ready to sand and paint on Monday. You got any more of this green?"

"What? I don't know."

He trotted down the back stairway and unlocked the new door's thumb-turn.

Meridith stopped at the top of the steps, sighing. The sooner he finished, the sooner he'd be out of her life. Out of the house, she corrected herself. That man was not in her life. From the base of the stairs she heard the scraping sound of the putty knife against the wall.

Feeling eyes on her, she turned to see the children standing in the doorway of Noelle's room.

ॐ   ॐ   ॐ

Jake flattened the knife against the wall, filling the crevice. It was all he could do to smother a grin. He didn't know which he'd enjoyed more, spending a couple hours alone with the kids or finding new ways to provoke Meridith. And to think he was getting paid.

Maybe once she went back outside, the kids would come down and pretend to play a game at the kitchen bar while they talked.

He could hear Meridith talking to them now, asking them about the game they'd supposedly been playing, acting all interested in their activities. If she really cared about them, she wouldn't be ripping the kids from Summer Place just so she could go back and live happily ever after with her fiancé. And he was pretty sure that's what she was planning.

Their voices grew louder, then Jake saw them all descending the steps. Noelle led the pack, carrying her Uno cards, followed by the boys, then Meridith.

Noelle winked on her way past.

Little imp. The kids perched at the bar, and he heard the cards being shuffled. Dipping his knife into the mud, Jake sneaked a peek. Meridith was opening the dishwasher. Great.

Ben kept turning to look at him, and Jake discreetly shook his head. Even though Meridith faced the other way, no need to be careless.

"Noelle, you haven't said anything about your uncle lately. He hasn't e-mailed yet?"

He felt three pairs of eyes on his back. He hoped Meridith was shelving something. Jake smoothed the mud and turned to gather more, an excuse to appraise the scene.

Meridith's back was turned. He gave the kids a look.

"Uh, no, he hasn't e-mailed."

"Or called or nothing," Max added.

Noelle silently nudged him, and Max gave an exaggerated shrug. *What?*

"Well, let me know when he does. I don't want to keep pestering you."

"Sure thing," Noelle said, dealing the cards. Her eyes flickered toward him.

"I was thinking we might go for a bike ride this evening," Meridith said. "Maybe go up to 'Sconset or into town. You all have bikes, right?"

"I forgot to tell you," Noelle said. "I'm going to Lexi's tonight. I'm spending the night."

"Who's Lexi?"

"A friend from church. You met her mom last week."

A glass clinked as she placed it in the cupboard. "Noelle, I'm not sure how things were . . . before . . . but you have to ask permission for things like this. I don't even know Lexi, much less her family."

"*I* know them."

"Have you spent the night before?"

"No, but I've been to her house *tons* of times."

He heard a dishwasher rack rolling in, another rolling out, the dishes rattling.

"Why don't we have her family over for dinner one night this week? I could get to know them, and then we'll see about overnight plans."

"This is ridiculous. They go to our church, and her mom and my mom were friends!" Noelle cast him a look. *See?* she said with her eyes.

Did Meridith think Eva would jeopardize her daughter's safety? The woman was neurotic. Jake clamped his teeth together before something slipped out.

"Just because they go to church doesn't necessarily make them safe, Noelle. It wouldn't be responsible to let you spend the night with people I don't know. You never know what goes on behind closed doors."

"My mom would let me."

The air seemed to vibrate with tension. Jake realized his knife was still, flattened against the wall, and he reached for more mud. Noelle was glaring at Meridith, who'd turned, wielding a spatula. Was she going to blow it?

To her credit, the woman drew a deep breath, holding her temper. "Maybe Lexi could stay all night with you instead."

"Well, wouldn't that pose a problem for *her* family, since they don't know *you?*"

Despite his irritation with Meridith, Jake's lips twitched. Score one for Noelle.

"I suppose that would be up to her family."

He heard Noelle's cards hit the table, her chair screech across the floor as she stood. "Never mind." She cast Meridith one final glare, then exited through the back door, closing it with a hearty slam.

Eleven

A week later Meridith ran her hand over the new door trim and surveyed the paint job. The sunny yellow matched the rest of the kitchen, and the finished wall was smooth as glass.

Ben touched the wall too. He hadn't left her side since he finished his homework.

"It's a beautiful day outside, Ben. Why don't you go enjoy the fresh air?"

He shrugged.

"Max is outside. Maybe he'll play Frisbee with you."

Silently Ben ambled toward the door and slipped through it.

Meridith turned her attention to the new partition, stepping back. You couldn't tell it was new. The trim had been painted white to match the old trim, and hard as she tried, she couldn't find a paint run anywhere. Not bad.

"Everything okay?" Jake appeared at her side.

"Would you stop sneaking up on me?" she said, unwilling to admit that the insanely loud washing machine may have disguised his entrance.

He nodded toward the partition.

She forced her eyes from his. "It's fine." She wasn't about to admit she'd been admiring his handiwork. He might raise his price. "How's the gutter coming?"

It was falling off the back of the house, its angle leaving a small pond off the back porch steps when it rained.

"All done. Have to run to the store for a few things." He placed his hands on his hips, just above his tool belt.

She checked her watch. "You might as well call it quits for the day." She was ready to have the house back, at least until her guests arrived.

He nodded once. "Just let me gather my—"

A sharp cry split the air, then was silenced by a thud. Meridith was out the door the next second.

She crossed the porch and found Ben near the puddle on his side. He pulled his knees into his belly, bawling.

"Ben!" Meridith pushed Piper aside and squatted beside the boy, carefully rolling him over. "What happened?"

"He fell off the ladder!" Max dropped to his knees beside his brother.

"You left the ladder up?" Meridith glared at Jake, but he was running his hand over Ben's head.

"Don't feel any bumps."

"My arm!" Ben wailed.

Jake reached toward it.

"Don't touch it!" Meridith said. "Can you move it, Ben?" She touched his arm lightly.

"Nooooo . . ."

"What happened?" Noelle appeared at her side.

"He fell," Meridith said. "I need to get him to the ER." Then she remembered. "The guests . . ." How were they going to get in? Someone needed to greet them. She couldn't think with Ben howling.

"It's okay, honey," she said. "We'll get you taken care of."

Jake gathered Ben in his arms. "I'll drive you to the ER. Noelle, stay here and check the guests in. Max, you stay with her."

A thirteen-year-old running the inn? She didn't think so. "Call Rita and see if she can come," she said, following Jake.

"I've checked in guests lots of times."

Meridith tossed a look over her shoulder. "*Call* her."

Noelle glared. "Fine."

Meridith followed Jake around the house to his truck. Piper followed silently, head low as if sensing the trouble.

"You don't have to do this," Meridith said. "I can drive myself."

"Get in," Jake said.

Once she was settled on the cracked leather seat, Jake placed Ben on her lap. The boy curled into her, cradling his arm.

"He needs to be buckled in."

"He's fine."

Jake hopped in the driver's side and backed down the lane.

Ben had quieted, his breaths coming in shuddery spasms. She had a bad feeling his arm was broken.

"How you doing, little man?" Jake asked once they were on the main road.

"Fi—fine." The word wobbled pitifully.

"How far's the hospital?" Meridith asked.

"Seven, eight minutes."

Meridith gripped the door as Jake took a corner fast. She nearly told him to slow down, but Ben's whimpering stopped her. She hoped they'd give him something for the pain immediately.

It was nice of Jake to give them a ride, but she wondered how they'd get home. She'd have to call a cab or ask Rita to come after them.

It seemed like an hour later when Jake swung into the hospital parking lot. She tightened her hold on Ben as he screeched to a halt at the ER doors.

Jake put the truck in park, and Meridith fumbled for the doorknob.

"I'll get him." Jake rounded the truck, opened her door, and pulled Ben carefully from her arms.

Once inside, she approached the admissions desk while Jake set Ben in a chair.

"I'll park the truck," he said. "Be right back."

Jake stood when Meridith entered the waiting room. A nurse wheeled Ben to the door, which opened automatically. Ben's cast looked wet and heavy. His eyes were closed, his head lolling against the chair back.

"How's he doing?"

"He's nicely sedated," the nurse said, then turned to Meridith. "Here's the prescription, and you'll need to make an appointment with his pediatrician."

Meridith nodded. "What about school?"

"He should be able to go back Monday. Is he right-handed?"

"Uh, yeah."

"That's good. He might need those painkillers the next couple days, and remember to keep the cast dry."

"I'll get the truck." The chill in the air felt good against Jake's heated skin. He'd hated waiting in the lobby while Benny was so upset, but he could hardly insist on going back. Besides, it had given him time to pray for the kid. As if the boy hadn't already suffered enough, now this.

He felt awful about the ladder. Guilty. And he hated the way it felt. Like he'd let Benny down again.

The kid was fine now, though, he reminded himself. Resting peacefully. He was glad they'd given him pain meds. Meridith had probably insisted. He'd been surprised she already had the kids on her insurance. But on second thought, he expected no less.

When he pulled the truck to the door, the nurse wheeled Benny out. Jake picked him up and set him in the middle. By the time he was behind the wheel, Ben was slouched across Meridith's lap.

"He's sound asleep," Meridith said. She set her hand on the little boy's shoulder awkwardly, as if she didn't know where to put it.

"Best thing for him." He turned toward the pharmacy.

"Where are you going?"

"Pharmacy."

"You don't have to do that. We've kept you out late enough."

"He'll need the pain meds in the morning." Jake turned on the heat. Meridith was probably cold in that short-sleeved sweater.

While they waited for the prescription, she called home and checked on the kids again. He could tell from her end that the guests had arrived and retired to their room.

She was still on the phone with her friend when he pulled out of the pharmacy parking lot. "No," she was saying. "You go on home. We'll be there in a matter of minutes . . . Did he ask me to return his call?"

Lover Boy must've called. Jake eased around a corner, then flipped off the heat.

Meridith closed her phone.

"Your friend headed home?"

"Yes. Her daughter needs help with math."

As silence settled around them, he reviewed the evening for

the dozenth time, remembering the grimace on Meridith's face when Ben had fallen, the worry lines etched across her forehead. If he'd doubted she cared about the kids, those doubts had faded. Maybe she went about it wrong, but there'd been no mistaking her concern.

All that time in the waiting room had given him too much time to think. She seemed far too normal to be bipolar. Some quirks, sure, but nothing dangerous or crazy. But, he reminded himself, a person with bipolar disorder could have frequent and extended periods of normality between the depressed and manic phases. He had to remember that. Couldn't let those sea-green eyes beguile him.

"Thanks for the ride. That was above and beyond."

"Wanted to be sure the little man was okay. My fault anyway." He'd be more careful in the future. No ladders left standing, no nail guns left on.

"I shouldn't have said that."

"Shouldn't have left the ladder up."

"Let's just call it an accident. The doctor said it was a minor break. Should heal in three to four weeks."

Ben shifted, heaved a deep sigh, then settled.

"Just glad he's not in pain anymore. He'll have fun drawing pictures on the cast, getting autographs. When the itching starts, tell him to use a blow drier set on cool to blow air inside it."

"You've broken an arm?"

"And a leg and a wrist."

"Oh my. You must've been a handful."

He chuckled. "And then some." He had a feeling some of his escapades would shock the stockings right off her. But with the kind of childhood he'd had, he was lucky he wasn't rotting in jail.

"Never broke a bone?" he asked.

She shook her head.

She'd probably never stepped in a mud puddle, much less broken a bone. The same could probably be said for her anal-retentive fiancé.

Not fair, Walker. You don't even know him.

He glanced at her hand in the darkened cab. The diamond glimmered under a passing streetlamp—an ordinary solitaire diamond. Boring. He'd buy his woman something unique, something that suited her, something different and special. Not that he had a woman.

"Sit tight," he said after he pulled into the drive and put the truck in park. He came around and opened Meridith's door, then eased Ben into his arms. Even with the wet cast, the kid weighed nothing. He was small boned like Eva, but Jake was sure he'd lost weight in the weeks since his parents died.

The house was quiet and dark except for a lamp in the living room. Meridith set the pharmacy bag on the kitchen island and unlocked the door to the back stairs. Ben slept soundly through it all.

"That room," Meridith whispered when they reached the landing, reminding Jake he wasn't supposed to know the way.

The moonlight flooded through the sheers, offering a beam of light.

"Top bunk." She dashed around him to pull back the covers.

Jake lifted Ben over the railing and set him down gently, supporting his casted arm.

Meridith climbed two rungs up the ladder and eased Ben's Nikes off his feet.

Jake drew the covers to the boy's chin. He hoped Ben would sleep through the night. The arm was going to hurt like the dickens when the meds wore off. He wished he could stay and tend to him.

From the bottom bunk, Max let out a noisy snore. Jake turned to smile at Meridith, but she was gone. She appeared two seconds later with an armload of bedding, which she dropped on the floor.

She gestured for him to follow her from the room. The stairs creaked loudly as they descended.

"Thanks again for your help," Meridith said once they reached the kitchen.

"No problem."

She fetched a glass and filled it with water. With her back turned, Jake studied the way her dark hair shimmered in the stove top's night-light, the way it swung easily with each turn of her head.

"Maybe you shouldn't come tomorrow," Meridith said. "The noise and all. Ben will need his rest."

Jake pocketed his hands. He needed to make sure the kid was okay. "I'll work on something quiet. Maybe outside. Besides, you're not going to keep that little boy in bed all day."

"I guess that would be okay." She ripped open the pharmacy bag, removed the amber container, and set it by the water. Looked like she was preparing for a long night.

"I'll get out of your hair." He walked toward the back door.

"Where are you going?" She followed him.

"Taking the ladder down like I should've hours ago."

"Oh." She folded her arms against the chill in the air, and he noticed again how little she was. Barely to his shoulders. Her chutzpah made him forget her small stature.

Her chin was a pixielike triangle, and her eyes were like a shadowed forest. Deep. Mysterious.

"Well. Good night," she said.

What was he thinking? He cleared his throat. "Night."

As he retrieved the ladder and carried it to his truck, he reminded himself of all the reasons why he shouldn't be noticing her hair or her chin and most definitely not her deep-green eyes.

Twelve

Meridith was thrilled to have the house to herself after a hectic weekend with guests, church, and helping Ben adjust to his cast. He was down to Tylenol, had slept through the night, and this morning had been eager to show off his new cast at school.

With Jake working outside it was almost like having an empty house. Today, she decided, she would clean out Eva and T. J.'s room. Clearing out their belongings would help the kids adjust and move on. Leaving the room as some kind of shrine wasn't healthy.

She spent the morning packing clothes. Eva's taste had been simple, mostly jeans, tunics, and T-shirts. T. J. had a few nice things hanging in the closet, but the casual clothes in the chest seemed to be the staples of his wardrobe.

When the clothes were packed away, she set the boxes on the porch for the charity that was picking them up, then she stripped the bedding and washed it.

She'd found a large box of photos and mementos in the closet and carried it to the living room to sort. As she set the box by the hearth, she decided a roaring fire would be relaxing. She'd seen a stack of logs at the side of the house.

After carrying them in and finding a lighter, Meridith poked around until she found the flue. Pushing it upward, she felt the draft and set to work lighting the fire, starting with the kindling she'd gathered and placed at the bottom of the stack.

When the kindling caught, she rolled up yesterday's newspaper and encouraged the flame. The logs were dry and should make for an easy light.

But the smoke was going the wrong way. She leaned over the tiny fire, closed the flue, then opened it again.

The fire grew, and smoke rolled past her. What in the world?

Maybe she had the flue closed instead of open. She pulled the handle and waited for the smoke to drift upward.

The log caught fire, and the smoke increased, pouring into the living room.

She moved the handle back the other direction. No change. Was something blocking the opening? She turned, coughing.

Maybe she'd better extinguish it before the smoke detectors went off. She went to the kitchen for the fire extinguisher she'd seen in the cupboard.

"What the—" Jake's voice carried from the living room.

"I know, I know," she exclaimed, grabbing the extinguisher. So much for a nice relaxing fire. Why did everything in this house have to be so difficult?

She pulled the pin as she rushed back toward the living room through the thick wall of smoke, coughing and waving her hands as she approached the fireplace. She aimed the extinguisher and pulled the handle. Nothing.

She squeezed again to no effect, then noticed as the smoke cleared that the fire was already out. Jake was pulling up the old window sashes.

"You trying to burn the place down? That fireplace hasn't been used in years."

"Well, how was I supposed to know that?"

"The inch of dirt in the grate?"

"I thought it was ashes." She set down the extinguisher and opened another window, coughing. "What's wrong with it anyway?"

"Bird's nest, cracked flue pipe, who knows?"

The smoke was slowly rolling out the windows, the air inside clearing. "Shouldn't the smoke detectors be going off?"

He opened the door, heedless of the bugs that were probably coming in. "Count your blessings."

Great. Something else wrong. Maybe they needed fresh batteries.

"I'll have a look at the fireplace later if you want."

"The smoke detectors are priority one now. Start on that next," she said, still stung by his tone.

He gave a mock salute and left the room.

Meridith carried the box of photos into the kitchen and set it on the island. Not as comfy in here, but at least she could breathe, and she had plenty of room to sort.

She opened the window and door to air out the room, then settled on a stool. The photos had been tossed into the box haphazardly. She found pictures of T. J. and Noelle in the Galaxie for some parade, mixed with photos of Christmas and Ben's birth.

As she sorted, an idea formed. She'd make an album, one for each of the children, something to remember their parents, their family. As the idea settled, she became excited as she anticipated their responses. She would buy special acid-free albums and use scrapbooking decorations as she'd done for her own high school scrapbook. It would be a keepsake the children would treasure all their lives.

Meridith began sorting the photos by child. She'd worry about chronology later. She found a photo of Max when he was younger, sitting on a motorcycle with a man who could only be Uncle Jay, but a black helmet covered the man's head. Too bad. She was curious to see what this paragon looked like. And there didn't seem to be any other photos of him. Strange.

She paused over a recent photo of Noelle with her mother cuddled on one of the Adirondack chairs down by the shore. It must've been spring or fall. Eva, wearing a periwinkle hoodie, had her arms wrapped around Noelle and smiled with her whole face. Noelle's head rested on her mother's shoulder, and she turned a shy smile toward the cameraman—her father?

Meridith felt a tweak of jealousy. The photo captured a moment of contentment between Eva and Noelle, and Meridith knew instinctively it was the norm, not the exception. Noelle was a lucky girl to have been loved that way.

The second the thought formed, she chided herself. How could she be jealous of a relationship that had just been stolen from the child? She was certain Noelle didn't feel lucky at all. Though maybe someday, when they were on better terms, she'd articulate how blessed Noelle had been to have loving parents.

Meridith laid the photo in Noelle's pile and pulled a small shoebox from the larger box. She opened the lid and found the box filled with more memorabilia.

A smoke alarm beeped loudly. At least Jake was working on them.

She withdrew a paper from the shoebox and unfolded it. It took a moment for the words to register, for the title to ring a bell.

The heading read *Restaurant Hospitality Magazine* and below that was an article on food safety in restaurants—her article. It was printed off the computer. Her photo was centered on the page.

She stared at the paper as if it would explain itself. How had her father acquired it? Why? Maybe Eva ran across it while doing research for Summer Place and printed it out.

Meridith set the article aside and grabbed a rubber-banded stack of greeting cards. Maybe she should turn the children's albums into scrapbooks, so she could include the cards and pictures they'd drawn.

She removed the rubber band and opened the first card. Her hands froze as she read the signature. *Love, Meridith.* The writing was large and sloppy, the size of the letters inconsistent. It was a birthday card. She opened the next card. Father's Day, her signature.

Her heart drummed out a hard, heavy beat. Christmas. Father's Day. Birthday. At least twenty cards, some with a sentence or two accompanying the signature. *I love you, Daddy. You're the best.* Then the later ones. *I miss you, Dad.*

She closed the card in her hand, bundled them back into the rubber band. So he'd kept her cards. Big deal. Would've been nice if he'd picked up the phone and asked if they had grocery money. If they'd been evicted. If her mother was conscious.

She wanted to toss the shoebox aside, but she forced herself to finish. A few coloring-book pages; a cheap ring, warped and tarnished; school photos; a poem written on pale-green primary writing paper:

> *Daddys give hugs and kises*
> *Daddys make hambergers on the gril*
> *Daddys read bedtime storys*
> *Daddys love*

Meridith wadded up the paper and threw it into the wastebasket. Daddies don't leave their child with an incompetent parent.

Daddies don't remarry and forget their firstborn child. She'd written him letters, waited for him to contact her. Sometimes she'd nearly picked up the ringing phone, praying it was him, even though her mom had forbidden answering it because of the bill collectors. Eventually she stopped writing, stopped hoping. Her mom said her daddy had left her, too, and it was best she just put him from her mind.

Her first year in college she'd finally gotten a few letters from him. But it was too little too late, and she'd discarded them unread.

She looked down at the stack. But he'd saved all these as if he cherished them. Was it possible . . . what if he had written her, and her mom had disposed of his letters? What if he'd called, and she'd told him Meridith didn't want to speak to him?

Meridith forced herself to grab the last few things in the shoebox. Then she could throw it away and forget what she'd found. Forget these memories and the questions they stirred.

The photos took her by surprise. She flipped through them, four all together. They were of her. Her high school graduation. Her college graduation. How did he . . . ?

Maybe her mother had taken them, sent them to her dad. But no, she would never have done that. And her mother hadn't even attended her high school graduation.

How had he gotten them? No one had attended her high school graduation. But there she was in the picture, walking across the stage. And there she was afterward, clutching her diploma, her long hair fluttering in the breeze. The college graduation pictures were taken from a distance, zoomed until the shot was grainy.

Was it possible . . . ? But he couldn't have been there. Why would he come so far, get so close, and not speak to her? Why wouldn't he hug her and tell her he was proud of her? Because she hadn't responded to his letters and calls? Because he thought she didn't want to see him?

Her breath seemed trapped in her lungs by the knot that swelled in her throat. She had to get out of there.

The stool squawked across the floor and she fled outside, across the porch and down the steps toward the beach. The air nipped at her flesh, raising goose bumps, and she curled her arms around herself.

She stopped at the edge of the lawn where the grass gave way to the sea oats and sucked in air like it would clear her lungs. It was the smoke. That's why her eyes burned, her throat ached.

Had her father come to her graduations? She let time rewind, reliving her high school ceremony. She'd waited in the folding chair for her name to be announced, wishing, not for the first time, that her last name didn't put her near the end of the alphabet.

"Meridith Elaine Ward."

Returning to her seat among the 212 graduating seniors, Meridith felt lonelier than she had in all her life. If it were true, if her father really had been present that day, had come all that way and watched her receive her diploma, she wasn't sure which she wanted to do most: hug him or hit him.

Not that it mattered. It was too late to do either now. Her eyes fell to an old piece of driftwood just inside the sea oats. Some time in the past it had been pulled from its home by a storm and spent heaven knew how long drifting aimlessly before reaching shore. Only to lay here, discarded for months or years.

"Meridith."

The sound of Jake's voice startled her, made her heart jump into the next gear. Why was he always sneaking up on her? She turned, glaring.

"Sorry, I—" He stopped a car's length from her.

She realized belatedly how she must look. Her eyes still burned, were no doubt red. She faced the shore, cleared the knot from her throat.

"I—checked out the smoke detectors," he said. "Batteries are old."

The wind whistled through the budding trees, stirred the wind chimes on the front porch. "Great. Thanks." She rubbed her arms.

"The ones upstairs are working." His voice was closer. "Need to run to the store and get more nine-volts and some other things."

"Okay." She wished he'd leave, go get the stupid batteries. She drew in a deep cleansing breath. Salt, grass, and Jake's woodsy scent filled her nostrils.

"Sorry if I was out of line in there," he said. "I get testy some-times—was having trouble with the porch spindles, shouldn't have taken it out on you."

He thought she was teary-eyed because he'd snapped at her. If she were that sensitive, Noelle would have her in tears on a daily basis.

She waved away his apology. "Don't worry about it."

The muted ring of the phone saved her from an explanation. "Excuse me."

She hurried to the phone, catching it on the fourth ring.

"Meridith, hi. It's Rita."

Meridith greeted the woman and thanked her again for staying with the children while she ran Ben to the ER.

"I know it's late notice," Rita said, "but it's turning into a nice day, and I wondered if you'd want to have a picnic lunch at Brant Point. You probably haven't had much chance to see the island."

"No, I haven't." She could go. She trusted Jake alone at the house now, but she also preferred to keep to herself, especially where this island and friends of her father and Eva were concerned.

The back door closed as Jake entered. She heard his heavy footfalls across the kitchen floor. He was going to get batteries, but that wouldn't take long. Suddenly she longed to get out of the house, away from Jake and the memories she'd long since thought dead and buried.

"Actually, lunch sounds great," she said.

Thirteen

The wind flipped the blanket's corner, and Meridith anchored it with the basket. "You should've let me bring something." Beside her, the solid white structure of Brant Point Lighthouse squatted, guarding the harbor. Out on the sound, a lone sailboat drifted by.

"You have enough on your plate." Rita set her can of Diet Coke in the sand and brushed the crumbs from her hands. "How are the kids doing? Noelle seemed distracted Friday, but she was probably worried about Ben."

"I think they're okay, all things considered. Noelle's a little sassy, but that's typical teenager behavior, right?"

Rita chuckled. "If mine are anything to go by."

Meridith finished the chicken salad sandwich, washed it down with a sip of Diet Coke, and leaned back on her elbows. "The sun feels heavenly." She'd spent too many hours cooped up in that house. With Jake.

"Wait until summer. It's a different island come July."

Meridith didn't mention that she wouldn't be around then. Rita might not understand her reasons for returning, and she didn't want to spoil the day with conflict.

"Tell me about your life in—St. Louis, is it?"

Meridith nodded. "I'm a health inspector for restaurants and hotels. Well, I was. My boss wasn't happy about my leave of absence, so I'll be looking for another job when I return."

Three seagulls flew overhead, their cries piercing the air.

"You'd think he'd be more sympathetic. Any family back home?"

She remembered the last time she'd seen her mom. Buzzing around the bedroom on a cleaning spree, her auburn hair awry.

Meridith shook away the thought. "No, there was just my mom, and she passed away a couple years ago."

"I'm so sorry. You're awful young to lose both parents. But you have your siblings."

"That I do, though I'd never met them until now."

"Wow. This must've been quite a shock. I can't help but notice you have a man in your life." Rita tapped Meridith's ring with the pad of her index finger. "That is some ring."

"Stephen's an accountant. We met four years ago at one of the restaurants I was inspecting."

A seagull set down at the shoreline.

"Love at first sight? Oh, I love a good story."

Meridith smiled. "Not really. We sort of—grew into love. He proposed on Christmas Day."

"What a great present! When's the big day? Getting custody of the kids must've thrown a real kink into the works."

"We haven't set a date yet. I never was one for a big wedding, but Stephen and his family want one. And now we—need time to sort things out." She needed to change the subject. "Are you a stay-at-home mom?"

"Oh, heavens no, our mortgage doesn't allow that. I own the Broad Street Gallery."

"You're an artist?"

She laughed. "Uh, no. I just appreciate fine art and buy the pieces I like, mostly from local artists. In fact, that's how I met your father."

"He was an artist?"

"You didn't know?"

"We weren't very close. In fact, I hadn't seen him in years."

"Hmm. Well, boat repair work kept him busy during the warm months, but in the winter he created driftwood sculptures. He was good, one of my more popular artists."

"The sculptures at the house must be his, then. They're very unusual."

"I asked him once what inspired him to take up such a unique craft. He said he enjoyed taking something so carelessly uprooted and making it into a thing of beauty. That really stuck with me."

"Hmm."

"He must've trusted you a great deal to leave the kiddos in your care. Has Eva's brother been reached yet? I know they were close."

"We haven't heard from him. Do you know him?"

"Our paths haven't crossed, but Eva talked about him a lot." The wind caught Rita's hair, and she shook it from her face.

"I was surprised he wasn't their first choice for guardian, frankly," Meridith said.

"Well, they must've had their reasons. He seems to travel a lot and, well, he's a bachelor. If he hasn't called home in all these weeks, that tells you a lot. I'm sure T. J. and Eva knew what was best for the kids."

"Most days I don't feel like I have a clue."

Rita chortled. "Welcome to parenthood."

Meridith returned her smile. Maybe that's just the way it was. The thought was liberating and daunting at the same time. Would things never settle down? Would she always feel powerless to help Ben and Max, unable to handle Noelle?

No, her life would calm down when she was back in St. Louis where she belonged. The children would settle in and make friends. It would be fine. Meridith tilted her head back and closed her eyes and let the sun warm her face. The sounds of the rippling water disquieted her. The wind tugged her hair this way, then that. Was it ever quiet and still here?

"Things will be easier once you and the kids get familiar," Rita said, echoing her thoughts. "Plus you're learning to run a new business, honey. And Noelle said you were having work done on the house?"

Meridith opened her eyes, watched the seagull hop down the shoreline into the foamy water's edge. "I hired a guy to fix a few things, trying to get the place up to code."

An image of Jake formed. Jake on the ladder, thick arms stretched overhead. Jake on the kitchen floor fixing the leak, his long legs extended. Jake carrying Ben into the hospital, cradling him against his chest.

What was wrong with her?

"He, uh, seems competent."

Rita eyed her strangely. "Well. That's good."

"He fixed the dishwasher leak, and the gutters are back where they're supposed to be, and he's going to replace the boiler and fix the fireplace. I made the mistake of starting a fire this morning and filled the house with smoke. I don't know what's wrong with it, but Jake will figure it out. It's a shame to have a nice stone fireplace and not be able to use it." She clamped her lips closed. Why was she running off at the mouth?

"Jake, huh?"

"Mm-hmm." Meridith drew her knees up and dug her toes in the cool sand.

"Is he good-looking?"

Meridith's laugh wobbled. "I don't know." She pictured Jake's crooked smile, his strong jawline with that perpetual stubble. "I suppose, if you like the—the rugged mountain man kind of thing." She turned tables on Rita. "Why do you ask?"

"I have a single sister. I've introduced her to every man at church, and none of them are cute enough or funny enough or Christian enough."

Cute was the wrong word for Jake, and he was *funny* only if you counted sarcasm. He had mentioned going to church though. She considered having Rita and her sister over one day when he was there. Maybe they'd hit it off. It was the heavy thump in the center of her stomach that made her hold her tongue.

"He's kind of arrogant," Meridith said. "And stubborn." But the picture that formed in her mind was the one of Jake lifting Ben into his bed, of the look on his face when he'd come outside earlier and caught her on the verge of tears. "I don't think your sister would like him."

"Hmm. Well." Rita let the word hang.

The seagulls screeched, filling the silence, and Meridith dug her toes deeper until her feet were buried in the cool packed sand.

Fourteen

"My goodness." Meridith examined Ben's cast. "There's hardly room for another signature."

The kids had just come through the doors, slinging book bags, shrugging out of jackets. Max and Noelle had gone upstairs as usual, but Ben was eager to show off his cast. Meridith felt refreshed after her picnic with Rita, more relaxed than she'd felt since her arrival.

"What's this?" Meridith pointed to a flower in red ink.

He rolled his eyes. "Heather Taggart drew it. I'm gonna scribble it out. I can't have a *flower* on my cast."

Meridith laughed, but the sound was cut off by a scream from upstairs. *What in the world?* Meridith took the steps two at a time, then ran through the hall to the family wing.

Noelle stood at her parents' bedroom door, her chest heaving, her expression something between horror and anger.

"What? What is it, Noelle?"

Max was in his parents' room, pulling drawers. Ben appeared at her side, cradling his cast.

"What did you do?" Noelle yelled, her face turning red.

"Noelle, calm down. I just cleaned out your parents' clothes. I thought—"

"Where are they?" She ran into the room, into the closet. "They're all gone! What did you do with them?" She appeared at the closet door, tears coursing down her face.

A stone lodged in the pit of Meridith's stomach, hard and heavy. "I—I gave the clothes away to people who need them. I kept the important things—"

"It's all important! Where are they?"

Jake appeared beside her, frown lines pinching his brows. "Everything okay?"

"What did you do with their things?" Noelle said.

Meridith wished the boxes were still on the porch, but they'd been gone when she'd returned from the picnic. "I gave the clothing to the thrift shop. I saved a couple—"

"You had no right!" Noelle screamed. Her arms stiffened at her side, her hands fisted.

"Where is it?" Max mumbled, still rifling through the drawers.

It took Meridith a moment to hear his quiet question. "What are you looking for, Max?"

"Dad's hat. His special fishing hat. Where is it?" His face was turning blotchy, his hands searching frantically.

What had she done? She'd only meant to help.

"You threw out their parents' things?" Jake asked.

"No, not *threw out*—I gave them to the thrift shop. Not everything." She stepped closer to Noelle. "There's a whole box of things downstairs . . ."

"You had no right!" Noelle flew past Meridith, grazing her, running into her room. Her door slammed so loudly the glass pendants on the chandelier rattled. Prisms of light sliced across the walls.

The sounds of deep wrenching sobs carved a hole in Meridith's middle. She stood immobile. Should she try to comfort Noelle, explain to Max that his search was futile, or put an arm around Ben, who stood like a frozen statue?

"You shouldn't have done that." A hard edge lined Jake's calm words.

Ben darted two steps toward Jake, threw his arms around the man's middle. His face disappeared into Jake's tool belt somewhere between the hammer and caulk gun.

Meridith's eyes flitted up to Jake's. His eyes widened and his mouth slackened, then he curled his arm around Ben's head.

The twinge of betrayal twisted into a hard knot.

A slamming drawer drew her eyes to Max. She stepped into the room. "Max, I'm sorry, but it's not here. I only kept a couple items of clothing, and I didn't keep the hat."

She remembered it, though. It had been navy blue with a bird or waves or something. The bill was frayed and stained with dirt, and she'd nearly tossed it into the trash pile.

Max turned to her, his eyes brimming with tears. "It was his special hat."

Meridith felt another slug to her middle. "I didn't mean to hurt you, Max. I was only—"

He rushed past her, fleeing into his own room. His door clicked shut. Noelle's sobs could still be heard from across the hall.

"Maybe you should've asked them first."

"Maybe you should mind your own business," she said, still stung by the children's reactions, still reeling with her own guilt. What right did he have to judge her? She'd had only the best intentions.

She thought of Max's quiet, desperate search for the hat. Maybe she could get it back.

She looked at Ben, still in the protective cradle of Jake's arms. That wasn't good. Not healthy. The man was a virtual stranger, for goodness' sake. She supposed the trip to the ER had bonded them, and the boy was no doubt missing his father. Still, Jake was a transient in Ben's life. It would do him no good to get attached.

"Come on, Ben," she said gently. "Let's go downstairs and have a snack." She pierced Jake with a look. "Jake has work to do."

A shadow flickered on his face, and he stared back, defiant. Ben didn't budge.

What right did the man have? Who did he think he was? She gave him a pointed look.

A moment later Jake released Ben. "Go on, little man." He rubbed Ben's head as the boy turned away.

Ben ambled down the back stairs, and Meridith turned to follow.

"Wait." Jake's eyes were dark as midnight in the hall's shadows, the chandelier at his back.

"What?" she asked.

He waited until the sounds of Ben's footsteps faded. "I know you think this is none of my business, but you can't just clean their parents out of their life. They need to remember them, not forget them."

T. J. had been her parent, too, or had Jake forgotten that? "You're right. It's none of your business." She turned to go.

Jake grabbed her arm. "They've been hurt enough."

"I didn't mean to hurt them."

Noelle's sobs filled the gap.

"You don't know anything about loss, do you? Well, I know all about it, and these kids need help." He jerked his head toward Noelle's room. "She needs comfort."

"She won't let me, I've tried!"

"You think you can just walk into her life and expect her to confide in you? You're a stranger. You have to earn her trust. And Max spends too much time cooped up in his room, working on his models."

"He enjoys it."

"He needs to talk."

"He talks plenty."

"And all Ben does is cling."

Meridith shook off Jake's hand. "He's just affectionate."

Jake put his hands on his hips, looked away. He pressed his lips together.

From behind door number one Noelle dragged in a shuddery breath. If Meridith thought for one second it would do any good, she'd go in there.

Jake faced her again, his eyes snapping.

Meridith didn't wait around to hear what else he had to say.

Meridith couldn't sleep. The children's reaction, combined with Jake's, left her shouldering a heavy load of guilt and remorse. She turned over and stared at the dark ceiling. She wondered what Jake had meant when he'd said he knew all about loss. What kind of childhood had he had? What kind of pain had he suffered?

She could almost feel pity for him, except for his other comments. *You don't know anything about loss, do you?* Especially that one. He didn't have a corner on the loss market. She'd lost plenty, starting with her dad. The losses with her mother were more complicated. Loss of childhood, loss of security, loss of stability.

She remembered waking to a loud noise one night when she was ten. A loud clank jerked her from sleep. Her digital clock read 3:21. She pulled Emily, her Cabbage Patch doll, close into her side, listening, eyes wide in the darkened room.

A soft clatter sounded. Her heart thudded against Emily. Maybe it was her mother. But Mom had hardly been out of bed for weeks. Only for work, then she came home and disappeared under the covers until morning.

Meridith wanted to shut her door and lock it. But didn't burglars have special tools to open doors? Besides, her door was old rickety wood. A grown man could kick it in if he wanted. That's what happened in apartment 4B last year.

She had to get to the phone and call 911. If she could just make it to the living room . . . Meridith slipped out of bed, set Emily down, and tiptoed across the stiff carpet.

Her mother's room across the hall was dark, the door half shut. A glow came from the kitchen, and Meridith crept along the wall. The noises increased as she neared the living room. She became aware of a smell.

Something sweet. Cake. The smell of it filled her nostrils, made her stomach grumble.

She rounded the corner. Her mother swept across the linoleum in her floral nightgown, waving a spatula. She cradled a bowl against her stomach and was stirring ferociously.

A buzzer rang, and Mom set down the bowl, pulled a pan from the oven, then set it on the counter with what looked like two hundred other cupcakes. Bags of flour, sugar, and chocolate chips were scattered everywhere.

She saw Meridith. "Oh, honey, I'm glad you're up. Come, sit down. Mommy has wonderful news!"

Meridith moved slowly across the sticky carpet. She climbed onto one of the bar stools overlooking the sea of cupcakes. Chocolate ones, vanilla ones. Some of them iced with pink, others as naked as her Totally Hair Barbie doll.

"I'm going to start a bakery business! I quit my job. Who needs that lousy, boring job anyway? I'm going to make cupcakes and cookies and, here, taste this."

She handed Meridith a cookie, and Meridith slid it into her mouth, chewing tastelessly.

"Awesome, huh? I can't wait until morning, I'm going to call all the local grocers and restaurants. I'm going to call it Simone's Sweets, don't you love it?" Her blue eyes glittered under the bright kitchen lights. "Don't you like that name, Simone?" She said it with a foreign accent. "I'm going to change it tomorrow—so much more elegant than Susan, isn't it? Aren't you happy, baby, what's wrong?"

"Nothing, Mommy." Her mother's auburn hair hadn't been washed in days, and it stuck to her scalp at the top, but the rest was tossed and ratty like she'd just roughed it up good.

"Once all the grocers and restaurants around here start carrying my baked goods, I'll open my own shop, and we'll make a fortune! No more living in this run-down apartment, no sirree! I'm going to buy my baby a house in Lindonwood Park with the rich folk, what do you think of that? And once my sweets hit it big, I'm taking it national! A whole chain of Simone's Sweet Shops!"

"But—but what about your job, Mommy?"

"Ugh, you sound like your daddy. Don't be such a spoilsport! This is my new job, and it'll be so much more fun! You can help me bake—here, stir this—and we'll build it together. Tomorrow you can help me make fudge and candies, and then we'll take samples around to every grocer in St. Louis, and once they taste our awesome sweets, they'll order up a big batch—all of them!"

"Tomorrow's Wednesday, Mommy. I have school."

"Oh! That's right. Well, you can help me when you get home. We'll have so much fun together and make a fortune, just you wait and see!"

Meridith set the bowl and spoon down and looked at the stove clock. "I think I'll go back to bed."

She thought her mom might argue, but she was already scooping batter into the baking cups and humming "Achy Breaky Heart."

Meridith slid off the stool and returned to her room. How were they going to pay rent if her mom quit her job? She had slid under the covers and pulled them over her head, knowing she wouldn't go back to sleep.

Now, Meridith turned over and pulled the feather pillow into her belly. Simone's Sweets hadn't gotten off the ground, hadn't been picked up by the grocers or restaurants. Within a matter of weeks her mother was back in bed, her dreams of the bakery business fading as quickly as the leftover aroma of cupcakes.

Fifteen

Two days later Meridith returned home from the Nantucket Atheneum with an armload of books on grief and children. She sneaked them to her room, avoiding Jake, who was replacing the chandelier in the dining room.

Since the big blowout two days earlier, a new tension had invaded the house. Noelle was barely speaking, Ben clung to Noelle instead of to Meridith, and Max buried himself in his boat model project. Even though Meridith had gone to the thrift shop and retrieved the hat. Even though she'd offered to take the children and buy back anything they wanted.

It had apparently been the concept, not the clothing, that mattered. Meridith wished she could alleviate the children's pain. Her own guilt had morphed into a pervasive ache.

Jake had changed, too, growing more distant, speaking only when necessary. The mood in the house was stilted and awkward and made Meridith want to crawl into bed and pull the covers over her head. But she wasn't ten anymore.

A loud crash sounded downstairs, followed by Jake's grumbles. He'd been so grouchy. She did her best to avoid him, though it wasn't easy when he worked in the main living areas. She'd already run every conceivable errand. She'd stocked the cupboards, had the oil changed in the van, bought Ben some button-up shirts that allowed for ease of change with his cast. She'd even gone to the driving range and hit a bucket of balls, just to stay away awhile longer.

The phone rang, and she rushed down the main stairway to answer. She retrieved the extension, catching sight of Jake through the dining room doorway.

"Summer Place, may I help you?" She injected the words with an enthusiasm she didn't feel, watching as Jake ran the utility knife blade through the tape of the new light fixture's box.

"Hi, honey."

"Stephen. I'm glad you called. You must be on lunch break."

The utility knife paused for a beat.

"I realized it's been three days," Stephen said. "Time just seems to leak away during tax season."

"I miss you, too, sweetheart," she said warmly.

She could see Jake's muscles strain as he pulled at the fixture, but the box wouldn't release its contents. He set his foot on it and jerked.

Meridith's lips twitched.

Stephen was telling her about a new tax law, but the show in the dining room was more entertaining. As the box released the fixture, Jake's elbow connected with the table's edge. *Thwack*. He dropped the light fixture and kicked the empty box across the room.

Meridith pressed her lips together and turned her back.

". . . and then I said, 'Welcome to accounting 101.'" Stephen laughed.

In the other room she heard Jake slamming something down. Hopefully not her new light fixture.

"What's all the racket?" Stephen asked.

"That's the contractor. I'll go upstairs where it's quieter." Her feet were already moving in that direction.

"How's the one kid's arm—Sam?"

"Ben. He's coping, keeping it dry, and he's sleeping through the night. He's down to an occasional Tylenol now."

"You poor baby. You must be exhausted."

"You have no idea." She entered her room, shutting the door behind her, and told him about the fiasco with the clothes and the fallout with the children.

"You did the right thing. They might be upset, but they have to move on. The sooner they do, the easier it will be. Have you heard from the uncle yet?"

"No. I hope something hasn't happened to him."

Stephen gave a weak laugh. "I sure hope not. I want you back sooner rather than later."

She should tell him now—tell him she had to keep the kids. Tell him Uncle Jay wasn't fit to parent them.

"Oh, there's someone on the other line, a client. Gotta go."

"See you," she said, but they were disconnected before the last word left her tongue.

She'd tell him next time they talked. Stephen was the most rational, even-tempered man she knew. They were two of the qualities she appreciated most in him. He'd see how important keeping the children was, especially in light of her childhood.

But if she was so certain of that, she wondered, why did she continue to postpone the conversation?

ॐ ॐ ॐ

Stupid cheap bracket. Nothing was going right today. Or the day before. Jake had been so preoccupied earlier he'd forgotten to shut off the electric and had gotten zapped good. Then when he'd shut off the electric, he'd whacked his head on the corner of the fuse box door.

All he could think about was the fiasco that had shaken the kids and left them brooding. He kept seeing the look on Max's face when he talked to him after Meridith went downstairs, kept remembering the way Noelle's fists had clutched his shirt as she sobbed into it, soaking it with tears.

And then there was Meridith. The look on her face when she'd realized what she'd done, how she'd hurt the kids. That hadn't sunk in until after his anger had burned off. And the fact that Meridith's feelings mattered at all ticked him off.

Who was she but an interloper who'd usurped his rightful place? She had no clue what she was doing. Monday's debacle had proven it.

But that look . . . the way she'd crossed her arms over her belly like she was nursing a wound.

After he'd left for the evening, he'd gone tooling around the island on his Harley. He'd needed to clear his head, but all he thought of was Meridith and what she'd done. And then that look. Back and forth he'd gone. Anger and resentment warring with compassion and pity. It was about to drive him crazy.

Get on one side of the fence or the other, Walker.

Ever since he'd arrived that morning, he'd been aware of her every move. Her steps on the stairs, the creaking floor over his head, the quiet hush of running water in the kitchen. He was relieved when she left. And then the house felt empty. Too empty. He spent the whole time she was gone wondering where she was and when she was coming back.

But then she returned, and he reverted to tracing her every movement. Up the stairs, then back down to answer Lover Boy's call.

He'd been glad she'd taken her conversation upstairs. It bugged him to hear her crooning to her fiancé. Then it bugged him that it bugged him.

What was wrong with him? Maybe he'd whacked his head so hard he'd knocked a few marbles loose.

He finally got the bracket in place and set a screw. The powerful whirring of the screwdriver gave him a scrap of pleasure. He felt like doing something physical. He'd have to set up a game with Wyatt soon to blow off steam. And beat the pants off his friend. That would help, a little friendly competition.

When he set down the screwdriver, he heard the squeak of the floorboard at the top of the stairs and found himself wishing Meridith would leave again. She stirred something in him, and he wasn't sure he liked it. He had to keep his wits about him. Had to think of the kids, watch for signs of instability. Signs like throwing out their parents' belongings.

He set another screw in the bracket and drove it in. The bit slipped off the screw and rammed into his thumb. A deep growl escaped his throat.

He wished Meridith would leave so he could focus on the stupid light fixture.

He was setting the screwdriver down when he heard her light footfalls on the stairway. Then a wad of keys jingling. And the front door closing.

Sixteen

Meridith pedaled the bike down the lane. Her shallow breaths drew in salt-laden sea air. She was glad it was Friday. The kids would be home all weekend, and she could try some of the books' suggestions for coping with grief. She'd read on the beach all morning, had lunch at the Even Keel Café, but now it was time for the kids to return from school.

Even though Jake's demeanor had relaxed as the week waned, there was still a stiltedness to their conversation. He was all business now.

And that's just the way I want it. Meridith turned onto Driftwood Lane. Leaves were coming in on the trees, hiding the skeletal branches. A carpet of purple crocuses bloomed at the base of a mailbox. In the next yard, a line of daffodils edged the drive. Not yet blooming, their pale buds stretched over tongues of green leaves. Spring was underway, and she was ready. Ready for more time outdoors, ready for sunshine and golf. Ready for school's end when she could return to her home, to Stephen.

With her three siblings in tow. She envisioned Stephen meeting the crew at the airport.

Hi, honey, here we are, your ready-made family of five.

She tried to picture his reaction and failed.

Well, of course she couldn't. She hadn't told the man yet.

When she reached Summer Place, she turned into the drive, skirting Piper and Jake's dirty truck, then pulled into the garage beside the Galaxie. According to Mr. Thomas, the old car had been willed to the kids' uncle, along with T. J.'s tools. She was sure he'd be delighted, if he ever called.

She set the kickstand, entered the house through the front door, and checked the voice mail. No customers, but Max's teacher asked her to call back.

A scraping sound across the room startled her. Jake emerged from the fireplace grate. Soot covered his hands and streaked his cheek.

"Want to come look?"

Her mind still on the message from the teacher, she approached the fireplace. Jake made room on the hearth.

"See these cracks? Crumbling mortar, loose stone. Feel this." He reached for a river rock, and she touched it.

He placed his hand over hers and wobbled the rock, but she barely felt the movement for the jolt that went through her at his touch.

She jerked her hand away.

His eyes scanned her face, which grew warmer by the second.

She studied the blackened rocks as if mesmerized by them. "So the, uh, loosened rocks caused it to smoke?" Was that her squeaky voice?

"Right."

She still felt his touch on her hand, though it was now cradled safely in her lap. She ran her other palm over it and felt the protrusion of her ring.

Stephen. Wonderful, steady Stephen.

She still felt Jake watching her. She was probably glowing like hot coals by now. Confound it.

"So, you can, uh, patch it or something?"

"Or something."

She wondered if the amusement in his tone was caused by her question or the fact that she'd ripped her hand away as if he'd jabbed her with a poker. She flickered a glance at him, but it stuck and held.

The amusement slid slowly from his face, replaced by something else. Something that made her stomach feel as if it contained a batch of quickly rising dough.

You just had to look. Heat radiated off his arm, inches away, and flowed over her skin. She could smell the faint scent of pine and musk.

She looked away. Told her heart to stay put. Deep breaths. She sucked in a lungful of his woodsy scent. *Ix-nay on the eath-bray.*

Meridith jumped to her feet and put distance between them.

Jake cleared his throat, then leaned into the grate. "Don't see any daylight."

Back to business. "That's good, right?"

"Not if you want to use this thing. Flue's blocked. Debris or bird's nest, could be anything."

"You can fix it?"

He pulled out of the grate, wiping his hands on his jeans. "Sure."

Meridith hated how unsettled she felt around him. And the faulty fireplace only prolonged his presence. Why did he have to make her feel this way? Why did she have to keep reminding herself this was business?

"Can you draw up a separate bid?" she asked.

"Sure."

She gave a nod, then returned to the phone to where she'd jotted Mrs. Wilcox's number and waited for her heart to get a grip. Thank God he couldn't read her mind.

She dialed Mrs. Wilcox, and the teacher picked up on the second ring.

"Thank you for returning my call, Ms. Ward." The teacher's voice was young and soothing. "I know Max has been through a trauma, and I've been keeping my eye on him, talking to him, giving him extra attention."

"Thank you. I appreciate your concern."

"I thought he was doing okay until today."

"What happened?" Meridith leaned on the check-in desk, listening intently.

"There's an event tomorrow night, Shining Star. I'm not sure you've heard. It's a parent-child talent show we're trying this year. I'm coordinating it."

"No, I hadn't heard."

"Well, I'm afraid I goofed. I printed the list of participants without checking it, and—well, Max is on there. He and his mother had planned a ballroom dance presentation."

"Oh. I didn't know." Poor Max. She wondered if he'd been thinking about it all week.

"The list was posted for participants to see the dress rehearsal order today. I heard some kids being cruel to Max at recess. I handled the situation, and the other boys are being appropriately disciplined, but I'm worried about Max."

Meridith closed her eyes, aching for the boy. "Thank you for letting me know and for handling the situation."

"Max was noticeably upset through the afternoon, and when I removed the list from the wall, I saw he'd marked out his and Eva's names. In fact, he scribbled through the names so hard it left a hole in the paper."

"Oh, I see."

"I tried to talk to him after school, but there wasn't much time before he had to catch the bus. I just wanted you to know."

Meridith thanked her, then hung up. She felt so bad for the little guy. So helpless. All those books she'd read had nothing about this sort of thing. How was she supposed to know what to do?

"Everything okay?" Jake's voice cut into her thoughts.

The screech of brakes announced the bus's arrival.

"Fine." Or would be. Eventually.

When the children scrambled through the door, she caught sight of Max's mottled face and red eyes. All the books had recommended helping children express their feelings, so maybe she could start there.

After she greeted them, she asked Max to follow her into the dining room while Noelle and Ben disappeared upstairs.

Max plopped into a chair, the weight of his body sagging downward. Someone had written on his pale arm in ink, though she couldn't read it upside down.

"Max, Mrs. Wilcox called and told me what happened today."

His eyes flashed at her. "Toby and Travis are stupid morons." He crossed his arms.

She'd expected sorrow, not anger. "Do you want to talk about it?"

He looked down at the table. "No."

Okay, now what? The books said children need affection when they're grieving. Not her strong suit.

She set her hand on his tense arm. "I'm sorry about the talent show." Did the words sound as awkward as they felt? She was no good at this touchy-feely stuff.

Max blinked rapidly. Maybe she'd said the wrong thing. Maybe she was making it worse. But she was doing what the books recommended.

She tried again. "Were you looking forward to it?"

Max sniffed, then nodded his head. In the next room she could hear the squawk of the flue opening.

"How did you learn to ballroom dance? That's quite an accomplishment for a boy your age."

"My mom taught me." He glanced at her. The anger had faded from his eyes. "I'm pretty good."

"I'm not surprised." She liked the way he'd perked up. It was good to see his confidence emerging. Too bad he couldn't showcase his talent for tomorrow's audience. She was certain it would be beneficial.

"Is there anything else you could do for the show? What other talents do you have?"

Max shrugged. "Nothing, really." His feet shuffled under the table. "'Cept being a goalie and building boat models, but I can't do those for a talent show."

"Is there some other kind of dance you could do?"

"It's too late to come up with a new dance. The show's tomorrow. Besides, it's for a parent and their child." His eyes pulled down at the corners, and he ducked his head.

"I wish I could help, but I don't know how to ballroom dance. I guess it wouldn't be the same without your mom anyway."

His head lifted. Hope sparkled in his eyes. "You could learn."

"Oh, I—I think it would take longer than a day, Max." Meridith laughed uneasily. "Especially for me."

His head and shoulders seemed to sink. "I guess you're right. I only know how to lead, and I don't know how to teach it."

"I know how." Jake appeared in the doorway, filling it with his broad shoulders and tall frame. "Didn't mean to eavesdrop."

"He could teach you!" Max's eyes widened. He looked back and forth between Jake and Meridith.

"Oh," Meridith said, "We couldn't ask—"

"I'm offering," Jake said. "I can be here bright and early tomorrow morning."

Max's dimple hollowed his cheek.

"No, I—you don't understand, the show's tomorrow night, and I'm a bad dancer."

Jake leaned against the doorframe, crossed his arms. "You said you wanted to help."

"Well, I do, but I don't see how—you know how to ballroom dance?" The notion suddenly struck her as unlikely.

"I can do more than swing a hammer."

"I didn't mean—"

"So you'll do it?" Max bounced on the chair.

She hadn't seen him this excited since she'd arrived. She looked at Jake. At his wide shoulders, thick arms, sturdy calloused hands. She remembered the look in his eyes just minutes ago and imagined herself trapped in the confines of his embrace for as long as it took her to learn the dance. Which would be about, oh, a few years.

"And why would you do this?" It wasn't as if he owed her anything. Unless he was punching the time clock on the lessons.

"Let's just say I was picked on a time or two myself."

Max rubbed his hands together. "Toby and Travis, eat your heart out!"

"Now, hold on. We already missed dress rehearsals. I don't know if Mrs. Wilcox will let us slip in last minute."

"Call her," Jake said.

He had all the answers, didn't he? She spared him a scowl as she slid past on her way to the phone.

"Hi, Mrs. Wilcox? This is Meridith Ward again." She looked over her shoulder.

Max waited, Jake standing behind him, thumbs hooked in his jeans pockets, looking all smug.

"I was wondering. If Max can get a replacement for the dance, could he still participate?" *Please say no.* "I know he's missing dress rehearsals and—"

"That would be no problem whatsoever." Mrs. Wilcox sounded delighted. "We'd fit him in and be glad to have him. Have you found him another partner?"

"Uh, looks like we have."

She thanked Mrs. Wilcox and hung up, then turned to face a hopeful Max.

"What did she say?" he asked.

Meridith swallowed hard. "She said they could work you back into the schedule." She cast Jake a plea. "But I don't know if I can do this. I wasn't kidding, I have no rhythm whatsoever."

"Look at the kid. You can't say no to that."

Max was grinning from ear to ear.

It was Meridith's shoulders that slunk now. Heaven help her. She winced and forced the words. "All right. I'll do it."

Max let out a whoop and threw his arms around her.

Seventeen

"What if potential guests stop in?" Meridith asked.

Max and Jake moved the sofa against the wall. The living room was quickly becoming a dance studio.

Jake straightened to his full height. "That happen often?"

"Almost never this time of year." Ben unplugged the lamp and moved it aside.

If Meridith had been anxious the night before, it was nothing compared to her response upon seeing Jake at her door. His hair was damp, like he'd just stepped from the shower, and he spun a roll of blue painter's tape around his index finger. He wore a black polo, fitted jeans, and a furtive grin. How had she gotten herself into this?

"Noelle, grab the stuff on that table," Jake said.

Surprisingly, the girl complied. Maybe she was glad her little brother was getting his chance onstage.

After moving the coffee table, Jake rolled up the rug, Ben assisting from the other side. Only one week with a cast and he was one-handing things like he'd done it all his life.

"Be careful, Ben," Meridith said.

She watched them prepping the room with a sense of impending doom. The thought of dancing for an audience in ten hours was almost as distressing as the thought of being in Jake's arms all morning. Maybe ballroom dancing would be easier than she thought. It was just a few steps, and Max had learned it, right? How hard could it be?

"You know, I don't have any music," she said. They couldn't dance without music, right?

Jake whipped an iPod from his jeans pocket. "I'm sure one of you kids has a dock."

"I do!" Noelle bolted off, taking the stairs two at a time.

Wasn't she the eager beaver.

Jake knelt on the floor, pulled a strip of blue tape, and tore it with his teeth.

"What are you doing?" Meridith asked.

"Taping off a square."

"Won't it mar the wood?"

"It'll come right off." He tossed her a look that let her know he saw through her excuses. "Are you done?"

She pressed her lips together, hating the heat that crept into her neck. She rubbed it with her sweaty palm as if she could massage it away.

By the time he finished the box, Noelle had reappeared with her iPod dock, and Jake set it up on the hearth.

"Okay, we're set," Jake said.

Noelle perched on the displaced sofa, leaning forward, a smirk curving her lips. "This should be good."

Now Meridith understood why the girl had been so eager.

"Don't think so," Jake said. "Off you go, all of you." Jake shooed the grumbling children from the room, and Meridith felt like kissing him.

She cleared her throat.

"Take off your shoes," Jake said after the kids disappeared up the stairs.

Meridith eyed her leather loafers. For some reason, she was reluctant to part with them. Not to mention she needed every inch of height.

"You're still wearing yours."

"I'm not planning on trampling your feet."

She removed her shoes and set them by the wall, taking her time. "You want something to drink? I made coffee. Or there's always tea or soda if you prefer."

He tucked the corner of his lip. "No, thanks. You want to come closer? I can't teach you from over there."

She inched closer. "I'm really bad."

"So you said." He gestured to the blue box. "We'll start with a basic box step. Ballroom dancing is counted off like this: one-two-three, one-two-three. Max said he knows how to lead, so I'll teach you to follow."

"Good luck with that."

"Stand right here." He placed her on the upper right corner of the box. "The first count, step back with your right foot. Good."

"Shouldn't we start the music?"

"Don't think you're ready for that. Bring your left foot back with your other foot, then sweep it to the other corner."

Meridith tried that. So far so good. She went back to the beginning position and did the entire step. "One-two-three. I did it."

"That's just the one and two count. The third step your feet are together on the bottom left corner of the box." He demonstrated slowly from where he stood. "One-two-three."

"Oh, I see." She mimicked the move with painstakingly slow movements.

"That's it."

Though the steps were right, she was sure she resembled an elephant in high heels. At least he wasn't laughing. Yet.

He showed her the next three counts, up and around the front left corner of the box and back to start. "So it takes two counts of three to complete the box. Why don't you try it?"

"Okay." She went to the start position and proceeded slowly. "One. Two. Three." And then she was stuck.

"Left foot forward."

"One. Two. Three."

"There you go. That's all there is to it."

She gave a wry grin. "Except ten times faster and in sync with a dance partner."

"Exactly. Do it again."

"Tyrant."

"What's that?"

"Nothing." She went through the steps slowly again. Then again and again until she could perform them at normal speed. Even though the steps were right, her movements felt awkward, more like she was on an espionage mission than a dance floor.

She stopped midstep, huffing. "Something's wrong . . ." Her voice came out in a whine. She knew she'd be no good at this. What if she embarrassed Max in front of his friends?

"Let's talk posture." He placed his hand in the small of her back. "Straighten your spine."

She arched her back, more to escape his touch than anything.

"Good. Shoulders back. Maintain this posture while you do the steps."

She tried the steps again, concentrating on her posture. It took all her focus to do both. She completed the box and started another one.

"Good posture not only makes the dancer look better, but is essential for communication between the—"

Her steps faltered. "Shush!" She glared at him, and was rewarded with a smirk. "I can't think with you yammering."

He motioned her on.

Back straight. Shoulders back. One. Two. Three. One. Two. Daggonit.

"Try again."

Meridith took the starting position and did a slow turn around the box.

"Good. Again."

She completed three more box steps, going a little faster each time.

"Posture," Jake said.

By the time she'd made a few more turns, she was beginning to feel like she might have a chance. She turned a satisfied smile at Jake.

"Not bad. You're getting there."

She practiced the move a few more times, then he turned on the music and counted it off for her. The song was mercifully slow, and she was able to move at the right tempo.

Ten minutes later Jake stopped the music. "You're ready for a partner."

It took no more than those words for her heart to go off like a jackhammer. "I'm not sure about that."

"We're on a time crunch here, and you need to practice with Max too."

"Where did you learn to dance? No offense, but you don't seem like the ballroom type."

"You stalling, or you really want to know?"

He'd see right through a lie. "Both."

He appraised her, then seemed satisfied with her answer. "Had a foster mom who was a dance instructor. She thought a boy should know how to dance."

She wondered what had become of his real parents, but he didn't offer and she wasn't asking.

"Haven't had much use for it till now, though. More of a Texas two-step kind of guy."

"Two-step? And you're teaching me a dance with three steps?"

"Fewer steps doesn't make it easier. All right, enough stalling."

His approach launched a nervous ripple through her. He stopped a breath away. She stared at the V of his open polo.

"The height difference will be a challenge. It'll be easier with Max. But for now, you don't want to stand toe to toe." He moved to her right until his foot was between hers.

"Put your hand here."

His upper arm was solid beneath her palm. The heat emanating off him made her own temperature kick up a notch.

"Thumb to the front, fingers to the back. Give me your other hand."

He curled his hand around hers, and her heart stuttered. Her eyes focused on his leather corded necklace that disappeared under his collar.

"Right, like that." He settled his hand on her back.

She got a whiff of his woodsy cologne and wondered how long she could hold her breath.

"This is the basic position. It's important to maintain your space. No noodle arms, got it?"

"Got it." She stiffened her arms, all the better to keep him at a distance.

"Let's go through the basic box step slow. I'll count it off."

She drew in a breath and blew it out slowly through her mouth.

"Five. Six. Seven. Eight. One-two-three. One—that was my foot."

"I *know* that was your foot." She pulled her arms away and rubbed the back of her neck with her cold hand. She couldn't think when he was so close. Didn't like the way he made her feel, all agitated and nervous and awkward. Why was she doing this to herself?

"Let's try again."

"I don't think I can do it."

"You'll get it." He took her in his arms.

Meridith took another calming breath. *Focus.*

He counted them off and took them slowly through the box step. This time she made it around without treading on him.

"You got it. Again." They repeated the box step a dozen more times, faltering a few times when she stepped on his foot or knocked him with her knee.

"Again," he said over and over each time she misstepped.

When they were almost up to tempo, Meridith started feeling more confident. She could do this. One-two-three, one-two-three. She *was* doing this.

"Straighten up, Quasimodo."

Did he have to be so rude? She shot him a glare. If it was posture he wanted, it was posture he'd get. She pulled herself up to her full five foot three.

In her concentration on posture, her steps suffered, and she trod on his foot.

He stopped. "Too much give in your arms. When they're loose, I can't lead you. You can't feel where you need to go. Close your eyes."

"What?"

"Close your eyes. Communication between partners is through subtle movements. I'm waiting."

She sighed hard but closed her eyes. Suddenly all the periphery details now took center stage. The feel of his fingers on her back, his thumb aligned under her arm. The roughness of his palm against hers. The manly smell of him.

"Maintain resistance."

No problem there.

"Your arms are like spaghetti, Meri."

"*Meridith*." She stiffened her arms. Her mouth felt as dry as sand. She didn't like that he could see her and she couldn't see him.

"Better. Let's go through the box step again with your eyes closed. Feel me guiding you with my arms." He counted them off, and they started around the box slowly.

Her feet knew what to do by now, and he was right. She could feel him guiding her if she kept her arms rigid. They went around and around the square. She never stepped on his feet, though she felt the slight brush of his thigh against hers.

He gradually picked up the tempo, then held it once they reached a reasonable pace. Her movements were starting to feel almost fluid, if not exactly graceful. She could do this. Max was going to be so happy. Those boys wouldn't have any reason to make fun of him when they saw him onstage tonight. She could hardly wait to see his face when—

Meridith didn't know what happened. One moment she was glorying in her achievement, the next their feet were in a tangle, and she was falling backward.

Eighteen

Jake caught Meridith as she stumbled backward, tightening his arms around her. He pulled her toward him instinctively, breaking her fall.

She clutched his hand, his shoulder, helpless against gravity.

He drew her upright and realized she was nestled against his chest. Then he realized something else.

He liked it.

His right arm had curled around her impossibly small waist. His other hand trapped hers against his heart. He wondered if she could feel its heavy thumps. If she knew it was more than her sudden stumble that caused it.

Her moss green eyes widened. Her lips parted as if she were surprised to find herself pressed against him. He could feel her breaths coming and going, feel the warm puffs of air against his neck.

Have mercy, he wanted to kiss her. Lay one on her and let the pieces fall where they may.

Sudden strains of music broke the silence. Meridith blinked, then dropped her arms and jerked away like he'd electrocuted her.

"My phone," she mumbled, racing for her purse on the check-in desk.

Jake's empty arms complained. He turned and made a production of looking for a song on the iPod.

Behind him, Meridith answered the phone. "Hi, Stephen."

He reveled in the breathless sound of her voice even as he cursed a man he didn't know.

"Oh, nothing, I—was just helping Max with a—a project. Dancing, actually. I'm going to be in a talent show with him tonight. It was kind of a last-minute thing, but I think . . . Yes, I said dancing . . ."

Jake flipped through the tunes, unseeing. She probably wished they were done, but he still had to teach her to travel, and she and Max had to practice together.

"Actually, I'm doing pretty well."

He grinned to himself, remembering the near fall she'd just had. Then he remembered what came afterward, and the grin slipped away.

"I am. Listen, I have to go. Klutzes like me take time to teach."

Jake placed the iPod back in the dock and turned.

"No, I'm not mad." She'd lowered her voice to a near whisper. "All right. Bye."

She closed her phone, then took an eternity tucking it into her purse. When she turned, her face was the bland mask usually reserved for customers. "Now. Where were we?"

꒱ ꒱ ꒱

Jake dribbled the ball toward Wyatt. Score was thirteen to six, and he was on the winning end. Somehow that wasn't as gratifying as he'd expected.

The afternoon sun glared off the white concrete pad outside Wyatt's house, and when Jake sucked in a breath, the smell of freshly cut grass filled his lungs. Little early in the season to mow, but who was he to question?

He gave his watch a quick glance. He had fifteen minutes before he had to shower. He wasn't missing Max's moment for anything, even if it did mean hiding at the back of the auditorium.

He had time to put up at least four or five more shots.

"So let me get this straight." Wyatt hunched down, lowering his center of gravity as Jake approached. "This Meridith chick has custody of your niece and nephews."

"Yep."

"And you want custody."

Jake faked a left and spun, then drove the ball in for a clean layup. "Yep. Fourteen."

"Yeah, yeah." Wyatt ran his forearm across his forehead, making his curly bangs stand out at an odd angle. He caught the ball and took it out. "And she's engaged."

"Yep."

"She possibly has bipolar disorder."

"Uh-huh."

"And you ended up in an embrace today when you were teaching her to dance."

"Did I stutter?"

Wyatt drove the ball in, but Jake headed him off, using his height to his advantage, and forced Wyatt to back off.

"Just saying." Wyatt dribbled the ball to the other side.

Jake followed his every move, eager for a chance to pounce. He swiped at the ball, but Wyatt swapped hands.

"You're supposed to let a guy win on his own court, didn't anyone tell you?"

"I pay rent."

"Barely."

"What do you expect for that dinky little garage apart—"

Wyatt took advantage of his distraction to drive the ball around him and put it up. *Swish.* Wyatt took a lap, feigning the sound of a roaring audience.

"Get a grip, dude, you're losing bad."

"Depends how you look at it."

"Only so many ways to look at a fourteen-seven score."

Wyatt shrugged, palming the ball in both hands. "Way I figure, I have a beautiful wife inside, and you're playing footsie with your engaged, possibly mentally ill adversary." He chucked the ball at Jake, grinning. "You do the math."

Nineteen

There weren't enough calming breaths in the world to settle Meridith's attack of nerves. She and Max took their spot behind the curtain and waited for the trumpet duet to end.

"I'm scared." Max's hand was cold and clammy.

"Relax. You're a great dancer, and you look very handsome." They'd practiced the dance over and over until Meridith was sure she was going to dance in her sleep tonight. If she made it through this.

A squawk sounded from a trumpet, then a second later a note resonated and hung in the air.

It was their turn.

Max had his eyes closed, his lips moving silently. *Say a prayer for me too*, she thought. What if she stepped on his toes? What if she stumbled backward as she had with Jake? What if they ended up sprawled on the dusty stage floor with strains of music flowing by them?

The curtain parted, the mechanicals squeaking as the curtain *whooshed* open. The noises were lost in the applause for the trumpeters as the girl and her father disappeared stage right.

Mrs. Wilcox appeared at the microphone set off to the side. "And now we will enjoy the elegant ballroom dance of Maxwell Ward and his sister, Meridith."

Meridith turned toward Max, but her eyes caught on someone deep in the darkened auditorium. It looked like . . . but it couldn't be.

Before her eyes found him again, the spotlight switched on, bathing her and Max in a warm puddle of light.

She gave him a confident smile. *Breathe, Meridith, breathe.*

The music began, and they counted off six beats silently. Then together they moved in harmony through the first box step. Once they made it around twice, she began to breathe again. Her feet remembered the steps. Thank God.

Spine straight. Shoulders back. Arms rigid.

Max led her around the stage. She felt the swish of her dress against her knees. One-two-three, one-two-three. The spotlight seemed to spin in her periphery. She kept her eyes on Max, just a few inches beneath her line of vision.

His hand clutched hers, squeezing the blood from her fingers. Nerves. She remembered to smile, performing the steps carefully. She was doing it. They were doing it. Round and round they went. Just another minute or so and it would be over.

As they whirled to the right, Meridith caught sight of Noelle and Ben in the front row. She hoped they were cheering their brother on.

One-two-three, one-two three. Spine straight. Shoulders back. Arms rigid.

Max was a good leader. Not as good as Jake, not as firm, but his height made the movements less awkward. The spotlight lost them, then found them again.

A few more times around. One-two-three, one-two-three. She made eye contact with Max, a silent signal that the end was coming.

One-two-three, one-two-three, and . . . the big finish and . . . done! The music ended as her skirt settled around her knees.

The audience began to applaud, and Meridith shared a relieved smile with Max. They took their bows, the curtain drew closed, and they were shrouded in darkness as they trotted offstage.

꒰ꓴ   ꒰ꓴ   ꒰ꓴ

After the show, Meridith and Max met up with Noelle and Ben in the foyer.

"Nice job, little bro," Noelle said.

"Yeah, you guys looked like pros," Ben said.

"I'm so proud of you, Max," Meridith said.

Max flung his arms around her, and Meridith staggered backward. "Thanks, Meridith."

Meridith put her arms around the child. "You're welcome, honey. You did really good." He was a soft cuddly bear. His hair, freshly washed, smelled like oranges and sunshine.

When the crowd thinned, they went to The Soda Fountain for ice cream to celebrate. Riding home in the van later, Meridith got the first real slice of success since she'd arrived. They'd made it through the dance with flying colors, Max was happy, Ben was noticeably proud of his big brother, and even Noelle seemed to have put her dislike for Meridith aside for the night. Maybe things would work out after all. She caught a glimpse of a possible future with the children, happy and settled in her St. Louis home, and she smiled, content.

Back at the house, they exited the van. Max put Piper in the garage, and Meridith grabbed the mail.

"Up to bed, guys. It's late." She smothered a yawn. What a long day.

There was a message on the machine, but it could wait until morning. She flipped through the mail and was ready to set the stack down when she came to the last one.

It was from the tax collector's office. She slid her finger under the flap, dread kindling in the pit of her stomach. She shook the feeling away. It was probably concerning the transfer of ownership.

She pulled out the letter and unfolded it. Her eyes skimmed the words, the dread in her stomach spreading like wildfire. *Nonpayment of taxes . . . delinquency . . . taking of said estate . . . fourteen days.*

Fourteen days? Her eyes dropped to the amount due on the last line, and the breath left her lungs. How could she not have known?

Why would her father and Eva have all that money in the bank and not have paid their taxes? She'd gone through their business files and hadn't seen anything regarding back taxes. But then, it had been a disorganized mess, with papers filed under the wrong headings, many of them old or irrelevant. Eva may have been a hospitable hostess, but she'd lacked in business acumen.

Meridith took the inherited checkbook from her purse and opened it to the register. After paying Jake for the repairs he'd completed last week, she barely had enough to pay the taxes. It would leave her with . . .

She did a quick mental tally. One hundred and twenty dollars.

Not enough for a week's groceries, to say nothing of all the needed repairs. The house would never pass inspection.

She looked back at the letter and the words *taking of said estate* stole the decision from her hands. Pay the taxes and take her chances at the sale of Summer Place, or don't pay the taxes and lose the property.

It wasn't much of a decision.

Twenty

Jake climbed the apartment stairs, unlocked the door, and shrugged off his suit coat. It was all he could do to focus on Pastor Owens's sermon. Every time he closed his eyes for prayer, he saw Meridith whirling around the elementary stage, her dress drifting behind her like an afterthought. Max had looked debonair and so grown up in his suit. Eva would've been proud.

He sure had been. Proud of both of them. At least when it was finished. Until then, he'd been a basket of nerves. But then they were taking their bows, and he'd never seen Max so proud. Or Meridith so radiant.

And that's about where his thoughts were when he realized the prayer was over and he still had his head bowed.

After church he'd eaten out with Wyatt and Willow and a few friends from church, and now he found himself free for the afternoon. Maybe he'd take his cycle across the island and enjoy Surfside. Or he could ride up to the cemetery and freshen the gravesites. He'd put out fresh flowers a week ago when he couldn't get Eva off his mind. He missed his sister so much. He'd sat there for over an hour, thinking of her, missing her, grieving for her.

But he didn't want to go there today. What he really wanted to do right now was get the kids and take them fishing at Hummock Pond. But he couldn't do that. He couldn't even call them or visit them. This undercover operation had its drawbacks. And yet, what information had he found in his two weeks at Summer Place?

He was going to have to step it up. Start snooping. He hated the thought of rooting through Meridith's private things. It wasn't his style. Maybe he could get to know her better, cajole information from her. He hadn't quizzed her about her future plans for the kids. Not that it was going to help him get them back.

He needed definitive information that proved she was incompetent. Something so severe that the state would go against Eva and T. J.'s will. He'd done some digging at the library and had found that keeping children in their school district was important to judges. Ripping them not only from their school but from the island would surely not be favorable. If only he could find out if that was her intention. But would that be enough?

He wasn't sure he'd find anything worse. Even if she were bipolar, maybe it was under control with medication. The more he knew Meridith, the more he realized she wasn't the freak Noelle had claimed. Controlling and paranoid, yes. Repressed, certainly. But incompetent? Not even close. She wasn't exactly the nurturing type, but she wasn't cruel.

Still, why was she putting her life on hold to raise three kids? It was obvious she hadn't been around children much, and she'd never met her siblings before she arrived . . . so why did she want guardianship?

Even if she wasn't a natural with kids and didn't understand their grief, he'd have to do better than that to convince a judge she was unfit.

He'd have to get closer to her. It wouldn't be easy, but he did have his charms. And if the opportunity for a little snooping arose, he wouldn't turn it down.

A light flashed on his phone, and he punched the button as he unfastened his shirt.

"Hi, this is Meridith. I—uh, have some unfortunate news." There was a pause.

The kids . . . Jake walked back to the phone as if he doing so would hasten her words.

"There's been a change in my financial situation, and I won't be able to finish the house. Effective today. I'm sorry for any inconvenience. But thank you for the work you've done."

Another pause. What had happened? What financial situation? Were the kids okay?

"Oh, I also wanted to let you know the talent show went well. We didn't so much as falter, and I wanted to thank you for that as well. So. Thanks. I guess that's all. Bye."

What was going on? She'd given him no useful information. Maybe he could get hold of Noelle. But he couldn't risk an e-mail, and a phone call was out of the question. Besides, Noelle wasn't likely to know what was going on with Meridith's finances.

Okay, Walker, think.

Meridith didn't have the money to finish. He couldn't offer to work for free.

But he could offer a trade . . . Jake felt the weight lift from his shoulders, and as the idea gelled in his mind, a smile pulled at his mouth. Maybe this setback was really an opportunity in disguise.

Twenty-one

Meridith watched the school bus roll from the curb and went to the check-in desk to look over the registry. The tax bill, leaning on a homemade clay pencil holder, mocked her.

She'd go to the treasurer's office in person and pay the bill today. After that, she'd develop a budget. She'd have to get into her account back home, her personal savings. She hadn't mentioned that to Stephen when she'd called him the day before, but she didn't have a choice. They had to eat. She had to keep the electric on, such as it was.

She prayed business would increase as spring progressed. There was a family of four coming late in the week, thanks to spring break, and a couple coming for the weekend. The extra money would help. Seeing how sparse guests were off-season, she realized how costly it was to keep Summer Place running. No wonder they were in arrears. Still, it would've been nice knowing that before paying Jake for two weeks' work.

She'd been thankful he hadn't answered the day before. Leaving a message was cowardly, but she couldn't resist taking the easy way out.

As she hung up, a weight she'd later defined as sadness enveloped her. Maybe a little disappointment too. And though she told herself it was the unfinished house that plagued her, deep down she knew it was more.

All the more reason to be glad Jake was out of her life. She was an engaged woman. She didn't need the distraction of some arrogant man who made her feel . . . things.

Her mind unwittingly flashed back to Saturday when she was whirling around the living room in his arms. When the feel of his shoulder, rock solid, did things to her insides . . . when the stumble had left her crushed against his chest . . .

And there was that feeling again. Drat the man. Even when he wasn't there he vexed her.

She removed a notepad from the desk and made a to-do list. The house was quiet this morning. No buzzing of saws or pounding of nails, no high-pitched whine of an electric screwdriver. No slam as Jake had a hissy fit over some snag.

She almost missed that part.

A loud knock sounded at the door, and Meridith set down the pen and went to answer it. *Please, God, a customer.* Though it was early in the day for tourists seeking shelter. Maybe she could raise the rates to offset her financial woes. She made a mental note to check her competitors' rates.

She opened the door. "Jake. I—didn't you get my message?"

Why had she left a voice mail? Now she'd have to explain in person.

"Can we talk?"

"Uh—sure. Come in." She didn't owe him more money, did she? She'd cut him a check on Friday, and he hadn't worked on Saturday— unless he was counting the dance lessons, but surely not.

He followed her into the living room, and she sat on the armchair, leaving him with a choice between the sofa and love seat. He chose the love seat, perched on the edge, elbows propped on his knees.

"I left you a message yesterday." She couldn't seem to get any further.

"Got it. You had a financial setback."

She didn't know why that humiliated her, but it did, even if it wasn't her fault. It was one of those issues related to her childhood, she supposed, taking her right back to the calls from bill collectors. But unlike her mom, she was meticulous with her finances.

"I had an unexpected bill," she said.

"I guess you inherit the bad with the good."

Was that sarcasm flickering in those brown eyes? One moment Meridith thought she detected it, the next second she was sure she'd imagined it.

Well, her finances were none of his concern. And if he'd received her message, why was he here?

She clasped her hands around her knee. "What brings you here today?"

He took his time responding. Stretched his legs out. Leaned into the sofa like he was settling in for the winter.

She looked away, over to the fireplace. The damaged, no-good fireplace. Yet another item on a long list of things wrong with the house. When she had a buyer, inspection was going to be a nightmare.

"Had an idea, a solution to your problem."

Meridith cocked her head. "Do tell."

"You have a lot of things needing fixed. The place isn't up to code."

"No secret there."

"The boiler could go out at any time, and you won't find parts for it."

"You said something about a solution."

He crossed his ankle over his knee. His foot looked huge in the boots. Size twelve? Thirteen? Virtual barges. No wonder she couldn't help but step on them when they danced.

"Thought maybe we could trade."

Meridith knew what she needed from Jake, but what did he need from her? The only skill she had was in the health safety industry, and he had no use for that, did he?

Her fingers clutched the collar of her shirt together. "What—what kind of trade?"

One of his eyebrows lifted. And that smirk.

"Nantucket isn't cheap, as you've no doubt discovered. My rent is eating a hole in my pocket, and I was thinking if that were eliminated, it would help me out."

"Your rent . . ." She wasn't connecting the dots.

"You run a B-and-B."

A trade. Oh.

"See, I was thinking if I moved in here—"

"Moved in here?"

"Temporarily." He spoke slowly, as if to a child. "In exchange for my labor."

"I have children here. I can't have a man moving in—"

"I'm not your live-in boyfriend. Just think of me as a long-term tourist." He grinned. "Who works on your house by day."

She shook her head. She didn't like this. It was difficult enough having him here during daytime hours. How would it be to have him around twenty-four/seven? She shuddered. "I don't think so."

"It's the perfect solution."

For whom?

"You get the work done with very little out-of-pocket expense."

"But even if you're working in trade, there'll still be costs." Some that had nothing to do with a bill from Marine Home Center. "There's not enough cash flow right now for extras."

"You paid for the new furnace when I ordered it. It arrived on Saturday, and it'll cost next to nothing for me to get it running. Just time. And one tiny little bedroom."

Jake sleeping down the hall . . . it wasn't something she wanted to contemplate. And what would Stephen say?

"I don't know. It doesn't seem proper. I'm engaged."

"You think Lover—your fiancé's going to object?"

Stephen wasn't controlling or possessive. Not at all.

"It's a B-and-B. You have male guests here all the time, how's this any different?"

Because the other male guests didn't look at her like Jake did. Because other male guests didn't make her feel bothered and agitated.

"Wait, what about your employer? Comfort Heating and Plumbing wouldn't make a dime if you traded out your services."

"Owner's a friend. Already cleared it with him. At least let me stay long enough to install the furnace, run the ductwork. You've already paid for it—what are you going to do, install it yourself?"

She shot him a look. She was as good with tools as she was on the dance floor. Still, he didn't have to be sarcastic.

"How long would it take?"

"A week. Two at most. And fixing the wiring problems will be cheap. You don't want the fire hazard, I'm sure."

How could she say no? The wiring was a safety concern, and she couldn't waste the money she'd paid for the furnace. It would save her a lot of trouble come sale time.

"How long will the new fuse service take?"

"Several days to a week."

"Isn't that a lot of hassle, to move your things for less than a month?"

"Don't have much. Apartment is furnished."

"Won't your landlord rent out your place if you leave?"

"He'll save it. He's a friend."

Everyone was a friend. She wanted to say *If he's such a friend, why is he charging you so much*, but she kept it to herself.

"What are we supposed to do without heat while you're working on it?"

"Got any space heaters? Forecast is warmer than usual, but it'll get chilly at night."

She'd seen several space heaters in the basement. She could put one in each bedroom.

"I have guests coming in a little over a week."

"I'll do my best to get it done by then."

There were still a couple more issues to settle. "When we do have guests—"

"I'll stay out of the way."

"And our personal lives here—"

"Are none of my business."

He was saying all the right things. He looked sincere, his brown eyes wide, his shoulders shrugging innocently.

Innocent, my fanny.

Still, she was getting a new heating system for next to nothing, and it was going to save her a ton in the end. She'd just have to put up with a week or two of . . . Jake.

Twenty-two

Meridith worked on Noelle's scrapbook in her room all morning. She'd already bought the albums, special tape, and other supplies. In the background she could hear Jake working. The buzz of a saw as he cut out the old boiler, the sound of his tromping up the basement steps, taking parts to his truck. The thing was mammoth. It would probably take all day just to remove the beast.

Her stomach growled at noon, but she waited until almost one, when she heard the rumble of Jake's truck backing from the drive, to leave her sanctuary.

It was silly. She couldn't hide in her room all week. She fixed a sandwich, started a load of bedding, and was upstairs again before Jake returned.

The house was getting chilly without heat, and she needed to get moving. She made a room ready for Jake—the seashell room, located in the guest wing and farthest from her bedroom door. The pale blue and coral décor didn't suit him at all, and she hoped that would make him eager for his own apartment.

Meridith knew she'd have to tell the children Jake was staying a few weeks. She dreaded informing Noelle of any changes, and mentally prepared herself for the possibility of a conflict ending with Noelle crying on her bed.

She hated that the girl upset so easily, hated that Noelle's agitation always led to her own. Since living here, Meridith had become so adept at counting backward by twenty-threes that she had to vary the number to challenge herself.

When the school bus squealed to a halt at the curb, she tucked the scrapping supplies in her closet and met the kids at the door.

When they entered, Meridith asked about their day, then helped Ben remove his jacket. Before they could disappear upstairs, she asked them to sit down in the living room.

"What's wrong?" Max asked.

"Nothing."

Noelle plopped on the sofa. Ben curled up on one side of her, Max on the other. They eyed her warily.

Meridith sat on the armchair. "You know how Jake's been working on the house."

The kids stared back blankly, still as statues.

Strange. "Well," Meridith continued. "There're going to be some changes that I wanted to make you aware of."

They weren't so much as blinking. She could swear Noelle was holding her breath. Meridith had a feeling this wouldn't end well.

"Jake and I worked out a trade." *Be firm. Take no flack. You're the adult here.* "While he's fixing the furnace, he'll be living here as a guest. It won't be but a few weeks or a month at most, and I put him in the guest wing, of course."

Only when she finished did she look at them again. Their expressions had changed, but Noelle's was the one she watched. The frown lines disappeared. Her lips lifted at the corners.

Then just as quickly her smile slipped, and she shrugged. "Whatever."

"Cool," Max added calmly, though his heel beat a nervous tattoo on the floor. "We're cool with that. Right, Ben?"

They exchanged a look.

"Oh. Sure. Yeah, whatever."

"I'm going to do my homework," Noelle said.

"Me too." Max sprang from the couch after her.

"I have math." Ben grabbed his book bag with his good arm.

"I can help you," Meridith said.

"I'll help him," Noelle called from the top of the stairs.

Ben disappeared up the stairs behind his brother and sister. Meridith watched them go and wondered if she'd ever figure out those three.

"Ben, can you set the table, please?" Meridith finished chopping the tomatoes and tossed them into the salad. Spaghetti boiled on the stove, and garlic toast browned in the oven.

"Mmm, smells good." Max entered the house from the back door.

"Wash your hands," Meridith reminded him.

She drained the spaghetti, poured the meat sauce over the top, then removed the bread from the oven and turned it off. The children helped her carry the food to the table.

Once seated, she tapped Noelle's arm. "Your iPod?"

Noelle rolled her eyes but took out the earbuds and turned it off.

"My turn," Ben said.

They bowed their heads and Ben said the prayer, then they dug in like they were starving.

Meridith was dishing out her salad when she heard Jake's boots on the basement steps. He was finished for the day.

A moment later he appeared at the doorway and stopped short. "Sorry. Just passing through."

His hair was flecked with sawdust, and black stuff covered his bare arms and stained his jeans.

"You can eat with us," Noelle said. "Can't he?" She turned innocent eyes on Meridith.

Meridith flashed her a look, pressed her lips together. It wasn't really a question, and it was the last thing Meridith wanted.

"I'm a mess," Jake said.

"Might as well eat with us if he wants," Max said. When Meridith shot him a look, he added, "I mean, we got plenty."

"*Have* plenty," Noelle said.

"He has to eat anyways," Ben said.

Jake looked at her, silently asking permission.

Oh, for heaven's sake. "Fine." She stabbed her lettuce with her fork. "Just need to wash up real quick."

Meridith was no fool. They'd just set a precedent. Now the man was going to be at their dinner table for weeks. She felt a headache coming on. A very long one.

Later that night, Meridith lay in bed reading one of the books on grief. As she flipped a page, she heard the muted thumps of Jake's steps on the main stairs. He'd gone to collect his things after dinner and had settled into his room.

The kids were safely tucked away for the night. She'd had just enough space heaters and had set them up after dinner to make their rooms cozy before bedtime. She hoped they were having better luck than she. It was hotter than a frying pan in her room. She adjusted the heater's thermostat again and crawled back into bed, kicking the quilt down.

After the stressful day, she was grateful for a moment's quiet to read and relax.

As if the very thought jinxed her, the cell rang. Meridith reached for her phone, charging on her nightstand, disconnected the cord, and answered without checking the screen.

"Hi, honey," she said.

"Just because we're living together doesn't mean you can call me honey." Jake's deep voice rumbled across the line. Meridith sprang upright and pulled the sheet over her bare legs.

He can't see you, goofball.

"Jake. Why are you calling—you're right down the hall—and how did you get my number?"

"There's a locked door between us—quite sturdy, I might add—and you called from your cell Sunday. I saved your number just in case."

She sighed hard. "Just in case what—you needed fresh towels?"

He laughed, deep and throaty. She resisted the pull of it.

"My towels are fresh and abundant, but thanks for asking."

Her heart was all up in her throat, and she didn't know why. She knew this was going to happen. Knew having him here would be a constant pain in the—

"Meridith?"

"What do you need, Jake?"

"Forgot to tell you a friend's coming at seven to help bring the furnace in. Just didn't want you to freak out when you came down the stairs and saw a stranger."

"Oh. Okay." She was glad he'd told her, but she wanted off the phone. Wanted to pretend Jake wasn't on the other end of the line. Wanted to pretend Jake wasn't just down the hall. "Anything else?"

"Nope, that's it."

"All right. Well, good night."

"Night, Meri."

She didn't bother to correct him before turning off the phone and plugging it back in.

Still hot, she kicked the sheet back down and settled into her spot just in time for her phone to ring again. What now? Something else he'd forgotten to mention?

She sighed hard, grabbed the phone, and flipped it open. *"What?"*

"Meridith? You okay?"

Stephen. Jake was making her lose it. "Sorry. I thought it was—the guy doing the repairs on the house."

"Why would he call so late?"

Tell him about the trade. Tell him Jake's staying here. "He just called a minute ago to let me know about a delivery in the morning."

"I thought you cancelled the repairs."

Tell him now. "Well, I'd already paid for the furnace, so it seemed a waste not to have it installed."

"Oh, well, I hope he's not putting too much stress on you. Between the kids, the household problems, and financial woes, you've got enough to deal with."

If you only knew. "I'm fine." A subject change was in order. "How was your day?"

"Busy, but good. I miss you, though."

"You're too busy to miss anything."

"True, true." He chuckled, a high-pitched *haw, haw, haw.* She remembered Jake's deep throaty laugh, then chided herself for comparing.

"Any word from the uncle?"

"No, and it's making me angrier by the day. How dare he fall out of contact with his loved ones for so long, you know? It's supremely irresponsible."

Stephen sighed. "I wish he'd just hurry so you could come home."

She had to tell him, at least give him a hint. "Stephen, I'm not sure their uncle is suitable. The more I hear about him and the longer he stays away, the more I worry." There, she'd said it. Well, not *it*, but she'd dropped a clue. She waited a full three seconds for his response.

"He's the only option though, right? I mean, there's not some other relative hiding in the woodwork, is there?" He gave a wry laugh.

"No. He's the only other one." She threw in that word, *other*, to remind him she was a relative too. He had to start seeing her, seeing *them*, as a viable option, because she was not deserting these kids. Surely he'd understand that. Even though they weren't related to him, surely he'd see it was the Christian thing to do.

"Well, he'll have to do, then." He missed the clue completely.

She rubbed her temple. Her Jake-headache was morphing into a Stephen-headache. "I can't hand the children over to some incompetent, irresponsible uncle, Stephen. They're my siblings." She lowered her voice in case one of the children was able to hear. "And he might not want them."

"I know how stressful this is for you, but have faith. God'll work this out."

"Faith without works is dead, Stephen."

"Meridith . . ." The tension in his voice was like a tight wire being snapped. *Ping.*

"I'm not saying anything right now. Just that we need to keep our minds open and see how things go."

"See how things go . . . ? Meridith, I see you might feel a sense of responsibility for them, really, I do. But children are a huge commitment."

It was late. He was tired. She shouldn't have brought it up tonight when he was so swamped leading up to Tax Day.

"It's late, honey. Let's revisit this later. Maybe we won't even need to. Uncle Jay could show up at the door tomorrow and prove me wrong." Meridith cringed. Why was she backing down? She knew that wasn't going to happen.

"You're right. I'm sorry if I seem on edge."

"Perfectly understandable. I'll call you tomorrow?"

"Sure. Night, Meridith."

"Night." Meridith closed the phone, turned off the light, and pulled the covers over her head.

Twenty-three

As Jake entered Meridith's room, the fresh smell of citrus assaulted him. The scent of soap or shampoo or lotion or whatever it was that made Meridith smell so good. It transported him to the moment he'd had her in his arms. Okay, so it was only because she'd stumbled. A man could pretend, couldn't he?

Pretend? What was he thinking? *Get a grip, Walker.* He was here to do a job, and not just the renovations.

He'd been living in the house now for three days and had been waiting to install the cold air return in Meridith's room. Waiting for her to leave the house, and finally, five minutes ago, the opportunity presented itself.

But as soon as he stepped into her room and took one whiff, he wondered if he could do it. Rifle through her things? Her personal belongings? Open drawers, rummage through her closet? Not his style.

A gaping hole opened in the pit of his stomach, and it wasn't hunger. He'd come to respect Meridith, if not see eye to eye with her.

But this was the only reason he was here. He had to think of the kids. If Meridith was bipolar, he needed to know. And if she was selling Summer Place, he needed to know that too. If she planned to uproot the kids, take them away from their friends, their memories, their home . . . that was unacceptable.

Jake scanned the dresser drawers, shut up tight as a beach house during a hurricane. She couldn't have left one drawer open? Just one?

He set down the saw and peeked out the window one more time to confirm she hadn't returned. The driveway was empty, except for his truck.

Half disappointed, he walked across the small space and entered the bathroom. He didn't have to like it. He just had to do it.

One little peek in the medicine cabinet was all he needed in here. The door sqeaked as he swung it open. He scanned the rows of shelves. Lotion, floss, hair spray, deodorant, toothpaste, eye drops, mouthwash. Not one single amber bottle of medication. Maybe she was as normal as she seemed. Or maybe she kept her medication in her purse. He was so not going there, even if he had the opportunity.

Jake exited the bathroom and opened the bedroom closet. If he thought the room smelled like her, it was nothing compared to the scent that wafted toward him when he swung open the closet door.

Her belongings were sparse. One rod hung across the small space, maybe twenty occupied hangers. She probably had the rest in drawers. On the floor a suitcase, a few boxes, shoes. Lots of shoes.

He was tempted to shut the door and move on. But it would be stupid and careless to waste the opportunity. He squatted on the floor and rooted through the boxes, trying not to disturb things. A plastic bag held a bunch of stickers, scissors, ribbons, and stuff.

He lifted the lid on the last box, a white glossy thing. There was an album on top. He lifted it to find two more, and under those, photos. Rubber-banded in three separate piles. He lifted them out. Photos of the kids. Family pictures, some that Jake had seen. Meridith must've found them when she'd cleaned out Eva and T. J.'s room. What was she doing with them?

Were there photos of him? He fanned through the stacks. Near the end, he found one of him on his Harley with Ben. Thank God he was wearing his helmet. He studied the photo. No, nothing to give him away here. Where were all the pictures of him? Then he remembered the school poster Max had done last fall. He'd had to make a photo collage of his hero. Jake smiled, picturing the poster that now hung on his bedroom wall. The kid had pilfered every last photo of him. *Thank God.*

He picked up a photo of Eva and remembered the way her eyes lit under the afternoon sun, the way her smile brightened every room she entered. He felt a catch in his breath at the feeling of emptiness and loss that settled over him.

Enough of this. He had to focus on the task at hand. He swallowed hard and placed the photos back where he'd found them. As he replaced the albums, curiosity got the best of him. He lifted the cover of the first one. Centered on the page and surrounded by decorations was a hospital photo of Noelle in Eva's arms with T. J. standing over her shoulder. A little pink bundle. Eva looked so proud. Seeing his sister so alive and happy made his throat ache all over again. He turned the first page and then another. The album stopped when Noelle was six or seven.

Had Meridith found these albums? He couldn't see Eva making these. She wasn't creative, and organization had been a foreign concept to her.

He touched the bag of ribbons and stickers. Was this Meridith's doing? Was she making the kids albums? Why else would these things be in her closet? He replaced the lid and stood, then shut the closet door. She really did care about the kids. Probably wasn't even planning to sell Summer Place. And he was rooting around in her things for nothing.

You're a real jerk, Walker.

Turning, he surveyed all the drawers in the chest and dresser. How could he make himself finish?

He dug his hands into his pockets. If she was planning to move the kids, surely there was evidence in here somewhere. If he found nothing, he'd assume the best, and he wouldn't do this again. He'd give her the benefit of the doubt. Maybe even settle for shared custody, if the bipolar wasn't an issue. As if it were up to him.

Feeling justified, he moved to the chest and began pulling drawers. The entire thing was empty. That was easy.

The dresser was next. Each drawer held a few neatly folded items, divided by clothing type. Sweaters, jeans, rolls of socks, then a drawer he knew he had no business in.

Nothing here. There was only one drawer remaining, and he'd saved it for last. The nightstand drawer where people kept personal things. He'd just give it a pull, a quick glance, then he'd be done. Back to cutting holes in the walls.

He approached the white table. A photo of Meridith and Lover Boy was propped in the corner beside a lamp. He picked it up and looked at the guy. Neat haircut, weak jawline, practiced smile. He shook his head and set it down.

An alarm clock topped a stack of library books. He tilted his head and scanned the titles. *Kids and Grief, When a Child Loses a Parent, 25 Ways to Help a Grieving Child.*

He really was a jerk.

Jake forced himself to reach for the vintage knob and pulled. The drawer squawked at him as he pulled it. *Yeah, yeah, I know.* When he released the handle, it settled at a cockeyed angle.

If he'd hoped to find it empty, he was disappointed. A copy of *Restaurant Hospitality Magazine* topped a stack of papers. So much for a quick glance. He looked out the nearby window and down into the empty drive. Still gone.

No excuses now. Just get it done.

He lifted the stack and scanned the bottom of the drawer. A pen, a CD entitled *Soothing Classics*, Carmex, a packet of tissues, and a paisley printed eye mask. The scent of lavender wafted from the drawer.

Nothing there. He'd sift through the papers and be done. He grabbed the stack and flipped through. Papers from the attorney's office, a copy of Eva and T. J.'s will. He stopped at the last group of papers, stapled together. He scanned the top sheet. She'd had an inspection done on the house. The date confirmed it had been after her arrival.

The papers listed the repairs needing done on the house—the ones he was in the process of doing.

A feeling he didn't like settled in his middle, heavy and unyielding. People had inspections before they sold a property, to avoid delays and problems during closing.

But people had inspections done for other reasons as well. A new owner wanting to get the place up to snuff. An overcautious safety inspector wanting to avoid mishaps and lawsuits.

He blew out a shaky breath, and as he returned the papers to the drawer, his eyes caught something he'd missed earlier. A white rectangle stuck in the groove against the drawer face. He slid the business card out. He recognized the woman's name and face from local advertisements, as well as the logo across the top of the card. Jordan Real Estate.

He flipped the card over. A message was scrawled in blue pen.

"Thanks for your call, Meridith. Let me know when you're ready. Lora"

The card blurred in his hand as his thoughts raced. It was true. The thing he'd been convincing himself wasn't happening, really was. She *was* planning to take the kids from the island, from their home. From him.

He slammed the drawer shut, picked up his saw, and left the room. His feet took the stairs quickly, and he was out the door in a matter of seconds. He dropped the saw on the porch and followed the flagstone path to his truck, sucking in gulps of cool air.

Inside his truck, he turned the key. He wanted to scream, wanted to hit something. He banged the heel of his palm on the steering wheel for good measure.

She was taking the kids away. Of all the stupid, selfish things . . . and he was helping her. Helping her ready the house so she could sell it out from under the kids. Keeping it a secret from them, on top of everything else.

But it would all work in her favor because she'd profit from the sale. The place was worth a bundle even if it wasn't in perfect condition. He had no idea what Eva and T. J.'s mortgage was like, but surely they'd managed to accumulate equity in all the years they'd been here.

He jammed the gear in reverse and backed from the drive. He wished he were on his cycle right now. He'd head for Milestone Road and open the throttle until the landscape was nothing but a blur. He pressed the gas pedal on his old truck and settled for a spinout on the shelled lane.

How could she even think of doing this? Sure, she was awkward when it came to people and relationships, it didn't take a genius to see that. Maybe she'd initially come here planning to sell the place, he could even accept that.

But now she knew the kids. She'd read a few books, and surely they told her what would be obvious to the average person: you don't uproot children from all they know when they've just lost their parents.

She'd been here a month. Long enough to bond with the kids. Long enough to know better.

He smacked the steering wheel again. His mind's eye saw her and Max box-stepping carefully around the elementary stage. Saw Benny clinging to her side as she read to him. Saw the stack of photo albums in Meridith's closet. How could she not see that this would destroy them?

If she were going to be their guardian, she had to put them first. It would mean putting her old life behind, her old home, even her fiancé, if necessary.

But maybe he was the problem. Maybe he didn't want the kids. Maybe he didn't want a life on Nantucket. If Lover Boy didn't want the responsibility, the money from the sale of the house would be a nice salve, wouldn't it? It would go a long way toward smoothing his ruffled feathers.

Was that why Meridith was doing it? He turned away from town, needing time to think, not wanting to return to the house in case she was back. He could drive all day, spin this a dozen ways in mind, but in the end, it didn't matter. All that mattered was that Meridith was planning to take the kids from Summer Place, and he couldn't let that happen.

Twenty-four

"Thanks for staying with us," Meridith told the Evans family. "I hope you enjoyed your spring break."

"We did, very much." Mrs. Evans handed over her key and took the receipt. On their way out, their kids fussed over who had to carry the heavy suitcase, and finally Mr. Evans scolded them and took it himself.

When the door closed, Meridith was torn between relief and dread. It was good to have the house back, but that meant the barrier between her and Jake was gone.

It had been almost two weeks since he'd come to stay, but he'd been distant recently. More than distant. He seemed hostile, moody. At first she'd wondered if something had happened. But she knew little of his personal life and wasn't about to ask. Then she'd noticed he was fine with the kids and friendly with the guests. The Evanses had commented on what a nice man he was.

Finally Meridith had asked him if she'd done something to upset him, but he denied it. Still, his attitude reeked, and she was tiring of the silent treatment.

As if her thoughts beckoned him, Jake's steps sounded on the basement steps. She tensed, wishing he were finished so she wouldn't have to deal with the extra stress.

She checked the schedule again, as if she didn't know she had three college students booked starting Monday. She had the weekend to ready the rooms and clean the house.

The children burst through the door. She hadn't heard the school bus. Piper tried to squeeze in with them, but Max held her off, petting her while the other two entered. Meridith was greeting them when Jake entered.

Ben slung his book bag off with his newly uncasted arm.

"Careful of your arm."

"Hey, little man." Jake stopped by the check-in desk. "Got your cast off just in time for spring break."

"My arm feels so light, and Meridith said we're gonna celebrate."

"That so?"

Jake didn't look at all upset now, smiling at Ben.

"Where we going?" Max asked.

"It's up to Ben," Meridith said. "It's his big day."

"Atlantic Café!"

She remembered passing the place in town. "All right. Does anyone have homework?"

"Not even *my* teacher is that cruel," Noelle said.

"Okay then, let me grab my purse and we're ready to go."

"Can Jake come?" Max asked.

Meridith's hand paused on her purse. She pressed her lips together. Maybe if she pretended she hadn't heard.

"Yeah, he drove me to the hospital," Ben said.

So much for not hearing. Meridith pasted on a polite smile. "I'm sure Jake's busy."

"Actually, I missed lunch." His lips tilted in a cocky grin, and his eyes challenged hers. "I'd love to go."

The kids whooped and were out the front door. Jake followed, and Meridith locked up behind them. They all stuffed into the van, a loud, excited bunch in the back. In the front, nothing but silence.

She hated having someone upset with her, and though Jake denied it, the signs were there. The way he spoke only when necessary, the way he avoided eye contact. Just like now. Being with him was always awkward, but now a new tension hovered.

Fortunately, the ride was short, and when they reached the restaurant, it was loud and busy enough that the children wouldn't cause a distraction. The hostess led them to the tall booths at the back. Meridith and Jake scooted in first, opposite one another, then Max and Noelle, and Ben on a chair at the end.

Meridith studied the menu, finally settling on the spinach salad as the server approached.

"Hey, Jake, how you doing?" She flashed a dimpled smile.

"Hey, Dawn."

"How you doing, kiddos?"

Meridith asked a question about the salad, though Dawn seemed more interested in making eyes at Jake.

"That sounds good. I'll have the spinach salad."

"Wow, taking a walk on the wild side." Noelle rolled her eyes. "I'll have the Brownie Supreme."

Jake ordered buffalo wings, and Max and Ben each ordered a Brownie Supreme.

"Wow, that's a lot of ice cream, kids," Dawn said. "Sure you can handle it?"

"I got my cast off today," Ben said.

"We're celebrating," Jake added.

Dawn's eyes lingered on Jake longer than necessary and said clear as a bell she'd like one private celebration to go, please.

"Well," Dawn finally said, "seeing as how your arm is newly healed, how about coming back to the kitchen and scooping your own ice cream?" She lowered her voice to a whisper. "I might even let you have an extra scoop."

"Sweet!" Ben said.

"Can I come?" Max asked.

"Me too?" Noelle asked.

Dawn tucked her order pad into her back pocket, though Meridith wasn't sure how she squeezed it in. "Aw, sure, why not?"

Because it was a health code violation?

The children bounced from the booth and trailed behind Dawn, leaving Meridith fully aware that she and Jake were alone. Painfully so. Not even a water to sip.

She tucked her hands in her lap and twisted the engagement ring around her finger. Pretended to be fascinated by the restaurant's décor. Green vinyl booths. Framed Nantucket photos. Nautical artifacts. Lantern-style hanging lights. Behind her, someone's silverware clattered to the tile floor.

She focused on her breathing. Three seconds in—the smell of fried onions and savory seafood—three seconds out.

"How are the kids doing?"

There was that confrontational tone again. What was up with him?

"They're fine. You see them yourself. It'll take time—grief is a process—but we're managing."

"How's your fiancé feel about taking on three kids?"

None of your business was on the tip of her tongue, but she wasn't making Ben's celebration more tense than it already was. Besides, maybe if she made casual conversation, he'd drop his attitude.

"I haven't exactly told him yet." She flickered a look at his face, but he gave nothing away.

"Really."

"You know, I just felt maybe I could ease into it."

"Don't think you can ease into parenting three kids. What did he think you came for, if not to take guardianship?" Jake spun the saltshaker in circles on the wood table.

"I came because there was no one else. I wasn't planning to assume guardianship initially."

The saltshaker stopped. "What do you mean?"

He'd lost the attitude. Those eyes bore straight into hers. The light overhead cast a warm glow on his face.

"They may be my siblings, but I'd never met them, and I knew they had an uncle they were close to. I only planned to stay until he returned." She could hardly believe she'd been there almost six weeks. So much had changed.

"What happened?"

She shrugged. "He never returned, never so much as called. And the more I heard about him, the more I realized he wasn't suitable. I mean, his own sister has been dead for almost two months, and he hasn't a clue."

Jake looked away. His jaw hardened, and a shadow danced in the hollow of his cheek. She felt spurred on by his reaction.

"The children could've used some familiarity, you know? Some-one who knew and loved their parents. Clearly, he's self-absorbed and irresponsible. I can't leave the children with someone like that."

She felt better just saying it. Better than when she'd told Stephen, who only seemed interested in the bottom line: when was she com-ing home?

"So you"—he cleared his throat—"initially planned to give him guardianship, then changed your mind when he didn't show."

"Well, that's part of it. I don't think he's suited for the responsibility of three young children. He goes gallivanting over the states all summer, and what kind of life would that be for the children?"

"Maybe he'd settle down."

"Eva and my father apparently didn't think so. Besides, he hasn't even called in two months. Why would I think he'd make a huge lifestyle change?" She twisted the diamond upright and folded her hands on the table. "Anyway, I've grown fond of the kids. It won't be easy, but I'm not putting these kids through—"

"Putting them through . . ."

She'd almost gone too far, said too much. He wasn't Stephen, she couldn't confide in him, trust her wounds to him.

"They deserve a safe and settled childhood. Every child deserves that, and I'm more than capable of providing it." Confident words from someone who'd often felt like she was crumbling these past weeks.

"What about your fiancé?"

The children were rounding the corner carrying their sundae dishes, mounded high with whipped cream.

"Stephen will come around." Even as she said the words, she whispered a prayer that it was true.

Jake put the ball up and watched it swoosh through the net. Around him, the night was dark, but fortunately Wyatt had left the porch light on when he and Willow left.

Jake dribbled the ball around the court, faking to the left, then put up another shot. The ball bounced to the ground as Wyatt's

Dodge Caliber pulled into the drive. Jake moved aside as the garage door lifted and waved at his friends as they passed. Willow stepped from the car, stunning in a blue dress. "Hey, Jake, how are you?"

"All right."

"Liar," Wyatt said. "I can see right through you."

"Come in for a while," Willow said. "It's chilly out here."

After a nice night out, the couple probably wanted to be alone. He should've left long ago. "No thanks, I need to get back." He tossed the ball to Wyatt.

"Be there in a minute, hon."

"Night, Jake," Willow said before entering the house.

Wyatt dribbled the ball to Jake. His sport coat flapped in the breeze. "Okay, what'd she do now?"

"How do you know it's Meridith?"

"Same way you knew 'she' was Meridith."

He had a point.

"HORSE?" Wyatt tossed the ball to him.

He couldn't usurp Wyatt's whole evening. "Make it PIG." Jake dribbled to the edge of the drive and put up a shot. Score.

He tossed the ball to Wyatt. "Meridith is selling Summer Place."

Wyatt put up the shot and made it. "She tell you that?"

"Not exactly." Jake dribbled the ball to the free throw line. *Swish.* "Found a Realtor's business card and papers from an inspection."

"'Found' them?"

He shrugged. "Launched a little investigation."

"You snooped through her private stuff. Dude."

"She's selling Summer Place." Jake planted his hands on his hips, watched Wyatt's shot bounce off the rim. *P.*

"What about the kids?"

"Isn't it obvious? She's taking them to St. Louis. I can't let that happen." Jake missed a long shot and tossed the ball to Wyatt.

"Wonder what her fiancé thinks about that. It's not every guy who would agree to raising someone else's kids."

"She hasn't told him."

"You find that out by snooping too?" Wyatt missed his shot.

Jake gave him a look. "I asked."

"Novel idea."

Jake lined up for a three-pointer and made it. "She was going to turn the kids over to 'the uncle' initially. But when he didn't return, she decided it was up to her to raise them."

Wyatt made the shot. "She was going to give them to you?"

What an idiot he'd been. If he'd just come back and told her he wanted the kids, maybe he'd have had a prayer of convincing her he was the best person for the job.

"Gotta say, you've risen to the occasion. Never thought I'd see the day you'd settle down, much less take on your niece and nephews."

"Thanks for the vote of confidence." Though obviously Eva had felt the same, as Meridith had so kindly pointed out. Shoot, even he hadn't realized he was capable of that level of responsibility. "I guess losing Eva showed me what's really important."

"Too bad Eva didn't see this side of you before. It's kind of shocking she agreed to leave them to Meridith."

"Not really. Blood was everything to Eva. After being raised in foster homes, she wanted her kids raised by a relative. That pretty much narrowed it down to me and Meridith. I guess I did a pretty good job convincing her I wasn't father material."

"Why don't you just tell Meridith who you are, man?"

"Because she thinks the uncle is irresponsible and self-absorbed." Jake missed.

Wyatt snorted. "She tell you that?"

Jake scowled.

Wyatt put up another shot, this one from the left side—Jake's weak spot. The ball swished through the net.

"Besides, after I've been there all these weeks incognito . . . I don't think it's going to go over well."

Meridith may have been skeptical of him at first, but she'd come to trust him. And not only with the repairs. Just that she'd opened up at the café was proof of that.

"Anyway, I still don't know for sure she doesn't have bipolar disorder."

"The kids want to be with you, though, right? That has to count for something."

Jake shot and missed, then passed Wyatt the ball. "You'd think. But kids have to be fourteen to make that decision legally. Noelle won't be fourteen until next February, never mind the boys. Maybe the fact that Meridith's planning to take them from their home would sway the judge?"

Wyatt dribbled to the free-throw line. "It's not going to look so good that you're working there under false pretenses."

The thought had occurred to him more than once. "I am a licensed contractor."

"Not to mention the way you finagled your way into her home. You're living there, dude."

"I wanted to be near the kids. It's for their own good."

"Not sure a judge would see it that way." He put up the shot, and it rolled around the rim before falling through the net. "I think you should wait until she tells her fiancé. I have a feeling it'll hit the fan."

Jake put up the ball. It hit the backboard, bounced off the rim, and landed in Wyatt's hands.

"PIG," Wyatt said.

"Tell me something I don't know."

Twenty-five

Jake entered his room and unbuttoned his shirt. Meridith and the kids weren't home from church yet, and he wondered if she'd keep them on the go all day again. Golf lessons, bike riding, a trip to Sconset. It had just been him and Piper the day before. He'd given the dog extra attention on his lunch break, and looking into her big brown eyes, he'd wondered if she missed Eva and T. J. Poor thing didn't even know what had happened to them.

He heard the front door open, then the kids clomping up the back stairs. He laid his dress shirt across the doily-covered dresser next to a shell-filled vase.

He hoped to sneak some time with them today. He was worried about Noelle. Her feisty behavior had changed. Rather than being excited about a week off school, she seemed sad. A normal part of grief, he knew, but she didn't have anyone to talk to.

By the end of this week he'd be finished with the two jobs Meridith had agreed to. He dreaded leaving the kids. Even if he didn't spend much time with them now, at least he was present. He could see for himself how they were doing. If he couldn't stay and work on the house, he wouldn't see them at all. The thought nearly tore him in half.

"Knock-knock." Noelle stood in the doorway, looking way too grown up in her bright pink sundress. Her hair was growing out, and her bangs swooped to the side, falling over one of her sad brown eyes.

"Hey, squirt," he whispered. "Where's Meridith?"

Noelle padded into his room and sat at the desk. "Downstairs making cinnamon rolls. She'll be awhile." Noelle's toes played with the rug's fringe. She'd painted her toenails the same pink as her dress. She and Eva used to paint their nails crazy shades like green and purple.

"Where are your brothers?"

She shrugged. "Outside, I guess."

"Church okay?"

"Sure."

Jake lowered himself to the bed's edge and planted his elbows on his knees. He studied his niece's face, so like her mother's. Her skin was still winter-pale, the freckles from last summer faded.

"Missing your mom and dad?"

Her lips quivered, and she nodded.

"Ah, honey. I am too."

She was in his arms in a split second. She held on so tight it brought a lump to his throat.

"It's okay."

"No, it's not." Her voice was muffled against his shoulder. "You're almost done and you're going to leave and we'll never see you, and Meridith is still here and the Daffodil Parade is coming up and Dad's not here."

How could he have forgotten about the parade? Noelle and T. J.'s annual tradition. It was one more loss.

Noelle pulled away and wiped her face. "I don't want you to leave. I like having you here."

"I like being here."

"Have you found anything that'll make a judge send her away?" Noelle plopped on the desk chair.

"Nothing conclusive." He couldn't tell her what he'd found when she was already upset. When her face fell he added, "But I haven't given up, and neither should you. In fact, I'm going to see if Meridith will let me stay longer. Let me work it out, okay? Do you trust me?"

She nodded, and it did his heart good. At least someone had faith in him.

"As much as I miss Mom and Dad, I'm glad they're together in heaven. They'd be really sad if they were apart."

"That's something to be grateful for."

"And you, Uncle J. I'm so glad you're here."

"Me too, munchkin. Me too."

Meridith kneaded the soft dough and checked the time. Less than a minute. As her hands worked, she watched Max and Ben toss a green Frisbee back and forth in the backyard. Piper played man-in-the-middle, making the boys laugh when she intercepted the disk.

Outside, the cloudless sky seemed to remember it was spring. The sun sparkled off the sound like a million diamonds. The daffodils in the yard had fully bloomed, coloring the yard with splashes of yellow.

The smell of yeast reminded her to check the time again. Done. She gave the dough one last turn, covered it with a towel, scrubbed her hands, then replaced her ring. Breakfast dishes still sat in the sink, plus the ones she'd used making the dough. It was Noelle's turn to wash. Maybe they could do them together. It would give them a chance to talk.

The girl had been too quiet lately, even through the golf lessons yesterday. Meridith was worried about her. She hung up the towel, checked on the boys one last time, then went upstairs to get her.

Noelle's bedroom was empty, the light still on, her church shoes lying where they'd been kicked off. She flipped off the light and noticed the door between the wings was open. Meridith had only been locking it at night, as Jake needed full access to the upstairs.

She walked through the doorway and down the hall. She heard Noelle's voice and followed it to the seashell room—Jake's room. At the doorway, her stomach did a flop.

Noelle sat in the desk chair, and Jake perched on the bed's edge.

Two sets of eyes darted to the doorway, and Noelle stopped talking midsentence.

The girl's eyes widened and her lips parted. She looked to Jake as if seeking help.

Meridith didn't like it. Not one bit. She made an effort to keep her voice calm. "Noelle, can you come do the dishes, please?"

Noelle sprang to her feet, then squeezed past Meridith. The fact that she didn't argue was proof something was up.

She couldn't believe Jake had let Noelle into his room. It was beyond inappropriate. She knew she should confront him, but she had no desire to get into it now. Or ever.

Jake stood, looking too attractive in his white T-shirt and bare feet. "I need to change."

Meridith headed back the way she'd come. Why had Noelle been in there? And why had she looked so . . . caught?

Meridith could hear her trotting down the back steps, setting off a cacophony of squeaks and groans on the old stairway. She had been smiling when Meridith entered Jake's room, a rare occurrence, especially lately.

Meridith's feet faltered on the first step. *Of course.* Noelle had a crush.

The child was going to get her heart broken—the last thing she needed. And Jake should know better. Surely he could read a girl's signals. She was sure he had plenty of them tossed his way—she'd seen it herself, with that server at the Atlantic Café.

But what if . . . what if he was . . . some kind of . . . ?

No, not Jake. He wasn't a pedophile.

But what if . . . ?

She recalled an article that had appeared in the *St. Louis Post-Dispatch* last year. The manager of one of her restaurants convicted of child molestation. He'd have been the last person she'd have suspected of such a horrible crime.

She stopped midway down the steps. She couldn't take any chances with Noelle. She didn't want to confront Jake, but this was nothing to be careless about. She had to lay down some rules. And get him out of the house as soon as he finished the fuse box, which she hoped would be soon.

She drew a lungful of oxygen and released it through her mouth. *Just get it over with. For Noelle's sake.* Turning purposefully on the stair, she retraced her steps.

When she reached Jake's room, he was shutting the door, wearing only his pants and his leather corded necklace.

Meridith's eyes fell to the floor. Her face was hot, and she knew her cheeks were blooming with high color. Great.

"Need something?"

"It can wait until you're—" She waved her hand in the general direction of his chest.

He opened the door fully and strutted back into his room, snagging his shirt from the dresser. He shrugged back into it.

Meridith stayed in the doorway. She crossed her arms. "I came back to ask why Noelle was in your room."

Jake leaned against the windowsill. "Think she just needed to talk."

"Odd that she chose you." With him silhouetted against the window she couldn't read his face.

"Thanks."

"You know what I mean."

"She lost her parents. She doesn't seem to have many people to confide in."

She tried not to take offense, but what was she, chopped liver? "I think there's more than that." She wished he'd step away from that window.

"What do you mean?"

Was he really so oblivious? "Surely you see it's inappropriate to have her in your bedroom."

He came off the sill, seemed to stretch taller and broader. "You are not thinking I'm some kind of—" He struggled for words.

She didn't have to see his face. The anger was right there in his voice. "She's a *child.*"

His anger eased her mind, and she went back to her first response. "It's not unusual for a girl to develop a crush on an older man. I don't want Noelle getting hurt. She's been hurt enough."

"The last thing I'd do is hurt that child. You're worried about nothing. She just needed to talk."

He seemed sincere. Now that he'd stepped away from the window she could see he was making eye contact with her. He looked as serious as she'd ever seen him.

"Nonetheless, Jake, I can't have her coming in—"

"I won't let her in here again. You're right. I wasn't thinking."

He had been helpful and honest so far. She had no reason not to trust him.

"Just be careful not to give her special attention. I don't want her misreading your signals and getting confused."

He held up a palm. "I understand."

"Just so we're clear." She gave him a final nod and retreated, glad that part was over. Now she just had to deal with Noelle.

The girl was not going to like Meridith prying around her private life. But maybe Meridith could use this as a chance to bond with her. Maybe, if what Jake said was true, she did need someone to talk to. Maybe Meridith could be that person. If Noelle would only give her a chance.

Meridith checked on Max and Ben on her way to the sink. They were rolling on the ground with Piper, who wasn't letting loose of the Frisbee. At least they'd changed from their church clothes.

It was only when she saw Noelle standing by the open dishwasher that she realized the girl was still in her dress. "You should probably change out of your pretty dress."

Noelle looked down as if just realizing she was still wearing it.

"On second thought, how about if you unload and I load?"

Noelle shrugged and began removing glass cereal bowls, stacking them on the counter.

Meridith turned on the tap and waited for the water to warm. When it did, she began scrubbing the dirtiest dishes and filling them with water to soak.

She had to broach the topic delicately or Noelle would go ballistic. Maybe if she shared from personal experience.

"You did very well with your one-iron yesterday. Your swing is coming along."

Noelle gave a barely perceptible nod as she placed the bowls in the cupboard.

"I worked at a golf course as a caddy when I was your age. That's where I learned a lot about golf."

"What's a caddy?"

"You know, those people who follow the golfers around, carry their bags and what-not."

"Sounds boring."

"It was interesting. There was this seventeen-year-old boy who worked in the pro-shop." Meridith sighed. "Jeremy Peyton. Had these golden curls and a smile that lit up my world."

Noelle flashed her a disbelieving look.

"What—you don't think I think about things like boys? I am engaged, you know."

"It's hard to imagine you were ever thirteen."

"It wasn't *that* long ago." Meridith scowled, but Noelle wasn't looking. "He was so cute. I remember wearing my most flattering clothes to work because I wanted to impress him. Oh, I knew he was too old for me, but he was so gorgeous, and he called me Peanut."

Noelle gave a wry grin. "Peanut? And you liked that?"

"I liked the attention. I didn't get much at home."

"Why not?" Noelle pulled the silverware basket.

"Oh, well, my dad wasn't there, and my mom was kind of . . ." How to put it? "Kind of sick." Meridith shook her head. She was getting off subject. "Anyway, I liked thinking about Jeremy, daydreaming about him. I used to pretend he was my boyfriend. Only in my head, of course—I'd have been mortified if he'd known!"

"That's weird."

"Not really. It's normal for girls to have crushes on older guys. Happens all the time."

"If you say so."

Meridith rinsed a cup and placed it in the top rack, then faced Noelle, leaning against the sink ledge. "I know we haven't gotten off on the best foot, Noelle, but I hope you know you can talk to me. About anything you want . . . even crushes."

Noelle's forehead wrinkled. "I don't have any crushes."

She was going to have to dig. It needed to be done, with Jake in the house and the kids off school all week. "I thought maybe you had a crush on Jake."

Noelle's hand stopped midair, her fist clutching a cluster of forks. Her lips parted, her eyes widened.

Then her whole face screwed up. "*Gross!* He's my—he's—*old*!"

It wasn't the reaction she'd expected. Was Noelle that good an actress? "He's hardly old."

"Not to *you*."

Touché.

Noelle stuffed the forks in the drawer.

"Well, you were in his room earlier, and I thought—"

"Well, you thought wrong. *Gross!*"

"Okay, okay, I get it."

"We were having a conversation."

"His bedroom is not an appropriate place for that."

"What*ever*."

"Noelle, I need to be clear on this. You're not to be alone with Jake or any male guests in the house. It's for your own protection."

Noelle stuck a bundle of spoons in the drawer, then the knives.

Her brows pulled together, and her lips were a tight line, pressed firmly together.

"Is that clear?"

Noelle slammed the drawer and tossed the basket into the dishwasher. "Crystal." She turned and charged up the steps, her dress billowing behind her.

Twenty-six

The three guys at the check-in desk, young and athletic looking, didn't resemble their usual guests. Meridith wondered why they'd chosen a quiet bed-and-breakfast instead of a happening hotel. But maybe every place was booked for spring break. Oh well, she could use the income. Three rooms were three rooms.

"Here are your keys." She handed them to Sean, who'd made the reservation. "Is there a particular time you'd like breakfast, since you're our only guests at the moment?"

The long-haired one laughed. "I'll be sleeping till lunchtime."

"Don't worry about breakfast," Sean said. He wore a University of Massachusetts ball cap and a polite smile.

"Speak for yourselves," the stocky one said. "I'm a growing boy."

Meridith smiled. "I'll put out a small buffet around ten and keep it warm. That sound all right?"

"Perfect, thanks," Sean said.

The guys headed up the stairs noisily with their duffel bags. She was glad the kids were on break, so she didn't have to worry about their sleep being disturbed by rowdy and possibly drunk college guys. She was doubly glad she'd had the doors installed.

Jake appeared at the base of the stairs in fresh clothes, his hair damp on his polo collar. "Young ones," he said referring to the guests he'd passed.

"I hope you're a heavy sleeper. I think they plan on keeping late nights."

"I'll manage."

Meridith tidied the desk. Dinner had been quiet with Noelle at Lexi's house. Meridith had taken the children to the cemetery earlier, and it had lowered Noelle's spirits even more. When Lexi called, it seemed like a good distraction.

"I was thinking . . ." Jake said.

"Uh-oh."

He gave a little half grin. "The electric will be done in a few days, and we agreed I'd be finished then. But some of the other projects wouldn't cost much." He nodded toward the fireplace. "All I need is some mortar, a few stones, and some time, and I can get that fireplace working."

He listed a host of other projects, but Meridith's mind was off and wandering. With her worries over Noelle and the havoc Jake created inside her, she was anticipating his departure. Not anticipating, exactly. Just desperately needing it to happen. For her own peace of mind.

He seemed eager to stay, and she dreaded turning him down, but extending his time was out of the question. The furnace and the electric would be done. Those were the two biggies.

"Jake, I appreciate what you're saying, but I think it's time we parted ways."

The relaxed grin fell from his lips. The light in his eyes was extinguished as if she'd doused his hope with a fire hose. More than just disappointment, he seemed surprised.

"I'd love to have the work completed, and you've done a fine job, but I really don't have the money, and I'm eager to—to move

on." She twisted the ring on her finger, then wondered if the action
was telling.

"Oh."

"I hope you—"

Max and Ben entered the front door, arguing over who got the
video game first. While Meridith settled the dispute, Jake slipped
quietly out the door.

When the house was quiet again, she picked up the current issue
of *Yesterday's Island* and sat in the armchair, browsing through it. A
photo in the events section caught her eye. It was a line of antique
cars, decorated with daffodils, driving down a cobblestone street.

She remembered the photos of Noelle and her dad in the Galaxie.
Meridith took the paper to her room, where she opened her closet
door and knelt on the floor. She flipped through Noelle's album,
pausing at the parade pictures. In one of them Noelle was preschool
age, in the others a little older. There were seven of them, each taken
a different year.

Meridith knew the Daffodil Festival was approaching. She had
a sudden recollection of something Ben had said about decorating
the Galaxie, and it all came together. It was a family tradition, and it
seemed to be particularly a tradition Noelle shared with her father.

Was that why the girl had been depressed lately? Because the
parade was coming, and it was one more thing she'd lost? Did she
feel like she was losing her dad all over again?

Noelle hadn't needed a trip to the cemetery this afternoon. She
needed a way to keep her father's memory alive. Meridith wondered
if she'd like to participate in the parade, or if that would only make
her sadder. There was only one way to find out.

*   *   *

Noelle called later and asked to spend the night with Lexi, and since Meridith had become familiar with her parents she felt safe saying yes.

It was a restless night's sleep. The guests stumbled in after midnight, and then Max had a nightmare at three o'clock.

When morning arrived, Meridith forced herself from bed to prepare eggs, bacon, and biscuits, which sat in the warmers until they were inedible. At one o'clock, she scraped the food into the trash, then told the children to grab their jackets. She needed out of the house, and the day was warming to a sunny sixty-five degrees.

The kids had wanted to show Meridith the other side of the island, so they decided to ride their bikes over.

"I wish we could take Piper," Max said as they wheeled their bikes from the garage.

"Why can't we?" Meridith kicked up the stand and straddled the bike.

"She's too well-trained on the electric fence," Noelle said.

"Ever since Mom trained her, she's afraid to leave the yard," Max said.

"What happens when you take her out?"

Ben shrugged. "She just freezes. Won't walk or nothing."

"Anything," Noelle said.

So they left Piper and took the Surfside bike path, riding in single file. The sun on her skin and wind in her hair felt good. The boys had worn their trunks, though Meridith wasn't sure about letting them in the frigid water. She'd brought a couple beach towels she'd found in the upstairs closet.

By the time the bike path opened to the beach, Meridith's muscles ached. They parked their bikes and kicked off their sandals. The boys ran toward the waves, Ben's eagerness making up for his shorter legs.

Meridith handed Noelle a towel, spread her own, then retrieved the sunscreen and slathered it on. "Want some?"

"We put it on before we left."

"We probably sweated it off."

Noelle shrugged, then stretched out on the towel, closing her eyes.

Meridith planted her palms behind her and watched Max and Ben frolic in the water. So far they hadn't gone more than ankle deep. The fresh, salty air blended with the scent of her coconut lotion in a soothing combination.

Above them, three seagulls drifted on the wind, their cries punctuating the shush of waves crashing the shoreline.

"Did you have fun at Lexi's?"

"Guess so."

The bike ride in the sun had made a few freckles pop out on Noelle's nose. She looked young and small lying on the oversized beach towel.

"The Goldmans are coming next weekend. Do you remember them? They said they come every year for the Daffodil Festival."

"Yeah."

"Ben said Mrs. Goldman helps decorate the old car in the garage for the parade?" She hoped phrasing it as a question would spark a conversation.

"Classic."

"What?"

"It's not an old car, it's a classic. A 1959 Ford Galaxie convertible with a V8 and a dual exhaust."

Meridith smiled, encouraged at the response in spite of Noelle's irritable tone. "I have no idea what all that means."

When Noelle said nothing else, Meridith tried again. "It was your dad's car?"

"Mm-hmm."

"Why does Mrs. Goldman decorate it?"

Noelle sighed hard, as if responding to a pestering preschooler. "There's a parade every year at festival time and the Goldmans come for it, and Mrs. Goldman arranges flowers and stuff for her work so she helps decorate the car."

Meridith tried to ignore the girl's *Are you happy now?* tone. "Oh, I see."

She watched Max wade into the water to his thighs. When a wave hit his belly, he squealed and ran for shore. Ben, who hadn't dared to venture in past his ankles, laughed.

Meridith considered how to continue the subject of the parade. "Would you and your brothers want to participate in the parade?"

The wind blew a strand of Noelle's hair across her cheek, and she smoothed it back without opening her eyes. "It wouldn't be the same." Her voice all but disappeared under the *shush* of a wave.

"That's true. But it's kind of sad to let traditions die."

They'd already lost so much, and this was their last chance to participate, though Noelle didn't know that. It might be cathartic to carry on this one last time.

Noelle blinked at Meridith, shading the sun with her hand. "I guess we could. The boys might like it."

It was good to hear a splash of hope in her voice. Meridith smiled. "All right then, let's do it."

"Oh, I forgot. I think something's wrong with the Galaxie. Last time Dad tried to start it, he couldn't. I don't think he got it fixed."

So much for that idea. Unless she could get it repaired before the parade. Her bank account back home was dwindling quickly. Meridith knew nothing about cars, but she had a feeling repairing a classic wasn't going to be cheap. But Noelle had sounded so hopeful, and now her face had fallen again.

"Maybe we can get it fixed. Let me look into it, okay?"

"Really?"

"We have a week and a half. Maybe it's something simple, just a twist of a wrench or something." Who said she wasn't Pollyanna?

"Okay." Noelle sprang upright, then scrambled to her feet. "I'm going in."

She watched the girl go, sand spraying behind her feet, and a satisfied smile tugged Meridith's lips.

"Noelle said you wanted to get the Galaxie running."

Meridith jumped at Jake's voice. She hadn't heard the screen door.

"You walk like an Indian."

"You were lost in thought. The Galaxie's not running?"

She tucked her feet under the Adirondack chair and looked out over the harbor where evening had turned the sky pink and purple. She'd tried to start the car when they'd returned from their ride.

"Something's wrong with it. You wouldn't know a good mechanic, would you? Someone that wouldn't break the bank?"

"I could look at it." He perched on the edge of the chair next to her. Too close.

She raised her brows at him. "You fix cars too?"

He shrugged. "I'm good with my hands." The arrogance was back. The cocky half grin, the bold stare.

She was sure he'd meant nothing by the comment. Still, heat climbed her neck and settled in her cheeks. She was glad for the dim lighting.

"Give me the keys, and I'll try and start it."

Maybe it was another ploy to stay. It would save money, maybe a lot, but was it worth it? "Already did that. It just clicks."

"Probably a dead battery."

"That would be cheap, right?"

"Depends. Old cars can be tricky, and if you take it to a repair shop, sometimes they don't know what they're doing. Unless it's a specialty shop, and then they'll charge you an arm and a—"

"Okay, I get it. How long would it take?"

"If it's just the battery, have it done tomorrow."

"What about the fuse box?"

"All set to go in."

One day on the car, one on the electric, then he'd be out of her hair. "Two more days?"

"Eager to see me go?" That knowing grin.

He did things to her insides, and he knew it. Meridith pressed her lips together and watched the sea grass bow against a breeze.

"Two days and you'll be rid of me," Jake agreed. "So long as it's just the battery."

Twenty-seven

Meridith woke to a fumbling noise. She opened her eyes and glanced at the clock. Twelve fifteen. The college guys were back. A loud laugh—Sean's, she thought—echoed through the hall. There was no way Jake was sleeping through that.

Meridith turned over and pushed down the covers. It was unseasonably warm, good weather for spring break. She and the kids had gone for another bike ride, this time to Sconset. They'd brought a picnic for lunch on the beach, then enjoyed ice cream cones from Siasconset Market before their ride back.

Stephen had called when they were on the bike path, but she'd let it roll over to voice mail and then forgot to call until it was too late.

Good news was, the Galaxie was fixed. When they returned from Sconset, Jake was closing the hood and the car was purring.

"You fixed it," she said.

"Needed a charge and some fluids, was all. She's good as new."

Jake had backed the car from the garage, then they'd scrounged up a water hose and some buckets and scrubbed until the aqua paint sparkled. Noelle had been all smiles, especially when Meridith asked if they wanted to take a spin around the block. They piled in the car, Jake put the convertible top down, and Meridith took the wheel.

Now, as she turned over again, the image of Jake, elbow on the open window, hair blowing in the breeze, taunted her. Tomorrow was his last day. He said he expected to finish the fuse box by evening, and there was no reason he couldn't move out then. No reason at all.

She wondered why, when she lay in bed at night, her thoughts turned to Jake. The realization that she didn't daydream about Stephen pricked her with guilt. It was only because Jake was a thorn in her side. But soon he'd be gone, and everything would return to normal.

Normal. She didn't know what that was anymore. Upheaval had become a way of life. She hadn't liked it as a child, and she didn't like it now. But when Jake left, it would be better. Then when she returned to St. Louis, everything would be okay. The kids would settle in and make friends, and she and Stephen could plan their wedding.

Stephen. She had to tell him soon. Trepidation stirred inside, produced adrenaline that would only keep her awake. She didn't want to think about it now.

She sighed hard. The house was finally quiet again, but she was wide awake.

After wasting two warm breakfasts, Meridith had made a batch of cinnamon rolls for morning. The guys hadn't even apologized, but they were the guests, she reminded herself. Besides, they were leaving in three days, and she needed the money.

Now that the repairs were finished—at least, as finished as they were going to be—she was free to put Summer Place on the market. But that meant telling the children they were moving to St. Louis, and she wasn't ready for that.

She placed the task under Things I'm Putting Off, along with Tell Stephen I'm Keeping the Children.

Meridith's stomach rumbled. Great. They'd eaten an early dinner, then gone for a walk along the beach. Poor Piper had whined from the property's corner, watching them go. They could hear her clear down to the point. When they'd returned, Meridith helped Max with the dishes, swept the back porch, and made the cinnamon rolls, and by that time, she was ready for bed. Her stomach missed the evening snack.

Her stomach rumbled again. *All right, all right.* She needed to check the front door anyway. The students had left it unlocked when they returned the night before.

Meridith slipped into the white fluffy robe she'd pilfered from a guest room. The back stairs creaked under her bare feet, sounding loud in the tomblike house. At the bottom of the stairs, she unlocked the divider door and stepped into the kitchen.

The oven night-light cast a dim glow over the countertops. Enough light to guide her to the peanuts. She poured out a handful and recapped the jar, replacing it quietly.

She checked the front door and found it unlocked. She turned the dead bolt and returned to the kitchen. Outside, beyond the porch, the moon shed a pale silvery light over the tops of the sea grass, over the darkened ocean.

Had her father liked to go out back on a night like this? Inspired by the moonlight? Her feet headed toward the door. She flipped on the porch light, stepped outside, then guided the screen door back into place. After popping the last few peanuts into her mouth, she brushed the salt from her hands and started down the steps.

The wind had picked up, and the chilly breeze tugged at her hair. She wrapped the robe tightly around her and padded over the flagstones leading to the beach. The briny smell of sea mingled with the tang of freshly cut grass.

Gritty sand stuck to the bottoms of her feet as she took the beach steps. When she reached the bottom, her feet sank into the cool layer of sand. She walked closer to the shoreline, staring at the cone of light the moon cast on the surface.

It was pale and silvery with blue flecks against the velvety darkness of the night sea. She closed her eyes and listened to the soft ripple of water kissing the shoreline.

A scraping sound startled her and she whipped around. Nothing moved on the dimly lit porch or in the shadowed yard except the shimmying sea grass. Maybe Ben had forgotten to put Piper in the garage.

"Piper?" she called over the rippling water. The wind answered with a gust, sending a shiver over her arms. Gooseflesh pebbled her skin.

Her eyes scanned the backyard again. Nothing. Probably just the wind rocking a chair or tree branches scraping the house.

She looked out to sea and focused on the sounds again. She'd become accustomed to the ocean's music. The repetition of the waves had a certain rhythm to it. She might even miss it when she left.

She thought of her father and the nice life he'd had here. So different from their life in St. Louis. While in the deepest part of her she couldn't blame him for leaving her mother, she did blame him for leaving her. Why hadn't he taken her? Why had he left her to suffer under her mother's erratic mood swings? Had he thought Meridith had any chance at happiness when he'd had to leave to find it himself? She'd been a child. A lost and lonely child.

A thump sounded behind her. Meridith spun.

The tall silhouette, so close, sent her heart into her throat.

"Heeyyy . . . Meridith . . ."

She stepped back even as she recognized the thickness of his neck, the curls at his nape, against the distant porch light.

"Sean."

"Thought that was you." He took two steps closer, the movement kicking sand over her feet. He reeked of alcohol.

Meridith clutched at the collar of her robe. "I was just turning in. But you stay and enjoy the moonlight. Good night." She tried to step around him, but he blocked her path.

"Waas your hurry? Enjoy it with me."

"No, thanks, I'm tired." She stepped around him.

He grabbed her arm. Even through the thick robe, his fingers bit into her skin.

A riptide raged inside. Her mouth was as dry as the sand under her feet. "Let go."

"Don't be like that." His grip tightened, digging into her flesh. "You know you want me." His voice was suddenly dark, his words clearer.

What did she know about this guy? Nothing at all. She could scream out here, and no one would hear. Her voice would be swallowed by the wind, by the ocean. Her heart was bursting from her rib cage. "You're drunk, Sean."

"And you're hot, but you know that, doncha? All pretty girls do."

She pulled away, dislodging her body from the robe he gripped. She made it two steps before he grabbed her. He jerked her into his chest.

His breath smelled like whiskey. Meridith turned her head, pushed against him. But his chest was like a brick wall, his arms like shackles. She grunted in her effort.

"Oh yeah, I like the spunky ones."

His laugh sent a shiver up her spine. He was too strong. "*Let go, Sean.*" She fought the lump of bile churning inside. Her lungs struggled to expand against the hard wall of his stomach.

She gave another push, stepping back, and he stepped forward, maintaining his hold. His feet tangled with hers, and Meridith felt herself falling backward, then the heavy weight of him crushing her.

Twenty-eight

Jake flipped over and punched down the feather pillow. Meridith's guests had stumbled in, waking him, and now he couldn't get back to sleep. Lying in the darkness, he listened to the house sounds. The heat kicking off. The ticking of the alarm clock. The squeak of the back stairs. Probably Meridith checking the front door.

All he could think of was that tomorrow was his last day at Summer Place. He'd leave, and then what? Did he have enough information to take to a judge, or should he try and convince Meridith that moving was wrong?

But who was he? Only a contractor, as far as Meridith was concerned. And if he told her the truth now, she wouldn't care about his opinion. She'd only care that he'd tricked her into working here, living here. She'd be furious.

And he couldn't blame her.

He flipped onto his back. Maybe he could talk to her again, convince her to let him stay and finish the list. What did he have to lose?

He lay quietly, listening, then realized he'd been waiting for Meridith's return, for the squeak of the stairs to announce she was headed back to her room. He sat up in bed, wondering what was taking her so long to check the door. Outside his window, a light glowed from under the porch roof, a halo reaching into the yard.

Meridith always turned off the light before bed, but maybe she was sitting on the porch, unable to sleep, just like him.

He perched on the bed's edge, tempted by the idea of joining her. The thought stirred something he didn't want to acknowledge. Wyatt was right. He was an idiot. He was falling for his adversary. His engaged adversary. Talk about self-sabotage.

Jake ran a hand over his face. Stay or go? He drummed his fingers on his leg.

A noise sounded outside his room. The clicking of a door. He listened. A squeak on the front steps. Meridith wouldn't come up that way, not with the locked door between the wings. One of the guests was stirring.

A new concern rippled through him. Jake stood and rooted for his T-shirt before remembering he'd hung it on the bed's spindle. He shrugged into it, opened his door, then peered into the hall. Two doors closed, one cracked open.

It was enough. Jake crept down the front stairs, his eyes scanning the darkened living room. When he reached the front door, he found it locked.

Where was she? A dim light glowed in the kitchen, but that was only the stove light. He padded through the living room and dining room, into the kitchen. The refrigerator hummed, breaking the silence. Light glowed from the porch through the kitchen window. A quick scan revealed nothing but empty chairs.

Had Meridith turned on the porch light and forgotten about it? Had she come up the back stairs without his hearing? She must have.

He breathed a wry laugh. Meridith was upstairs drifting off to sleep under a warm quilt while he traipsed barefoot through the house in search of her.

He flipped off the porch light and turned toward the living room. He could use a little sleep himself, if he could just stop thinking about—

A movement on the beach slowed his steps. He approached the window and peered out. The stove light glared on the window-pane, blocking his view. He reached for the doorknob and found it unlocked. He knew that wasn't an oversight. Meridith was on the beach.

But what of the guest? Jake knew he'd left his room. His origi-nal fear returned. He opened the door and traversed the porch in three steps.

He pictured Meri up against one of those boys, drunk and bel-ligerent. Alone and vulnerable on the beach. Jake felt the blood fire in his veins. Then he told himself he was crazy, jumping to conclusions. If they were outside, they were just having a little chat, a casual conversation about Nantucket or ocean tides or col-lege life.

But even as he reassured himself, his feet carried him quickly. The edge of a flagstone cut into the arch of his foot, but he barely felt it. He scanned the beach, his eyes adjusting to the dim moonlight.

There. A shadow moving. Two of them. Embracing?

They stepped from the moonlight's reflection on the water, dis-appeared in front of the water's inky blackness.

He took the beach steps slowly, questioning his gut instinct.

Their shadows barely visible, he strained to hear them over the wind. Maybe it wasn't Meridith at all. Maybe it was one of the boys with some woman he'd met in town.

"*Let go, Sean.*" Meridith's voice.

Something welled inside at her fearful tone. Jake darted forward, his feet digging into the sand.

The shadows clarified. Meridith went down hard; the guy came down on her.

Jake honed in on him. As he neared, he heard Meridith struggling.

He grabbed the guy's shirt, hauled him up. He heard a ripping sound, and then his fist found its mark. The loud *pop* was gratifying.

Sean hit the sand, moaning.

Jake braced his feet, ready—eager—to have another go at him. The kid only rolled to his other side.

A sound at his feet drew his attention. "Meridith." He dove to his knees beside her.

"I'm okay."

He helped her sit up. She looked impossibly small.

Behind him, Sean was standing, staggering.

Jake stood, placing his body between them.

Sean held up his hands, surrendering. "Hey, man, didn't mean nothin' . . . just flirting with the girl."

Jake took a step, ready to plant his fist in the guy's face.

A hand, surprisingly firm, on his leg stopped him. "Don't, Jake."

He took a breath. Tried to calm himself. He wanted to plow the guy down and show him what it felt like to be powerless. Make him feel as powerless as Meridith had. Jake had no doubt he could do it.

Apparently, neither did Sean. He was backing away toward the house. "Sorry, Meridith. Swear I didn't mean nothin'."

The words meant squat to Jake. He clenched his fists at his side. *Dirtbag.*

"Let him go."

Meridith's voice, all tired and shaky, was the only thing that stopped him.

He should call the cops and have the guy hauled off. Then he thought of the squad car pulling up to Summer Place, lights spinning. Summer Place didn't need the bad publicity. The kids didn't need the distress. He looked down at Meridith, huddled in the sand. She didn't either.

Jake glared at Sean. "Pack your things and get out of here. *Now.*"

Sean stopped and turned. "What am I s'posed to tell my friends?"

"Couldn't care less."

Sean shifted in the sand, grabbed the railing. Finally he turned and stumbled up the beach steps and across the yard.

Jake turned to Meridith. She'd pulled her knees to her chest, wrapped her arms around them.

He extended his hands and she took them. They were icy cold. He pulled her to her feet, then took her chin and turned her face into the moonlight. He scanned her face for damage and found none. Just dazed eyes and chattering teeth. "You okay? He hurt you?"

She shook her head.

He could feel her trembling. He remembered feeling something on the sand and stooped to collect a bulky robe.

Downwind, he shook out the sand, then draped the robe over her shoulders. The weight of it buckled her knees. He caught her around the waist.

She came into his arms willingly.

Jake tucked the robe around her, freed her hair, and the wind stole it from his fingers.

She shivered.

He could feel her cold fists through his shirt, tucked into his stomach. "You're cold." He wrapped his arms around her, turned his back to the wind.

Shallow puffs of breath hit his chest, warm and quick. He cradled her head in his palm. She was so small. Helpless. What would've happened if he hadn't come?

And where was Lover Boy when Meri needed him? Halfway across the country. He ground his teeth together, fighting the anger that had barely begun to simmer.

"The children." Meridith pulled away. "I left the door unlocked."

He nodded, taking her hand, and led her toward the house. Sean's friends would probably go with him, which meant they'd all be up and packing. And still drunk. They might even go on a rampage and decide to damage a few things in the process.

When they stepped inside, Jake locked the door behind him, then caught Meridith as she turned to go. "Check on the kids, then go to bed."

"I have to make sure—"

"I'll see to that, and I'll lock up behind them."

"Jake, I'm—"

"Not taking no for an answer. Go on, now," he said gently.

She opened her mouth one more time, an argument poised on her lips, as visible as the fire returning to her eyes.

He heard movement overhead, the guys, and played on her weak spot. "The kids . . ."

It worked. One last look at Jake, and she was darting for the back stairs. He heard the lock click into place and the squawk of the stairs as she ascended. Then he was off to offer his services as personal escort.

Twenty-nine

Meridith pulled the cinnamon rolls from the oven, savoring the sweet spicy smell. She set the rolls on the stovetop to cool, flicked off the oven, and poured a cup of coffee. The kids were taking advantage of the break by sleeping late.

Even Meridith had woken later than usual, her eyes heavy, her body achy. When her eyes fluttered open earlier, she'd stared at the clock's hands as the night before rushed back to mind. Her heart sped in response. She hadn't felt fear like that in so long. Never wanted to feel it again. Though her mother had never hurt her, there were the sudden change of moods, the euphoria, the yelling.

The waiting.

She'd waited for things to settle down, but they never had. When change came, it brought a different sort of fear. From euphoria to depression, the worry her mom wouldn't be there when she got home from school, would disappear just like her dad.

The night before she'd fought back futilely. Sean was so much stronger. The weight of him crushing her, leaving her breathless . . .

And then Jake arrived.

When Sean's weight left her body, she'd been confused. Then she saw Jake. He'd protected her, held her, taken care of her.

The concept was foreign to her. It left her feeling . . . confused.

Meridith sipped the strong brew, breathing the rich aroma. The college guys were gone, Jake had seen to that, and now the house was quiet except for occasional noises from the basement. Jake.

He was leaving tonight, and the realization stirred a new anxiety. What if she were attacked again? What if it were one of the kids? She was glad for the door between the wings, but they couldn't stay locked up there. And she couldn't watch three children every moment—that much she'd learned.

What if last night's scenario repeated itself—and Jake wasn't there? What was she going to do the next month and a half? Even after that, while she waited for Summer Place to sell. She should put it on the market now. The repairs were as done as they were going to be. Nothing was stopping her.

Except she'd have to tell the kids. She wasn't ready for that hurdle.

She sipped her coffee. Maybe she could kill two birds with one stone. If Jake stayed, they would be safe and the house would get finished. Plus, it would allow the children to bond with her before she broke the bad news.

When school let out in June, she'd tell them, then she'd put the house on the market.

Meridith drained her coffee, set the mug in the sink, then went to the garage to collect the summer decorations for the back porch. It was time to spruce up the exterior. She'd found boxes of chair cushions, conch shells, and knickknacks to decorate with.

She lugged the boxes to the back of the house, Piper wagging along behind her. Meridith beat the dust from the plaid cushions and set them in place along with the pillows.

Piper's reddish-gold coat gleamed from the sunny spot where

she'd settled. She watched Meridith for a moment, then laid her head on her paws with a heavy sigh.

Meridith rinsed the conch shells under the spigot, then placed them on the wicker table. Next she pulled out the long lantern strand. Dust rose, filling her nostrils, making her sneeze. She pulled a chair to the corner and began stringing the colorful lights.

The day was warming, no sign of a breeze, and Meridith was glad she'd chosen a short-sleeved top. Rounding the porch's corner, she looped the wire over the hook and looked back on her work, making sure the strand was secure enough to withstand heavy wind.

The clack of the screen door started her. She spun, and the rickety chair wobbled.

"Sorry." Jake rushed to steady her, but she'd already caught her balance.

He was always startling her, but how could she be mad after last night?

Jake scanned the porch appreciatively. "Nice."

Piper, always eager for attention, came running at the sound of Jake's voice.

Meridith stepped down from the chair and scooted it a few feet.

"Let me." Jake took the string and looped it over the hooks one at a time. It took him two minutes to finish the porch.

"Show-off," she said.

"Being tall has its benefits."

And being strong. Words of gratitude formed in her mind, but it took a moment to order them. "I never thanked you last night."

He scratched behind Piper's ears. "No need." He plugged the lights in the wall outlet, and they glowed dimly. "Hopefully there's a wall switch inside."

"I mean it, Jake. I don't know what I would've done." Heat worked into her cheeks. She pulled a cornflower blue pail from the box and set it on one of the tables.

"Your arms . . ."

She looked down, noticing the bruises. Brownish-gray blotches, Sean's fingerprints on her skin. She rubbed the spots, wishing she could wipe them away. Seeing them there, she could almost feel Sean's grip on her, feel the helplessness welling up.

"I should've beat the kid to a pulp." Jake's fists clenched.

"He's long gone. That's all that matters."

"He should've been arrested."

"I don't think he meant to—to attack me that way. We stumbled, and he fell on me."

"You're wearing evidence that says otherwise."

He had a point. And the night before, sand grinding into her back, she'd been convinced she was in danger.

"Don't like the idea of you and the kids here alone."

"Aren't you the one who thought the partitions were silly?"

"Never said that."

"Didn't have to." She gave a wry smile. She was pretty good at reading people. Like just now, he was thinking she was right.

"Maybe I did." He leaned a shoulder on the shingled wall, looking every bit as cocky as he had that first day he'd turned up on her doorstep.

It didn't bother her just this minute. "I know I said I was done with the repairs, but what would you think of finishing the ones that aren't too costly?"

His gaze intensified. "Really?"

Meridith collected a basket and began filling it with shells. "You mentioned the fireplace. I'd like to get it working again. We have tree branches hitting the house, a couple trees that a stiff wind would blow over—if you do that kind of work. Not to mention the other things on the list."

Jake walked to the railing, staring out to sea. When Piper joined him, Jake ruffled her fur.

Maybe he didn't want to stay now. Maybe having the kids under-foot all week had been a pain. Maybe he'd been offended at the way she'd confronted him about being alone with Noelle—a notion that now seemed ludicrous in light of the way he'd come to her rescue.

"I mean, if you can't, that's all right. You probably have other work lined up." It was only a couple months. They'd be safe that long, right? She saw Sean's hardened face, heard the bitter slur of his words, and shuddered.

"I'll stay."

"Are you sure?" Her words rushed out.

"Glad to."

She smiled. "All right then."

He straightened, winked, and she felt it down to her bones.

"Back to the fuse box. The electric will be off awhile today, that okay?"

"Sure, fine."

She watched him go, a new appreciation for those sturdy shoulders and thick arms. Now she wouldn't have anything to worry about.

But something stirred inside at the sight of him walking away that made Meridith wonder if she'd only exchanged one set of wor-ries for another.

Meridith pulled the sliding door and settled at the patio table with Rita. With the electricity off at Summer Place, she'd welcomed her new friend's invitation. The unseasonably warm weather had spurred the Lawsons to fill their pool early, and the kids had jumped at the chance to swim in the heated pool.

The smell of chlorine and sunscreen filled the air. Squeals of laughter and the splashing of water as Max did a cannonball made Meridith smile. Noelle sat on the curled ledge kicking water at Rita's fourteen-year-old son.

"The kids seem to be doing well lately," Rita said. "I think Brandon's flirting with Noelle. Look at that."

"Noelle's flirting right back." After worrying about a crush on Jake, Meridith was relieved to see Noelle interested in a boy her own age. Yet another part of her knew that would only make leaving the island harder.

"Brandon and I are singing in church Sunday. I think he's nervous. Who am I kidding? I'm the nervous one."

"I'm sure you'll do great. I'm looking forward to hearing you." She'd noticed Rita singing during the service. "You really love church," Meridith said. "Yours is a lot different from mine back home."

"I love church because I love God, you know? He's so good to me."

"Of course. We're very blessed."

"It wasn't always like that for me. When I met Lee, I was stuck in a rut. It was all just head knowledge."

"What do you mean?"

Rita sipped her Diet Coke. "Oh, you know. I believed in God, I knew Jesus was God's Son, knew I was a sinner. I knew it here." She pointed to her temple. "But I didn't know it here." She placed her hand on her heart.

Meridith watched Ben backstroke across the width of the shallow end. His arm seemed good as new. He wiped water from his face, smiled at her. Meridith gave him a thumbs-up.

"It's like you and your siblings. Before you came here you knew about them, right? Knew they existed?"

Meridith nodded. "Sure."

"But you didn't *know* them. There's a vast difference. I see the way you look at them."

"They're good kids."

"That they are. Ellie!" She turned her attention to her daughter. "Look before you jump. You almost landed on Max."

Meridith pulled her wrap more tightly around her.

"Go on in," Rita said, "The water's warm."

"Aren't you swimming?"

Rita chortled. "Oh, honey, my bathing suit days are long gone."

"I might get in later. I'm too comfortable to get up. How's your gallery doing?"

"It's slow. But it'll pick up soon. The festival weekend is usually busy. How are things with your fiancé—Stephen, is it? Must be hard to be apart."

"We're okay. Today's Tax Day, so his schedule will ease up."

"Maybe he can come for a visit. He needs to meet his new kids!"

Meridith grimaced. "Actually . . . I haven't exactly told him I'm keeping the children."

"Oh dear."

"I've hinted at it, but with the stress of tax season—well, I guess I have no excuse now, do I?"

"How do you think he'll react?" Rita tucked her glossy hair behind her ear. Her warm and caring eyes made Meridith want to spill it all.

Meridith shrugged. "He's a rational man. I think he'll under-stand, especially since there's no other viable option." But the tone in Stephen's voice when she'd mentioned it before belied her words. "I'll tell him soon."

She scanned the pool, accounting for all the children. The wicker crackled when she leaned back.

"Honey, what happened to your arm?" Rita frowned, reached over, and ran her fingers across the bruises. "Both of them!" she added, noticing the other arm.

The sleeves of her cover-up had ridden up. Meridith pulled them down. "Oh. It's nothing. A guest caught me by surprise last night."

"*What?* Did he attack you, Meridith?"

"Sort of, but Jake came and, well, kind of punched him, and everything's fine now."

"Jake . . . ?"

"The contractor I told you about."

"Oh, right. Thank God he was there! Did you call the police?"

"No. Jake booted him and his friends from the house."

"But are you okay? You must have been terrified!"

Meridith nodded. "I was. I was so relieved when Jake showed up. It was late at night, and I was alone on the beach—won't do that again." She gave a dry laugh.

"I'm just glad you're okay. This Jake guy seems like quite the hero."

She'd only vocalized what Meridith had been thinking. "We're lucky to have him around."

Thirty

It was Saturday night before Meridith got up the nerve. The kids were tucked in bed, their church clothes laid out on their dressers. Meridith had washed her face, brushed and flossed, and changed into her nightshirt. She could delay no longer.

She punched in the number on her cell and paced while it rang.

"Hi, honey," she said when Stephen answered.

"Meridith. I was just thinking about you."

She smiled. "That's nice to hear."

"I was watching the news, and it occurred to me that I never asked about your dad's taxes—did you file?"

That's what he'd been thinking? "My dad filed before he passed. I checked weeks ago."

"Oh, good. I was worried. Not that I thought you didn't have it covered, but you've been out of your element there."

"No kidding." She hadn't told him about Sean. No sense in worrying him, especially since Jake was here.

"No word from the uncle?"

"No." Meridith bit her lip. She had to tell him. He needed time to adjust to the idea before she brought the children home.

"I miss you. I want you to come home."

"I know, but I can't. You understand, right?"

He sighed. "You're going broke paying your mortgage without a paycheck coming in. You're losing your savings."

If only he knew Summer Place was draining it too. "When Summer Place sells, I'll get it back." At least she hoped she would. "Anyway, I wanted to talk about the children."

"What is it?"

She closed her eyes and plunged in. "When I come home, they're coming with me, Stephen." She waited for the response. And waited. Meridith's fist knotted, clutching her cotton nightshirt. Why wasn't he responding?

She continued, "Their uncle hasn't contacted them. He obviously won't be interested in guardianship, and frankly, I don't think he's fit anyway. And there isn't anyone else. They'd go to foster care, probably be separated, and I can't let that happen."

"But—we're getting married." He sounded stunned.

"They're my siblings."

"They were strangers two months ago."

"Well, they're not now. They're blood relatives, Stephen, and I care about them."

He gave a deep sigh. "I understand you feel a certain obligation. You're really caught in a bad spot. But where am I in this decision? It's *our* future, not just yours, and this isn't the kind of decision you make alone, Meridith. Not when you're engaged."

"I should've said something sooner, I know. But you were knee deep in taxes, and I—"

"We're talking about raising three children."

"You'll love them, I know you will. And the oldest is thirteen—four years, and she'll be off to college."

"You're missing the point. Don't I get a say?"

He was right, of course. But what if he decided he couldn't do it? "I'm sorry, Stephen, I know you're right. But what do you want me to do? They're my siblings. I can't abandon them. I thought you'd understand; you know about my childhood. How can I not offer them the stability of a good home?"

"It's very admirable of you, but—"

"You'd be a wonderful father, Stephen."

"I'm not ready for that."

The words, so pointedly spoken, made her reel. He hadn't gotten upset, wasn't yelling. He was calm and cool like always, but he wasn't budging.

"What am I supposed to do then, Stephen?" Even after three deep breaths, after closing her eyes and counting backward from ten, she wasn't ready for his response.

"I guess you have a choice to make."

Thirty-one

Mrs. Goldman made one last adjustment to the daffodil wreath and stepped back. Meridith surveyed the decorated Galaxie. The aqua finish gleamed under the April sky, having been washed and waxed by Ben and Jake. The color set off the garland of yellow daffodils and the spray fanning from a yellow bow above the license plate.

"It'll be the best one!" Ben said. Piper licked his hand, then sat at his side, tongue lolling sideways from her mouth.

"Thanks, Mrs. Goldman," Noelle said.

"Oh, honey, I look forward to this every year. So much fun. I'll be watching for it in the parade, but I have to go wake Mr. Goldman now, or he'll sleep right through the festivities." The woman scooted back into the house, her gray wispy hair and yellow tunic fluttering in the wind.

The wind chimes jangled, making a riot of noise.

Meridith checked her watch. "We should get the show on the road, kids."

"Wait, I have to get something." Noelle sprinted into the house.

"Me too," Max said.

Ben rubbed Piper behind the ears, and the dog gazed up at him with half-lidded ecstasy. "I wish she could be in the Daffy Dog Parade."

"Me too, honey," Meridith said. "When's the last time you tried to take her from the yard?"

Ben shrugged.

"Why don't we try again? Maybe she's outgrown her fear."

"Okay." Ben retrieved Piper's lead from the garage while Meridith removed Piper's computer collar and walked to the street. Piper stopped at her boundary line.

Ben returned with the lead. "Sit, Piper!" When the dog complied, Ben attached the lead. "Okay, let's go!" He pulled the leash and started walking, but Piper resisted the tug. "Let's go, Piper!" Ben tugged again.

Piper didn't look like she was having fun. Her eyebrows scrunched up, and she wouldn't look at them.

Meridith squatted at the edge of the street. "Come on, girl!"

"Let's go for a walk!" Ben said.

Piper squirmed, her tail almost wagging.

"She wants to come," Meridith said.

Ben tried pulling the dog with his hands. Piper's front paws dug into the ground, her back legs braced against the forward momentum. It would've been amusing if it weren't so pitiful.

"I don't think it's going to work, Ben."

"Dumb dog." Ben sighed.

"She's not dumb, she's just well trained. The last time she tried to leave she experienced pain, and she doesn't want to repeat it." Meridith replaced Piper's collar. "We'll work with her later, when we have more time."

The screen door slammed, and Jake appeared in jeans and a T-shirt. He padded down the steps and appraised the Galaxie. Piper ran to meet him.

"Not bad," Jake said when they neared.

But when Meridith looked at him, he was staring at her. His eyes still looked sleepy, his hair poking up at odd angles. She ran her hand down the length of her own hair.

Max and Noelle trotted down the porch steps. Noelle climbed into the convertible and hung a gold cross necklace from the rearview mirror.

"Mom's necklace," Ben said.

Max climbed in the other side and looped his dad's ball cap over the mirror. "And Dad's hat," he said.

Noelle fingered the cross. "They should get to come too."

Meridith swallowed around a knot in her throat. Jake was watching the kids with an expression she'd never seen. His tenderheartedness surprised her.

She cleared her throat, blinking against the ache behind her eyes. "That's a wonderful idea."

The kids piled into the car while Meridith retrieved her purse and the picnic basket. Jake was watching from the porch as she stowed it in the trunk.

"Can Jake come too?" Max said. "There's room."

Meridith was searching for an excuse when Jake jumped in. "Can't, guys. Haven't showered yet. I'll keep my eye out for you in the parade, though."

By the time they arrived at the car staging area, there were dozens of antique and classic cars in line. Once they had a spot, the children got out and found friends to talk with as they walked around checking out the decorations.

Meridith stayed in the Galaxie, surveying the festivities. Mrs. Goldman had told her Daffodil Weekend was a big deal, but Meridith hadn't anticipated the huge crowd, or the overwhelming sight of so many daffodils.

When her phone rang, she saw Rita's name on the screen. "Rita, hello."

"Good morning, honey!"

Meridith couldn't help but smile in response to her friend's sunshiny attitude.

"Are you lined up?"

"Lined up and ready to go." Meridith watched Ben and Max playing with a friendly black Lab. Noelle chatted with a friend three cars up.

"Do you have plans for the tailgate picnic? I made a ton of food, and we'd love for you and the kids to join us."

The picnic was held on the lush lawns of Sconset after the parade. "Our basket is in the trunk, but we'd love to join you."

"Great. Look for our car when you get there, and give me a jingle if you can't find us. I have to go, the gallery is packed!"

"We'll see you then." Meridith said good-bye and hung up. The children would be glad for the company. Especially Noelle, if Rita's son was present.

She was glad they'd decided to be in the parade. She knew from the books on grief that the festival was a milestone event, and the children were using it to honor their parents. She looked at the cross and cap dangling from the mirror. She also knew the festival could trigger a resurgence of loss, and she was glad they were joining Rita and her family. The distraction could be just what they needed.

A chilly breeze blew through the window, ruffling her hair. She took a deep whiff of the flower-scented air and relaxed into the white leather seat, letting the car glide toward Sconset behind a black antique Ford.

The children had settled in their seats, the excitement of the parade draining away as Nantucket town faded in her rearview mirror.

A For Sale sign in a landscaped yard caught her attention, turning her mind back to the previous evening when she and the Goldmans had sat on the porch sipping hot chocolate after the children turned in. They'd inquired about Summer Place's future, and Meridith had confided that she was selling.

"We've talked over the years about buying a bed-and-breakfast now that I've retired," Mr. Goldman said.

"Summer Place is like a second home to us. Wouldn't that be great if we could work something out?" Mrs. Goldman said.

They'd talked over an hour, and Meridith was thrilled. If the Goldmans bought it, she wouldn't have to put the place on the market, wouldn't have to pay a Realtor fee, and the house would go to familiar people. She thought that might help the children adjust to the idea of moving to St. Louis.

The thought of returning home brought her to Stephen. Though the topic of the children hadn't resurfaced all week, their conversations had been stilted.

When she answered his calls, a strange sensation welled in the pit of her stomach, a sort of weighted feeling she was eager to be rid of. She needed to clear the air. But every time she considered broaching the subject, she remembered Stephen's words. *I guess you have a choice to make.*

Maybe he was waiting on her. The real problem then was that there was no choice, no decision. She couldn't abandon the children. How could she let her siblings go to foster care, possibly separated? Why couldn't he understand that?

These thoughts had circled her mind all week, always ending in that heavy-weighted feeling and the realization that, regardless of the ring on her finger and the promise it implied, her relationship with Stephen might be over before it had hardly begun.

The car in front of her braked as they entered the town of Sconset, and Meridith pulled to the side of the road behind the long line of cars.

"There's the Lawsons' car." Max pointed across the street.

Rita had seen them pull up and was waving as they exited the car. The kids ran to catch up with the Lawsons, and Meridith retrieved the cooler from the trunk.

She made her way across the street and wove between cars and people, crossing the lawn. The weight of the cooler strained her arms.

Rita's son, Brandon, was jogging toward her, no doubt on a mission to take her load. But he was still twenty feet away when her foot hit a dip in the ground. Her ankle turned and her leg crumbled under the heavy weight of the cooler.

Jake wandered down the Sconset street. The smell of grilling burgers wafted through the air, tempting him. He scanned the crowd of people and tangle of parked cars and lawn chairs.

The kids had begged him to join them for the picnic, but it presented a challenge. What if someone mentioned his niece and nephews in front of Meridith? What if they mentioned his cycle or the fact that he usually wasn't back from the mainland in time for the festival? What if they offered their condolences on Eva's death?

"Hey, Jake! Come join us," Willow called from a knot of people clustered behind a black '72 Chevy.

Jake approached the group and shook Wyatt's hand as his friend stood. "Sweet ride."

"Wish it were mine," Wyatt said. "Got plenty of food." The smell of garlic and something sweet seconded his offer.

"And my cousin from Boston is here." Willow winked. "She's dying to meet you."

Before he could decline, a tall, honey-haired woman appeared. Willow introduced them, and they chatted a moment before the cousin went to help Willow set out the food.

"Pull up a chair," Wyatt said. "I wasn't kidding when I said we have plenty."

"Thanks, but I'm looking for Meridith and the kids. Have you seen them?"

Wyatt gave him a look. "They're over that way with another family." He leaned in close. "Dude." He gestured at Willow's cousin, who was fighting the wind with a checkered tablecloth.

Jake had already forgotten her name. "Kids are expecting me. I'll catch you later."

Wyatt shook his head.

By the time Jake stumbled upon Meridith and the kids, his stomach was rumbling. They were situated in a circle of lawn chairs, a red-and-white cloth spread in the middle. He was relieved when he didn't recognize the family sitting with them.

"Jake!" Max was the first to spot him.

"Did you see us in the parade?" Ben asked.

"Sure did, little man. It was the best car there."

"Have you eaten?" Meridith asked.

"No, ma'am." He noticed Meridith's foot propped on a cooler, a bag of ice over the ankle. "What happened?"

"Oh, she took a little stumble," the brunette woman offered.

"You okay?" Jake lifted the Ziploc bag. Her ankle was almost purple. "Ouch."

"Told you I was clumsy."

The word took him back to the dance lessons, and he could almost feel Meridith in his arms again.

"Don't think we've met." A bearded man stood, offering his hand. "I'm Lee Lawson."

"Jake. I'm working on Summer Place."

"I'm Rita, a friend of Meridith's." She shook his hand, then gave Meridith a peculiar look before introducing her two teenagers. "We've already eaten, but we have plenty of leftovers. Let me fix you a plate."

Lee set up another lawn chair beside Meridith, and Jake discreetly pulled it a few feet away, behind the Lawsons' car, where he could hide from anyone who might know him. He tugged his ball cap lower for good measure.

By the time Jake sat, Rita was setting a loaded plate in his lap.

"Thanks, appreciate it."

The turkey club hit the spot, settling his empty stomach. The group talked about the festival and which cars they'd voted for.

"There's Martin O'Neal," Lee told his wife. "Haven't seen him all winter." He went to talk with his friend.

"Can we walk around?" Noelle asked.

"Yeah, can we?" Ben asked.

Max and the Lawson girl stood.

Meridith scanned the crowd. "Oh, guys, I don't know. It's so crowded, and I can't go with you." She gestured to her ankle.

"I was about to suggest a walk." Rita stood. "Jake can keep you company."

The group was off and walking before Jake could finish chewing his bite of cranberry salad. He watched them go, watched the Lawson boy settle in next to Noelle. She elbowed him, laughing.

Rita took Benny's hand, and Max stole the hat from the Lawson girl's head. She chased him a few feet before recapturing it.

"I think they're going to be okay," Meridith said. She'd shaded her eyes with her hand, watching them. Despite the ankle that must be throbbing, she looked at peace.

He remembered when the Galaxie had come into sight earlier. He'd been standing in the crowd lining Main Street, catching up with people he hadn't seen since fall. They'd been near the end of the parade behind a black antique Ford. But once his eyes caught on the Galaxie, everything else faded away.

The kids waved at the crowd, all smiles. Even Meridith's face was wreathed in joy, obviously enjoying the Nantucket tradition. His breath had felt stuffed into his lungs for just a moment. They looked . . . like a family.

"Don't you think they're going to be okay?" Meridith's question belied her former confidence.

"Kids are more resilient than we give them credit for."

"What do you know about kids?" Meridith teased.

"Used to be one." He traded a smile with her. "Pretty cool what you did for them today."

Meridith took her hand down, looked at Jake. Those green eyes were downright mesmerizing.

"I didn't do anything." She shifted the ice pack. "I couldn't believe it when Noelle and Max brought out those mementos. Pretty smart kids."

"Pretty smart big sister." More and more he was coming to see it. If he could only understand why she'd take them from their home. But he didn't want to think about that today. Would rather think about the way the sunlight made copper sparkles in her hair. Or the way her nose turned up ever so slightly on the end.

"I worry about them, you know?" she said. "It's tough being a kid."

"For some. Others are more blessed."

She cocked her head at him. "Not you?"

He wondered how she knew that.

"You mentioned a foster mother once."

When they were dancing. He remembered now. "Not me." He tried not to think about it and mostly succeeded. "I was in foster care most of my childhood—parents died young."

"Like my siblings'."

He nodded. Being separated from Eva was the worst. He'd been too young to understand, but old enough to feel responsible, even if he was the younger one. At first they'd seen each other regularly, but busy schedules had gotten in the way, and soon he'd lost track of her.

"I was pretty tough, though," he said. "Made it through with only a few scars."

"That I can believe."

Her smile made him want to stare at her all afternoon. He thought of Willow's cousin. Her beauty was no rival for Meridith's pixie chin and guileless eyes.

"I'll bet you were a handful," she said.

"Got myself into a few scrapes."

"I knew it. You were a rule breaker."

"What do you mean, 'were'?" He shrugged. "I was good at not getting caught, made the most of it."

"I'll just bet you did."

Jake felt a smile pull his lips. She was almost flirting, but he wasn't going to point it out. The moment he did, it would be over. He scanned the crowd for people he might know and need to avoid.

"What turned you around?"

"Who says I turned around?"

She laughed, and the sound reminded him of the wind chimes on the porch, bright and happy.

"All right, I turned around. Or rather, God turned me around."

"God?" Surprise lined her tone, raised her brows.

"I'm not a heathen, you know."

"Sorry. Go on."

He'd have to be careful here. No mention of motorcycles, the mainland, or the motorcycle ministry that finally opened his eyes. "Met a friend about two years back who took me under his wing. Good man. I wanted what he had."

"Which was . . . ?"

He looked at Meridith. She took the kids to church faithfully each week. This wasn't news to her. "A relationship with God. He showed me how it's done." Actually, Eva and T. J. had planted the seeds, but he couldn't say that. He pulled the leather strip of his necklace, freeing the silver cross from his shirt. "This was his."

"Where is he now?"

"Died about a year ago after fighting lung cancer awhile." He'd been sick when he'd met up with Jake at a cycle hangout in Tallulah, Louisiana.

"No brothers or sisters?"

He thought of Eva and how hard he'd worked to find her after turning eighteen and heading out on his own. It seemed like the system had conspired to keep them apart. "Pretty much all alone in the world."

"I'm an only child too." She seemed to remember the kids. "Well, I guess I'm not. They feel more like my children than my siblings."

"Responsibility will do that."

"It is a lot of responsibility."

Two women he knew from church approached, waving.

"Jake, we've been looking for you," Sierra said.

The other one, Rowan, touched his shoulder. "A few of us are going out on my boat after the picnic, then back to my house for pizza and a movie. I hope you'll come . . ." Her blue eyes begged.

"Can I let you know later?"

"You have my number," Sierra said, her gaze flickering toward Meridith.

"Get a cell phone," Rowan said, sashaying away. "You are way too hard to track down."

Especially when he was hiding from the public at large.

"Girlfriend?" Meridith asked once the girls disappeared in the throng of people.

"Friends from church." Jake rubbed his jaw, unsure why he found the attention embarrassing.

"You should go with them—you don't have to babysit me."

"Nah."

Meridith removed the ice pack and put it in the cooler, then offered him a Coke. She closed the lid and propped up her foot again. The swelling had gone down, but it was still discolored.

"I can drive the car back," he said. "I rode up with a friend."

Meridith flexed her foot and winced. "That might be best. Thanks." She settled her elbows on the aluminum chair's arms. Her diamond ring glinted in the sun.

He wondered if she'd told Lover Boy about the kids yet. It was nearly May. School would be out in a month. Might as well ask, since she was so chatty.

He couldn't seem to pull his eyes from the sparkling rock. "You tell him about the kids yet?"

She followed his gaze to her hand. "Oh." She straightened the diamond, then cradled her hand in her lap. "I did, actually."

He tried to read her expression, gave up. "How'd it go?"

"Not so well."

Maybe Wyatt was right. Maybe it was about to hit the fan. He found himself irrationally pleased, and not just on account of the kids.

"You're still wearing the ring."

"It didn't go *that* badly. I think Stephen needs time to adjust to the idea. And once he gets to know the children . . ." Her voice trailed off, and she finally pressed her lips together.

Maybe if they called off the wedding, she'd move to Nantucket, keep Summer Place. As soon as hope began to swell, a sharp prick of guilt popped the bubble. Meridith obviously loved the guy. Who was Jake to wish a broken heart on her? Besides, while a breakup might mean she kept the kids here, it also meant he was up the creek with his identity.

"Jake! Hey, buddy!" Another acquaintance approached, transferring his glass of wine for a handshake.

"Mr. Stanford," Jake said, standing.

Did the man know about Eva? He prayed nothing would be said to give him away.

"You were right," Mr. Stanford said. "Those windows made a huge difference in heating costs this winter."

"Glad I could help. Mr. Stanford, this is Meridith . . ." *My employer? My friend? My late sister's stepdaughter?* He closed his mouth.

They traded greetings, and the man commented on Meridith's injury. Jake just wanted him to go, but he remembered how chatty the man had been while Jake installed his windows.

Mr. Stanford engaged them in a lengthy conversation about landscaping while Jake pocketed his hands, trying to think of a polite way to end the conversation. He was saved by the return of Rita and the kids.

Mr. Stanford said his good-byes, and Jake took his seat, relieved. The kids listed the friends they'd seen while Rita and Lee packed up. Jake gathered Meridith's supplies.

"Why don't you come back to our house?" Rita said. "We always cook out the night of the tailgate picnic, and since the pool's up and running we can swim. Unless your ankle's hurting too much, honey."

"Oh, can we?" Noelle asked.

Jake noted the way she traded looks with the Lawson boy and wasn't sure he liked it one bit.

"Well, I suppose we could," Meridith said. "We'll need to stop by the house for our suits."

"Jake, you're welcome, too, of course." Lee scratched his beard. "Otherwise, I'm overrun with women."

Jake glanced at Meridith—didn't want to wear out his welcome. But Meridith, seemingly undisturbed, was gently tugging her sock onto her foot.

"Thanks, don't mind if I do."

After running Meridith and the kids home for their suits, Jake drove the Galaxie to the Lawsons. The family lived in a mid-island home with a sloping front yard and a wide front porch lined with a plethora of daffodils.

The evening was so enjoyable, Jake forgot to return Sierra's call. He had no trunks, but the adults didn't swim anyway. They played spades on the patio, and he and Meridith won easily. By the time the kids were piling into the car to return home, Jake felt almost like they were a family. Meridith had, for whatever reason, let her guard down for the day.

He helped her to the car, and they started toward Summer Place in the dark. The wind blew across the open convertible, tossing his hair, and the kids huddled in the back complaining of freezing to death. Meridith pulled her blue sweater closed and hugged herself.

He wished she'd move closer so he could keep her warm. He imagined his arm wrapped around her shoulders, her face tucked into his chest against the wind. It was a picture he liked. Too much. Being near her all day, out of their element, had been revealing.

But it hadn't revealed something new about Meridith so much as it had revealed his own feelings. Not that he hadn't been aware of them; he just hadn't realized they were rooted so deeply.

If only she weren't already taken. And, okay, if she didn't believe he was someone else.

Wyatt was right. He was an idiot. He was in the middle of a mess, but it wasn't too late to ask for help—it was never too late. He sent up a silent prayer as he drove through the quiet neighborhood streets. Usually he made sound decisions and could calculate the outcome. This one had him baffled. And now that feelings were involved—his own—he had more at stake than he cared to.

He turned onto Driftwood Lane. The kids had quieted in the back, their teeth probably chattering too much to talk. Meridith had quieted, too, but when she carefully shifted her leg, he wondered if she was in pain.

"Ankle hurting?"

The night was too dark to read her expression. "I guess I need to keep it propped."

"Tylenol's worn off. You should take something before you turn in."

"I will. I was just thinking about the Goldmans and the Mowerys. I hope they're faring all right. I feel badly for being gone all day."

"The Goldmans seem to know what's what around here, and the

other couple seemed pretty autonomous. I'm sure they all had a full day at the festival and are tucked away for the night."

"You're probably right."

Jake pulled the car into the drive. "See, the house is dark." The engine hummed, accented by the pebbles popping under the wheels. "She's a sweet ride. Purrs like a kitten." He pulled the car into the garage. The familiar smell of mustiness and motor oil assaulted his senses.

He gave the house key to Noelle, knowing it would take him and Meridith a few extra minutes, and the kids took the short cut through the back of the house, probably eager to get into their warm pajamas.

"I'll be up to tuck you in," Meridith called after them.

Jake opened Meridith's door, and she swung her legs out, setting her foot down gently. Jake grasped her hands and pulled. She weighed nothing, a feather in the wind. He helped her navigate the car.

"The basket and stuff—"

"I'll come back for it. Come on, Hopalong." He took one arm, braced at the elbow, and put the other around her. Her skin was cool, the sweater a too-thin barrier against the chill in the air. She walked gingerly toward the front of the house, taking the route with fewer steps.

Piper circled them, barking.

"No, Piper. Back!" Jake said, fearing she'd trip Meridith. The dog sure was keyed up.

They navigated the flagstones slowly in the dark. When they reached the steps, a breeze stirred the wind chimes, stirred her hair, and the familiar citrus scent wafted toward him.

"Lean on me," Jake said as they took the steps. When they reached the top, a shadow by the swing moved. Jake dropped Meridith's elbow and stepped in front of her, the confrontation with Sean still fresh in his mind.

The shadow moved again. Too tall for Mr. Goldman or the other guests.

"Who's there?" Jake braced his feet, his guard up, ready to pounce.

Thirty-two

Meridith turned to see why Jake was suddenly alert, the muscles in his arms hardening. She peered around him, and a familiar form emerged from the shadows.

"Stephen!" Meridith hobbled forward and embraced her fiancé. "What are you doing here?"

"I missed you." He pecked her on the lips, but his embrace felt stilted. Then she remembered Jake.

She pulled away and cleared her throat. "Stephen, this is Jake, the contractor I hired. Jake, this is my fiancé, Stephen."

Jake extended his hand. The grasp seemed more like a challenge than a handshake. Or maybe it was her imagination.

"Nice to meet you," Stephen said.

"Same." Jake's voice seemed deep after Stephen's. "I'll turn in now," he said to Meridith. "You'll be all right with your ankle?"

"Yeah, thanks." Her laugh wobbled. "Good night."

She'd never gotten around to telling Stephen that Jake was staying there, and now she wished she had. Boy, did she ever.

Stephen would have questions. She wasn't blind to the way it must look, a cozy family returning from a day at the festival. Not to mention the way she'd been curled into Jake's arms as he'd helped her up the walk.

The screen door slapped into place, leaving them alone.

Meridith huddled into her thin sweater. "I can't believe you're here."

"He's staying here?" Stephen's voice had an edge she hadn't heard before.

"It was a trade. I couldn't afford the repairs, remember? Jake offered to trade for room and board."

"I'll bet he did."

"Stephen. This is a bed-and-breakfast. We have people here all the time. What's one more?"

His sigh filled the space between them. Piper sniffed at his pant leg, and Stephen nudged her away. "You're right. Sorry. I've been waiting a while, and I'm hungry."

There was the old conciliatory Stephen she knew and loved. She almost told him he could've knocked—the guests would've let him in—but mentioning it now was pointless.

"Well, let's get that taken care of." She hobbled toward the door.

"What happened to your ankle?"

She rolled her eyes, though he was behind her. "I was carrying a cooler and didn't see a dip in the ground. It's twisted, that's all."

"Did you have it looked at?" He set his suitcase inside the door.

"It's not that bad. Just a little swollen. Have a seat, and I'll fix you a plate." She remembered the picnic basket in the car. The trunk would smell by tomorrow, but she wasn't hobbling out there now.

Meridith prepared a salad and brought it to Stephen. He'd settled on the sofa's end beside the antique table.

"Here you go. I need to tuck the children in."

He took the plate. "Should I meet them now?"

That he was eager to meet them warmed her. "Why don't we wait until morning? They're pretty tired—might even be asleep already. I'll be right back."

Meridith limped up the back stairs. Ben and Noelle were already asleep, but she listened to Max's prayers. Downstairs again, she stopped in the kitchen for Tylenol. Remembering Piper, she let the dog in the garage and retrieved the picnic basket while she was there. The extra walking made her ankle throb.

Above her, she could hear Jake still stirring, and wondered for the first time what he thought of Stephen's arrival. Having the two of them there would be uncomfortable. It only proved what she'd been reluctant to admit. An attraction was one thing, but her feelings for Jake had gone beyond that. Leaving the disconcerting notion for later, she returned to the living room.

She limped to the armchair, then wondered why she'd chosen to sit catty-corner rather than beside Stephen. The time apart had made things awkward, she decided, multiplied by their disagreement over the children. Or maybe she'd only chosen the seat so she could prop her foot on the ottoman.

"Sorry we weren't here when you arrived. If I'd known you were coming . . ."

That he'd come without warning wasn't Stephen-like at all. He wasn't the spontaneous type.

He finished chewing a bite of salad. "I missed you. I know I should've called. Things have been a little strained between us this week, and I thought being together would help us find our footing again."

Meridith smiled. He regretted the way he'd handled her decision.

He didn't have to vocalize it; she could see it in the way his eyes turned down at the corners, the way his lips tipped up.

"You're right."

"Were the children still awake?"

"Only Max, he's the ten-year-old. Ben was curled into a ball in his top bunk, and Noelle was sprawled across the bed like she'd been there all night. It was quite the day. I'm sure they're tired." As if the mention of the word alerted her body, she yawned.

This visit would be a good thing. Stephen would get acquainted with the children and see why she couldn't leave them.

"There's some kind of festival going on, isn't there? The traffic getting here was atrocious."

"I hear it's worse in the summer."

He forked the lettuce and stuck it in his mouth. Meridith bit her lip. She shouldn't have brought up summer. It was a reminder of the vast gulf separating them, the question of when she was returning and whether she'd have the children with her when she did.

But of course she'd have the children. She'd already told him so. And he was here; that must mean he was willing to give the ready-made family a shot. She smiled.

The house was quiet, only the sound of Stephen's jaw clicking as he munched on the salad. Strange that she'd forgotten that about him. Her ankle throbbed, and she set a pillow under it.

"I thought you could show me around the island tomorrow," he said between bites.

Their first outing as a family. It was a good idea. "Maybe in the afternoon. I have to make breakfast first—we have guests here at the moment. The Goldmans are interested in buying Summer Place, but we can talk about that tomorrow. Then we have church. It's a lot different from ours, but I think you'll like it. When do you have to leave?"

"Monday morning, unfortunately. I was only able to get a long weekend."

"After all the hours you worked?"

He shrugged. "I tried to come in last night, but the flights were booked. Because of the festival, I guess."

"If I'd known you were here, I would've come home earlier."

"I kept trying your cell."

"It was noisy at the picnic, then it was dead by the time we reached the Lawsons'."

"The Lawsons?"

Meridith smiled, thinking of Rita. "You'll meet them at church. Rita's so kind. I'd be lost here without her."

"I doubt that. I don't know anyone as capable as you, Meridith."

"Thanks," she said, smiling. But the word wasn't the high compliment it used to be. She found herself wishing Stephen would say something else. *You're the most wonderful woman I know* or *You're so beautiful, Meridith.*

She shook her head. What was getting into her? She'd never cared about romantic declarations before. Stephen was a good fit. The best. Her aching ankle was making her irritable and critical. Meridith smothered another yawn as Stephen finished his salad and set his plate aside.

"It's late," Stephen said. "I should let you get to bed."

"Oh, you need a room." Meridith pulled her foot from the ottoman, already considering where to put him. The only room available in the family wing was Eva and T. J.'s, but she didn't want to upset the children. She'd put him in the nautical room beside Jake's.

"I can help get it ready." Stephen stood and pulled her to her feet. They were toe to toe in the same spot where she'd stumbled while dancing with Jake.

"The room's already made up."

Stephen's face was clean-shaven, his skin still pale from a long winter indoors. His baby-blue eyes smiled tenderly.

"I've missed you." His arms circled her. "It's so good to see you again. The phone just isn't the same." He kissed her, his lips moving slowly over hers. After a moment, he drew back with a smile, then turned toward the stairs and grabbed his suitcase.

Meridith's mind whirled as she negotiated the steps. Whirled because the kiss she'd missed all these weeks, the one that had once left her content and satisfied, had only left her shaken this time—and for all the wrong reasons.

Thirty-three

Meridith was restless all night. Between the aggravation of keeping her foot elevated and the disturbing realization that Stephen's kiss only stirred ambivalence, she found herself analyzing the relationship.

Was it the time apart? Their disagreement over the children? Or, more disturbing, her feelings for Jake? Maybe it was a combination of all three, a confusing cocktail that was even more unsettling.

By the time she drifted to sleep, she'd decided to put any reservations on hold and let tomorrow play out. Perhaps after a day together at least two of the issues would be moot.

Stephen had come to the island, wanted to be with her and get to know the children. That was all she could ask, and she knew the children would grow on him just as they had her.

When morning came, she pried open her eyes and forced herself to limp downstairs and fix breakfast. Her ankle felt worse, and she popped three Tylenol, hoping it would loosen.

Stephen kissed her good morning, his breath minty fresh, and helped her set the table. The Goldmans and Mowerys slept in, so Meridith put the food in the warmers and called the children down.

They trotted down the steps noisily and took a seat, so used to strangers at the table, they hardly noticed Stephen. Jake was conspicuously absent.

"Children," Meridith said, taking her own seat. "This is Stephen, my fiancé. Stephen, this is Noelle, Max, and Ben." She gestured toward each child.

"Hi." Noelle eyed him suspiciously. Max nodded at him, more interested in a big scoop of scrambled eggs, and Ben looked quietly between Stephen and Meridith.

"It's nice to meet you," Stephen said.

"Are you coming to church with us?" Max asked.

"I sure am."

"How's he gonna fit in the van?"

"There's plenty of room," Meridith said.

"I can drive separately."

"There's no need." Meridith dished out eggs for Ben and laid two strips of bacon beside it. "After church we're going to show Stephen the island's sights."

"Oh . . ." Stephen's fork stopped in midair. "I thought—"

Meridith questioned him with her eyes, but he looked away.

"Lexi invited me over after church," Noelle said. "We're going to start a blog, and we're setting it up today."

"You can go to Lexi's next Sunday, okay?" Meridith decided to table the discussion on online safety, but giving strangers open access to a teenage girl's life seemed unwise.

"We wanted to do it today."

Meridith pulled her lips upward. "Well, Stephen's here today, so you can do it next week."

"Can Jake come?" Max asked.

Meridith's smile wobbled. Heaven help her. She felt Stephen's eyes on her and wondered if he thought Jake tagged along on all their excursions—then cringed, because he often did. "No, Max, he cannot."

"Are you guys getting married?" Ben broke his silence.

"Duh," Noelle said. "What do think *fiancé* means?"

Meridith wanted to slide under the table and stay there, but she forced herself to referee the children's discussion through the meal.

Church, at least, turned out better than she hoped. They sat with Rita and Lee, who offered to watch the children that evening so she and Stephen could be alone. Meridith was about to refuse, wanting Stephen to bond with the children, but he jumped in with a gracious thanks, and Meridith realized it was reasonable for him to want a couple hours alone.

After church they went home to change. Meridith checked out the Mowerys and the Goldmans, who promised to be in contact about buying Summer Place.

After the children were ready, they piled back into the van and proceeded to argue over who had to sit in the backseat. Finally, Meridith moved Ben's booster to the back, and they headed toward town. Between driving and refereeing the children's arguments, Meridith found herself wondering where Jake had disappeared to. His truck had been gone when she'd woken and still wasn't back after church.

They children voted for lunch at the Atlantic Café, and throughout the meal Meridith reminisced about the evening they'd celebrated the removal of Ben's cast. After lunch they walked the brick sidewalks that seemed deserted after yesterday's parade.

By the time they were on their way to Sconset, Meridith became concerned by Stephen's silence. She tried to pull him into the conversation, but between Max and Noelle's bickering and Ben's questions, it was easy for Stephen to remain on the edge of the fray.

He did seem to enjoy Sconset, now serene after the bustle of the picnic and crowds the day before. The grassy lanes ran between the tightly spaced, gray-shingled cottages, offering views of small lush gardens that bloomed with daffodils and other early blooming flowers. Vines clung to white picket fences bordering the gardens.

"They look like dollhouses," Stephen noted.

"You wouldn't believe how much those dollhouses run," Meridith said. She'd cautioned him earlier, reminding him the children didn't know Summer Place was being sold.

From Sconset, they set out for Surfside, where she and Stephen sat on the beach while the children waded along the shore. It was there that a gust of wind carried Max's hat into the ocean. He had to wade in hip-deep to rescue his dad's old cap.

Max returned to the van for a long, soppy ride back to Summer Place to change and grab a quick dinner before they took the children to Rita's. When Meridith shut off the ignition in the Lawsons' driveway, she noticed Ben's pallor as the others exited the van.

"Ben, are you all right?"

He stepped down from the van. "I'm—not—feeling—" Ben's dinner made a repeat appearance, splattering onto the driveway and Stephen's shoes.

Stephen darted back, too late.

"Oh my goodness!" Meridith rushed around the van. "You're sick. Noelle, go ask Rita for a washcloth." She placed her hand on the boy's back. "Are you feeling better now?"

Ben nodded, wiping his mouth with the back of his sleeve.

"You'll have to come home and get some rest. We can't expose the Lawsons to an illness."

"I get carsick when I sit in the back."

Meridith sighed hard, torn between frustration and sympathy. "Why didn't you tell me earlier?"

"You told me to sit in the back."

"Well, I know I did, but—" Oh, what good did it do to argue now?

Noelle appeared with the washcloth, and Meridith wiped Ben's face, then handed the cloth to Stephen, who'd stepped well away. He took it between two pinched fingers, then dabbed at his shoes.

"Sorry," Meridith told him.

Rita welcomed Ben into the house and promised he'd be right as rain in minutes, then shooed Meridith and Stephen on their way.

By now Meridith was eager for time alone. She was exhausted from trying to make the children get along and playing middleman between them and Stephen. The day had been a disaster. If anything, she sensed Stephen pulling farther away.

When they turned into Summer Place's drive, alone for the first time since morning, Meridith noted Jake's truck in the drive. She didn't know how much more discomfort she could stand, and she had the sudden feeling things could get worse. Much worse.

Piper greeted her when she exited the van. "Hi, girl." The whole back half of the retriever wagged. Meridith's foot was better, but the medication was wearing off, and she felt a headache starting at the base of her neck.

"Want to sit on the beach?" she asked. "There are some nice Adirondack chairs out there, and we can enjoy the evening light." *And avoid Jake*, she added mentally.

"It's kind of chilly. What about a walk on the beach?"

"My ankle . . ." she reminded him. "I'll grab a nice, thick quilt, and we'll cozy up on the chairs."

"All right," he said, removing his shoes.

Meridith went inside while Stephen squatted at the spigot, rinsing his shoes. She took the medication, then retrieved a freshly washed quilt from the laundry room. Jake was in his room, she supposed, though she didn't hear him moving around. Was he giving her and Stephen space to work things out? She didn't know why the notion bothered her.

When Meridith joined Stephen, he was standing on the beach near the chairs holding a daffodil. He turned and held it out as she approached.

Meridith took the yellow flower, remembering all the daffodils she'd seen the day before. An image of Jake smiling as he teased her at the picnic washed across her mind.

Forcing the image away, she sat in the chair, and Stephen wrapped the blanket around her shoulders. He sat beside her and buried his bare feet in the sand. Piper whined from the edge of the property.

"I'm sorry about today," she said. "It's not normally like this."

Stephen took her hand. "Let's not talk about the kids." He kissed the tender skin of her palm. "I've waited too long to be alone with you, and I want to enjoy every minute."

He could be so sweet. He looked at her now like he was memorizing her face. "I wish you were going home with me tomorrow."

"I know." She nearly added *Me too*, then realized she didn't. Where would that leave the children?

Stephen turned her hand over and ran his thumb across the ring. The wind tugged her hair. A lone seagull cried overhead, floating on the wind, almost stationary.

"There was a part of me that hoped you would," he said.

"You know I can't." Hadn't they been through this before? "It won't be much longer. School will be out in a little over a month. And if the Goldmans buy the property, that'll expedite things."

"And then what?"

"The property would close thirty days from the signing. Maybe you could come for another visit between now and then."

"That's not what I mean, Meridith."

She knew he referred to the children coming home with her, to their being a family, and she wished so desperately the day had gone better.

"Today was a bad day. They're not normally so quarrelsome, and Ben's vomiting . . ." The memory was such a horrific end to the day, it was almost funny. She felt a laugh bubbling up inside. "Well, you have to keep your sense of humor around here, that's for sure."

"I don't find it funny in the least."

The bubble of laughter burst, unfulfilled. "I appreciate that you want to give them a chance. I'm just trying to say it isn't always like this."

He looked at her, his eyes intent with purpose. "I didn't come to bond with the kids, Meridith. I came to remind you what we have together." He pressed another kiss to her palm. "I love you. I want to spend the rest of my life with you."

Her breath caught, but not because he'd repeated the words he'd spoken when he'd proposed. The other words made a far stronger impression. *I didn't come to bond with the kids.*

She'd misread the reason for his visit. She'd taken her own wish and transferred it onto him.

"We have plans, good ones," he said. "Save for a home in Lindenwood Park while we focus on our careers for three to five years. By then we'll have enough to buy that dream home and start a family."

Meridith knotted the quilt material in her fist with the daffodil, clutching the stem against her chest. "I already have a family, Stephen."

His face fell. "They're not your kids, Meridith. And they're not mine."

"They're my siblings. And they have no one else."

"That wasn't our plan when I asked you to marry me. When you said yes."

"Life doesn't always go according to plan, Stephen. Things happen. Change happens. I didn't ask for this."

"I didn't either. And I'm asking you to put me first. To put *us* first." His grip tightened on her hand. "I love you. The future I want for us doesn't include someone else's children."

Meridith eased away from him, pulled her hand from his, and stood, even as he tightened his grip. If Stephen's future didn't include her siblings, then it didn't include her either.

She limped a few steps toward the water.

He wasn't interested in the children, and she wondered for the first time what this said of his feelings for her. How much could he love her if he couldn't consider her side? And what of her feelings for him? They now seemed vague and gray-washed, like they were lost in a fog rolling in off the harbor. When had that happened?

She realized what she had to do. Meridith turned. Stephen had followed her.

She released the blanket, and the wind tugged it from her shoulders, stole the flower from her fist. She eased the ring from her finger and extended it to him.

The frown returned, settling between his brows like claw marks in the sand. "Meridith. Put it back."

She opened his hand and placed the ring on his palm, the certainty growing roots. She looked at his clean-shaven jaw, the short-clipped hair that wasn't long enough for the wind to disturb, his high forehead and straight nose.

She was trading stability for chaos. Security for ambiguity. Predictability for uncertainty. In some ways, it would be her childhood all over again. But this time she was in charge. She was the one calling the shots. She was no helpless little girl swinging by the tail end of her mother's illness.

Even if he agreed in the end, what kind of father would he be if he didn't want the children? She wouldn't do that to her siblings. They deserved far more.

"It's over, Stephen."

"You don't mean that." He took her hand. "We're perfect for each other, you've said it yourself a hundred times."

She had said it, believed it. She wondered now if it was true. She couldn't deny the feelings that had sprung up for Jake, who was not at all what she needed, not at all the man for her. Still, if she truly loved Stephen, those feelings wouldn't be there.

"My future includes Noelle and Max and Ben. Things have changed since I agreed to marry you, and I'm doing what's right for these kids. I have to do what's best for them. That's my reality, but it doesn't have to be yours. I understand it's not what you want."

His jaw twitched. "It's that contractor, isn't it?"

"*No.*"

"I saw the way he looked at you."

The comment sent a pleasant warmth flooding through her. "This is between us, Stephen. My future's taken an unexpected turn. I can't leave the kids, and you can't accept them. There's nothing to do now but say it's over."

"Meridith . . ." His eyes pled, turned glossy. She'd never seen him get emotional, not even when his grandfather passed away last November.

She took his hands. "Our lives are taking different paths, but it's going to be okay." She knew it was true, knew to the bone she was doing the right thing, even if it pained her to hurt him.

"Maybe the uncle will come back tomorrow and—"

She shook her head. "It doesn't matter what the uncle does or doesn't do. I'm their guardian. For some reason, my dad and Eva left them to me, and they're my responsibility."

"This isn't how the weekend was supposed to go." The look on his face reminded her of Piper's when they were pulling from the driveway.

"I know." And yet, there was a feeling of inevitability deep inside that soothed her the way a thousand deep breaths couldn't. Meridith leaned forward and placed one last tender kiss on Stephen's lips.

Thirty-four

Through a slit in the curtain, Jake watched Meridith open the taxi door for Stephen. The driver stowed the bags, but Jake only had eyes for her. She wore a white gauzy top that fluttered in the wind and a pair of trendy jeans that showed off her figure.

Stephen turned to Meridith, and Jake's heart was like a jackhammer in his chest. What did she see in that guy? He was as tepid as day-old coffee.

Since Stephen had arrived, Jake had gone over and over the way Meridith had greeted him. The way he'd greeted her, with an apathetic kiss and a tame hello. If it had been him, missing his woman for weeks, he'd have swept her into his arms and kissed her until they were both breathless. He didn't get it.

Movement below stole his attention. Meridith leaned forward and kissed Stephen. Jake hardly had time to feel the prick of pain before she pulled away. She reached up, laid her palm against the guy's face. It was almost more than Jake could stand.

He started to release the curtain, let it fall into place, but then something caught his eye that made his fist clutch the sheer fabric.

ॐ   ॐ   ॐ

Jake swallowed the last bite of chicken alfredo and pushed his plate back. "Great meal, Willow."

"Thanks." She gathered his and Wyatt's plates.

Wyatt took them away, standing. "Oh no, you don't. You cooked, I'll get the dishes, baby." He laid a big wet one on her.

Jake turned his head, groaning. He stacked the remaining dishes, trying to ignore the couple.

"Should I leave?" he asked moments later, only half joking.

Willow stepped away from Wyatt, smiling innocently. "Of course not. I know a good dish washer when I see one."

Jake took her hand and kissed it. "At your service."

Wyatt flipped him with a towel. "Stop making a play for my wife and get your sorry rump into the kitchen."

Jake carried the stack of plates into the kitchen and set them in the sink. "Where's the dishwasher?"

"You're looking at 'em."

Whatever. It would give him a chance to talk to Wyatt, which was the main reason he'd accepted the invitation.

"I'll wash." Wyatt tossed him a towel, then rolled up his sleeves.

When the sink was full, Wyatt shut off the water, washed a glass, then rinsed it. "When are you coming back to work?"

"When I'm finished at Summer Place. Shouldn't be too much longer, a month maybe."

"It's getting pretty busy." He handed Jake the glass.

"Meridith's fiancé came to the island Saturday."

"Bummer."

"Stayed out of their way all weekend, and I'm glad I did."

"Because . . ."

Jake set the glass in the cabinet. "It's over between them."

"Seriously?"

Jake shrugged. "She didn't give me the details, but the ring's gone, and she said it was over."

"Is she upset?"

"Doesn't seem to be." *That was good, right?*

"Hmm." Wyatt handed him a plate. "You gonna make your move now?"

Jake elbowed Wyatt in the ribs. "She just broke her engagement."

"Or he did."

Jake frowned. "I prefer to think of it the other way."

Wyatt shrugged. "Just saying. She doesn't sound too distressed. Hey, maybe she broke up because she has the hots for you."

"Shut up." The thought was too ludicrous to entertain. Meridith might be attracted to him, but that was a far cry from what Wyatt suggested.

"It's about the kids," Jake said. "I'm sure of it. They spent the day together yesterday, and Max told me that Ben puked on Stephen."

Wyatt laughed. "Classic!"

"Yeah, I enjoyed that little tidbit." He was surprised the man hadn't gone running home the day before. From what Max said, Stephen hadn't been very friendly.

They washed and dried in silence for a minute, and Jake's thoughts turned to Meridith. She'd told him the engagement was broken so matter-of-factly. How could she love the guy and react so calmly?

"You know," Wyatt said, pulling him from his thoughts. "It's pretty remarkable, what she's doing. Not every chick would take on three kids at the expense of her engagement."

Wyatt was right, and it only deepened his feelings for Meridith. He hated that she was planning to take the children away, but there was no doubt she cared about them. And his suspicions about the bipolar illness had all but disappeared. He'd found no medications, seen no symptoms.

"You guys would make a cute couple," Wyatt said. "You could get married and have a ready-made family."

"You're forgetting one little detail."

"Ah, yeah. You're the uncle she called—what was it—self-absorbed and irresponsible?"

Jake scowled and grabbed the plate from Wyatt.

"So tell her the truth."

"Yeah, right. That'll go over well." She'd be furious. She'd kick him from Summer Place and might not let him see the kids anymore. His gut clenched.

"Gotta tell her eventually."

"When the house is finished."

"The longer you wait, the worse it'll be."

"Maybe not." Maybe he could change her mind about staying. Maybe he could make her see that he cared for her. Maybe they really could be a family.

Thirty-five

May arrived, bringing bright sunlight, clear skies, and colorful clusters of tulips. The warm temperatures drew people from their winter homes like bears from hibernation. Flags ascended poles, floral cushions appeared on patio furniture, and children flip-flopped around the neighborhood with pasty skin and freshly scabbed knees.

As the weeks passed, Meridith was surprised how little she missed Stephen's calls. While her finger felt bare at first, after a few days it seemed as if a ring had never graced the spot.

Jake continued to make improvements on Summer Place, and she was pleased with the progress. Island life grew more familiar, and Meridith began to wonder if it was feasible to stay, began to wonder if she could somehow keep Summer Place for the children. She scoured the business records—what there were of them—and calculated the income and expenditures.

It didn't take long to see that an additional income was needed to keep the place afloat. T. J.'s boat repair jobs and gallery sales had offset the cost of owning the place. Meridith wished she could make it work, wished she could keep the children on the island now that there was no future with Stephen. She even considered selling Summer Place and buying a smaller house, but real estate was outrageously priced. Even if she found a job, she'd never be able to support three children here on her income.

That notion extinguished, she reluctantly called the Goldmans. After several conversations they agreed on a purchase price, and Meridith hired an attorney to draw up papers. She was relieved to have it settled, but every time her thoughts turned to leaving, she felt a pang. She'd miss Rita and the people she'd met at church. And as much as she wanted to deny it, she'd miss Jake. And most of all, she hated taking the children from their home.

At times she'd think it was silly to return to St. Louis, when all that awaited her was an empty house, but then Jake would accidentally touch her in passing, and she'd remember how he stirred unwanted feelings in her. The kind of feelings she'd spent her adulthood avoiding. Or she'd come across a photo of her dad while assembling the albums and remember that he'd chosen this place instead of her.

His ghost seemed to haunt the place, from the sculptures on the tables to the furniture he'd selected. The father she didn't remember, hadn't known, was revealed to her daily, and it didn't fit with the villain she'd made him into. The discrepancy left her unsettled. Left her longing to return to a familiar place, where routine was a way of life, where reminders of her father were few. Having the children would bring new routines, but together they'd find a groove and settle in.

During the final weeks of school, Max slacked off, and she spurred him on toward the finish line. Ben began to talk more and only clung when he wanted a hug, then he was off to play in the yard like every other seven-year-old boy.

Guests came more frequently now that the days were buttery yellow, and the house often bustled with five or six visitors on weekends. Meridith frequently entered a room and found Jake chatting up the guests, giving them information about attractions or tips on finding the kind of beach they sought. He was good for business.

But bad for her sanity. She caught him staring at her so intently sometimes that a shiver ran down her spine. Though he was composed on the outside, she sensed a restrained passion. He made her feel things. Things that unsettled her. Things that felt out of control and left her longing for peace. But there would be no peace until Jake was out of her life, until she left the island.

At night she dreamed of serenity and counted down the final days of school even as she dreaded having to tell the children they were leaving.

When Mother's Day came, Meridith tried not to think of her own mother. They bought bouquets of daisies at the Flower and Garden Shop and took them to the cemetery, where the children laid them on the mound of dirt.

That afternoon, when Meridith heard Noelle crying in her room, she knocked, but Noelle claimed she was all right. While the girl hadn't allowed Meridith to comfort her, she hadn't screamed at her to go away either. A step in the right direction.

Later that night Meridith was in her room working on Ben's scrapbook when she heard a burst of laughter. Ben's belly laughs drew her from her room, toward the steps. What she saw brought a bittersweet smile.

Meridith lowered herself on an upper stair and peered through the oak spindles. Ben had Jake pinned to the rug and was tickling him. Jake moaned like he was in torture, which only made Ben laugh harder.

She'd never seen the child so happy. He was small next to Jake's mass, his wiry arms moving furiously, digging his fingers into Jake's side.

He twisted, straddling Jake.

Jake groaned. "Help! Someone help!"

Ben laughed. "You're doomed! If I had my ropes, I'd tie you up and toss you off a cliff!"

"No! Not that!"

Meridith smiled around the tears that gathered in her eyes. She wondered if her father had tussled with Ben. He surely missed the interaction. And while she was grateful for Jake's willingness to play with the boy . . .

What would happen when the repairs were finished and Jake left? She saw how attached Ben had become to him. Her mind flashed back over the previous weeks to other occasions. Jake helping Noelle fix her bike chain, Jake and Max working on Max's new boat model.

Jake, Jake, Jake. He'd become a fixture around the house right under her nose. Worse, he'd become a friend. A friend the children would lose.

The thought bottomed out her stomach. Another loss.

Meridith stood quietly and walked through the guest wing toward her room. Noelle was on her computer, and Max was painting a model in his room. Meridith descended the back staircase. Killing time, she unloaded the dishwasher, considering what she'd say to Jake. When the last of the silverware was put away, Meridith entered the living room. Ben was snuggled next to Jake on the sofa, watching a cartoon.

"Jake, can I talk to you a minute?"

"Sure." Easing away from Ben, he followed her out the back door and onto the porch. Meridith perched on the railing, too nervous to sit. It was nearly dark, and the string of lanterns cast a colorful glow on the porch.

Jake let the screen door fall into place and pocketed his hands.

His gaze trapped her for whole seconds. He really was a good guy. The image of him tussling on the floor with Ben was not one she'd soon forget.

"What's wrong?" Jake's voice, deep as thunder, unsettled her.

Why did he have to be so handsome? She wanted to fall right inside those brown eyes. "I saw you in the living room with Ben . . . earlier."

His lips pulled upward, no doubt remembering Ben's belly laughs. "He's a fun kid."

She hated to wipe the smile from his face. "I know you mean well, Jake, but I think it's best if you avoid spending time with the children."

The smile slid south. "We were just playing around."

"The children are getting attached to you. I don't think it's healthy."

His jaw flexed, his shoulders squared. "They need relationships now more than ever."

"Not from someone who'll soon exit their lives."

He flinched.

She hated to hurt his feelings, had a physical ache from wounding him.

"It doesn't have to be that way," he said finally. "I don't want to exit their lives. I don't want to exit *your* life."

Maybe he thought they could be some happy family or something. It was time to tell him everything. "I'm selling Summer Place. We'll be leaving the island soon. The Goldmans—our guests over the daffodil weekend—made an offer, and I accepted. I haven't told the children yet, so I'd appreciate if you wouldn't mention it. We'll stay through closing in late June."

Jake's lips parted. A second later they pressed together. He walked to the end of the porch and back. He reminded her of a caged tiger, constricted by the boundary of the porch.

She hadn't expected him to be so upset. When he passed, she set her hand on his bare arm, stopping him. The muscles flexed beneath her palm. He was so strong. She had the sudden image of him hitting Sean, using those muscles to protect her.

She pulled her hand away as if his skin burned her. "They've had enough loss. They've already become attached to you, and that's only going to hurt them more when we leave."

His face softened as he stared, his lips slackening, his eyes growing tender. His face had already darkened under the sun. Faint lines fanned the corner of his eyes.

He reached toward her and ran his finger down the side of her face. "Don't leave."

His touch left a trail of fire. She pressed her spine to the column. How could she want to dive into his arms and run away at the same time?

Inside a riot kicked up. She was back in the apartment on Warren Street, coming home from school, slipping in the door, unsure if she'd find her mom racing around the kitchen, slumped on the bathroom tile, or just gone.

The same uncertainty roiled in her now. "I have to."

"This is their home. Your engagement is over," he said gently. "Is what you're going back to as important as what you're leaving?"

He didn't have to say he meant them. *Us.* She shook her head, dislodging his hand. How had he turned this all around?

She slid past him, needing distance to breathe, to think. She thought of explaining her reasons, but the financial barriers now paled in comparison to the other one. She crossed her arms, a pathetic barrier between him and her heart.

"When you're finished with the repairs, you'll be leaving. Once that happens, I *will* sell Summer Place and we *will* move to St. Louis. And until then, I need you to keep your distance from the children. For their sakes."

Jake ran his hand through his hair, leaving it tousled.

Meridith had the sudden urge to smooth it down. His hair would be soft and thick between her fingers. She knotted her hands in fists before she was foolish enough to surrender to the impulse.

Jake's hand lowered to his neck and stayed there.

"Jake . . . ?"

He turned and set his palms on the railing, leaning toward the ocean. The wind ruffled his hair. "All right, Meridith," he said, finally.

The screen door clicked in place behind her. Jake wanted to punch something, but he forced himself to close his eyes and inhale the brine-scented air instead.

It seemed as if, piece by piece, the kids were being taken from him. First, Meridith was awarded guardianship. Now he wasn't allowed to interact with them. And in a few short weeks, they'd be taken across the country to St. Louis. Might as well be half a world away.

To make matters worse, he couldn't argue with what she said. If he'd wanted to be certain Meridith had the kids' best interest at heart, he had plenty of evidence. Given what she knew—or rather, didn't know—she was doing the right thing, protecting them from more hurt. But he didn't have to like the repercussions.

As bothered as he was by all that, it wasn't the only part of the conversation that made him feel like exploding.

All this time he'd thought it was her feelings for Stephen that kept Meridith at arm's length. But Stephen was gone, and still she held back. He'd seen the look in her eyes. She'd been putty in his hands when he'd touched her.

And then a wall had come up, shutting him out. What gave? And equally as baffling, how had Meridith, in two and a half months, gone from adversary to keeper of his heart?

Thirty-six

Meridith gathered the album decorations and returned them to the bag, then stowed Ben's album in the closet with the two completed albums.

After closing her closet door, she removed her socks and changed into her long nightshirt. Outside rain pattered the window and the wind stirred the chimes on the front porch.

Meridith brushed and flossed, then propped her foot on the sink ledge and smoothed on her favorite lotion. The past few days had been awkward between her and Jake. Being near him always put her on edge, but now that he'd made his interest clear, it was worse. Because she had feelings, too, and hiding them was hard.

Avoidance had become her MO, but it wasn't easy when he lived under the same roof. *Not much longer.* She could do anything for three weeks, right?

The lights flickered, then went out, leaving her in total darkness. The heat kicked off, and the only remaining sound was the rain tap dancing on the roof.

Meridith rubbed the lotion into her hands, then opened the door. Her room was a black abyss. No matter how wide she opened her eyes, there was not even a vague hint of a shadow, and the only flashlights were downstairs in the laundry room cabinet.

She felt her way across her room and looked out the window. It was like looking at a sheet of black construction paper. Maybe the whole neighborhood was out, but it was hard to tell since it was late and people were likely in bed.

She looked farther down Driftwood Lane and caught a distant porch light. The rain kicked up a notch, pummeled the window. It wasn't storming, so she couldn't imagine lightning had kicked off their electric.

What if something was wrong with the circuitry? At least they had no guests at the moment. Listening to the heavy downpour, she thought of the sump pump in the basement. If it continued to rain all night without the pump, she might awaken to a flooded basement.

She stared in the direction of her door. Should she get Jake? Could he do anything about it? He might be asleep, and she hated to disturb him, hated even more to be alone, face-to-face with him.

Maybe the electric would return on its own. She stared into the darkness waiting, as if her wish might make it happen. But a minute later there was still no bathroom light, no night-light in the hall.

Meridith sighed. She couldn't afford a flooded basement. She had to do the responsible thing. A floorboard squawked under her feet as she exited her room and shuffled down the hall. The wood was cold against the pads of her feet. The children's rooms were quiet. She felt her way along the wall to the doorway that separated the wings.

Having come to trust Jake, she no longer locked it when they had no guests. The doorknob turned easily, and the door swung silently open. She felt her way along the chair rail. The nautical room doorway, more chair rail, the guest bath, chair rail. Jake's door.

Her palm traced the glossy surface of the five-panel door. Closed. He must be asleep or he would've come to find her, or at least gone to check the breaker box or whatever he might need to do.

She let her fingertips rest against the flat panel, wondering if it was worth waking him. What was in the basement, really? Some old boxes and a concrete floor. But flooding brought mold, and mold wreaked havoc on health.

Stop being such a baby, Meridith.

She tugged her nightshirt down, then rolled her eyes at her own stupidity. She could be wearing a clown costume for all he'd know.

Closing her fist, she tapped lightly, not wanting to startle him. Her heart echoed the drumming of the rain on the roof. She was being ridiculous.

There were no sounds from the other side. She tapped again, harder. He'd surely hear that even if he were sleeping. She thought she heard the squeak of his mattress and turned her ear toward the door.

A thump sounded, then Jake's muffled complaint.

A moment later the door latch clicked. She felt the *whoosh* of air on her skin, smelled the woodsy, spicy smell of Jake. Before she could stop herself she drew in a lungful of the fragrance. Heaven.

"Meridith?" His voice was close.

"Sorry to wake you," she whispered, though the children were too far down the hall to be disturbed. "The electric went out."

"I noticed."

She thought she detected sarcasm and imagined his lips twitching. She hated not being able to read his face.

"It's probably just the storm," he said.

"There's a light on down the road, and I haven't heard any thunder. I'm worried about the sump pump."

He was quiet a moment, and she wondered if she was over-reacting. Maybe she should say never mind and slink back to her room.

"Sounds like it's really coming down. I'll go check. Where are the flashlights?"

"In the laundry room cabinet above the dryer. Is there anything I can do?" She moved aside so he could pass, but anticipated his direction incorrectly. A flash of bare skin grazed her fingertips. His stomach.

Jake went still. "I can handle it." His tone was hesitant, breathless.

Meridith's stomach tightened in a knot even, as the air around them seemed to pulse. His body heat warmed her skin, and his breath stirred the hair at her temple. A shiver shimmied down her spine.

He was there, so close. She could smell him, hear him, feel him. Of its own volition, her hand reached into the space. The pads of her fingers grazed the warm hard flesh of his stomach.

She heard his sharp intake of breath even as his muscles flexed under her fingers.

"Meri . . ." he whispered, a warning.

She should withdraw her hand, step away. Yet she couldn't seem to move.

She felt his work-calloused palms on her cheeks. A moment later his lips touched hers. He took her mouth, stole her breath. His lips moved with sureness, possessing her.

Her hands crawled up his chest, around his neck, into his hair. It was soft and thick between her fingers, just as she'd imagined.

He pressed her into the doorframe. His jaw scraped the tender flesh of her palms. His breaths were ragged. Or were those hers? They were melded into one and it wasn't enough.

His lips lifted a fraction. "Meri," he whispered.

She registered her complaint by closing the distance. She'd never felt such need. He was like water for her thirsty soul, food for her famished heart, and she took it all greedily.

He groaned, setting off an earthquake that rippled all the way through her.

"Meri," he mumbled against her mouth. The sound of her name on his lips was the sweetest of music. She wanted him to say it over and over again. She would never tire of it.

"Meri," he said, pulling back, a breath away. But this time, the hands framing her face held her in place.

Her heart was rapid staccato, stealing her breath. She gulped in air.

"I love you," he whispered.

His voice registered, but the meaning didn't sink through her foggy thoughts.

He gave her a little shake. "Did you hear me?" His thumb moved down her face, along the corner of her lip. "I *love* you."

His ardent tone cut through the fog, clearing a path for his words.

She shook her head.

"Yes."

She was so stupid. How had she allowed this to happen? Did she think because they were blind in the darkness that it didn't count? That there would be no consequences?

"Meridith?" Ben's small voice called from down the hall.

"Say something," Jake whispered, and she knew he wasn't talking about Ben.

Jake's hands, the ones she couldn't get enough of before, now felt like a vise. She pulled them away.

"Meridith," he said.

"I have to go." She whirled into the shadows before he could stop her. With trembling hands she felt her way through the darkness and she knew, come morning, nothing would be as difficult as facing the light of day.

Thirty-seven

Jake awoke late the next morning, a rarity. After finding his way to the basement the night before, he'd found nothing wrong and had called the power company to discover that an accident had taken down the wires. After being assured electricity would resume in a few hours, he went to bed.

But he didn't go to sleep. No, he lay for hours remembering the feel of Meridith in his arms, the feel of her lips on his. He remembered until he wanted to stride down the hall, knock on her door, and tell her something was wrong and it had nothing to do with the electric.

What was holding her back? The fact that she was leaving? That she was still in love with Stephen? Was it possible that she somehow saw Jake as beneath her? A mere carpenter . . . She'd never treated him that way, but what else was there?

His mind spun with possibilities, returning repeatedly to the fact that she didn't know who he was. He had to tell her, but he'd been hoping . . .

What? That he could win her heart first? Heaven knew discovering he was the uncle wasn't going to win him anything but her wrath.

Now that his feelings were involved, they muddied the waters more than ever. It wasn't only the kids he had to consider now. There were Meridith's feelings, not to mention his own, and he'd clarified those pretty well.

And he did love Meridith. Despite her response—to the words or lack thereof—he wasn't sorry he'd said them. It was the truth.

But now he realized his declaration had frightened her. What if she asked him to leave? In the middle of the night, he decided to start on the fireplace right away. He'd have half the stone chipped out, and then what could she do? She couldn't afford to pay someone else to finish.

Jake woke to a quiet house. The kids were at school, and Meridith was avoiding him—he had no doubt that's what she was doing. At least it gave him a chance to dismantle the chimney.

By the time she pulled in the drive, the fireplace was a mess. Mission accomplished. And now that she was home, he'd finally get the chance to talk to her about last night.

But when the door opened, the kids bustled through—a half-day at school, Noelle fairly sang. Great, now he just needed a dozen guests to arrive on their doorstep and they were good to go. And as it was a Friday, he realized that could very well happen.

All afternoon Meridith buzzed around the house, fixing rooms, mixing up a batch of something in the kitchen, vacuuming the rugs. Doing everything but speaking to him, making eye contact with him.

But she wasn't fooling him. The woman had wanted that kiss as badly as he had. Even now, as he chiseled away a loose piece of mortar, the memory stole his breath. He ran the back of his hand across his cheek, rubbing away the dust and grit.

His stomach growled, and he checked his watch. It was nearly dinnertime, and he needed to clean up his mess and shower. As he swept away the debris, he could hear Meridith and a newly arrived guest talking on the porch.

After dinner he was going to get a few minutes of her time. Surely she knew it was coming. Surely she knew she couldn't avoid him for two weeks. Not after that kiss, not after what he'd said.

An hour later Jake was seated across the table from Meridith. She chatted with the kids while Jake brooded about what he'd say when he finally got her alone.

After a long meal, the kids finally pushed back from the table. Meridith hopped up, no doubt to busy herself in the kitchen. But Jake was prepared.

"Meridith, a word?"

"I have to clear the table and do the dishes," she said without a glance.

"Max and Ben, clear the table, please. Noelle, the dishes?"

The kids agreed before Meridith could protest. Finally, she set down the casserole dish, apparently realizing she couldn't stop the inevitable.

He gestured toward the back door, and she exited the house. Not wanting the kids to overhear, he continued down the porch steps into the yard, stopping at the steps leading to the beach.

Dark clouds gathered on the horizon, and the wind tugged at Meridith's blouse. She'd known this was coming, had dreaded it all night and all day. Had lain awake for hours trying to put words to her feelings. Impossible. Instead, she'd felt Jake's lips on hers, heard those words that all but stopped her heart.

Jake turned to face her, leaning against the wood railing of the beach steps. She wasn't deceived by the casual pose—he was going to get to the bottom of this. Only Meridith didn't know what was at the bottom. She only knew this thing with Jake could not happen.

She couldn't bring herself to look him in the eye. Not after that kiss. It had been easier in the dark. Too easy. She felt a flush climbing her neck as she remembered deliberately touching his bare flesh. She'd made no bones about wanting that kiss. What had gotten into her?

Even now her skin warmed, her pulse sped as if preparing for a repeat. She wished she could hide the flush that climbed her cheeks. Wished he would say something. Anything.

"What's going on?" he said.

The wind breathed a cool breath across her skin, making her shiver. "What do you mean?"

"Come on, Meridith—that kiss . . ."

"It was just a kiss," she said feebly, but her mind replayed the embrace, refuting her words.

"You won't even look at me." His voice was strained. "Maybe we need to turn out the lights."

Her face burned. Even the wind couldn't cool it. The grass at Jake's feet shimmied and bowed over his scarred tennis shoes.

"I don't know what to say. I—I just can't do this." She wrapped her arms around her middle.

"Why?"

She searched the ground for answers like she'd find it among the blades of grass, pull it up by the roots, and hand it over. If only it were so easy.

When nothing materialized, she chose the only answer that sounded logical. "I just broke my engagement a month ago. You can't expect—"

"This isn't about him, and you know it."

An ache started behind her eyes. "I don't know what it is."

"Then there's nothing to stop us, is there? Unless you don't feel anything for me . . ." Self-doubt crept into his tone.

She let the sentence hang, unable to deny it. She prayed somehow he wouldn't remember her response to the kiss or at least not remember it the way she did. She took three cleansing breaths. Four. The briny air failed to calm her.

"No, it's there, isn't it." It wasn't even a question.

There was no point denying it. "All right, I won't deny an attraction. But that's all, that's all there can be."

"Why?"

She threw her hands up. "I'm leaving soon, moving hundreds of miles away, I've just inherited three kids, my engagement's broken, my future's uncertain . . ." Surely there was more, but her mind ran out of steam.

"Those are all things people work around." He took a step toward her, then another. "There's something else."

A memory flashed in her mind. Her mother, in manic mode coming toward her, slowly, just like this. She'd been no more than nine years old, had been wrapped in her mom's arms only an hour earlier, but an hour made all the difference. Now her mom's face was red and mottled, and she was yelling. Meridith had covered her ears with her hands.

Jake's movement snagged her attention. He was getting close. She stepped back. 974 . . . 948 . . . 922 . . .

"Why are you running?"

She knew he wasn't talking about the step. It hadn't put nearly enough distance between them. He was there, right in front of her. 896 . . . 8 . . .

"Meridith." He took her by the shoulders.

The motion drew her eyes to his, and she knew it with certainty: she was too far gone. As far gone as he, maybe more. What had she done? How was she going to escape with her heart intact? There weren't enough calming breaths to fix this. She could count backward from a million and still be where she was now. Hopelessly in love with the man who made her feel too many things.

"You're afraid." His own statement seemed to surprise him.

Was she afraid? She took a frantic survey of her vitals. Was it fear or just this . . . she struggled to find the word. Why was it so hard? And why did he have to torture her with the particulars? She didn't want to think about this. Why couldn't he just drop it?

"What are you afraid of?" He gave her a little shake. "What, Meridith?"

"I don't like the way you make me feel!" The words burst from her unbidden. It was as close to the truth as she could get. This inward searching was worse than feeling her way through the darkness. She felt like she'd just smacked into a wall.

Jake released her slowly.

She rubbed the place where his hands had been, hoping they were done. *Please let's be done.*

"Explain."

She should've known he couldn't leave it at that. "I don't know how."

"Try."

The wind blew her hair across her face. She welcomed the screen between them. "You make me feel . . . unsettled." It was as close as she could come to explaining, but it didn't do justice to what he did to her.

"That can be a good thing." She heard amusement in his tone. It reminded her of when she first met him.

"Not for me," she said, suddenly saddened to realize where they'd ended up all these weeks later. "I spent my whole childhood feeling unsettled. I'm done with that."

The wind blew again, pulling the curtain of hair from her face. He was like this wind, pulling her one way one minute, another the next, changing course without warning.

"So . . . what? You're going to live your life without love? What kind of life is that?"

"There are different kinds of love."

"Like what you had with Stephen?" He jammed his hands in his pockets. "That's not love, Meridith, that's settling."

A knot swelled in her throat. He could see it however he wanted, but that wasn't going to change anything. She was done here. She turned and walked toward the house. The wind sucked at her shirt.

"You gonna let your fears dictate your life, Meridith?" he called after her.

But she didn't stop. Didn't stop until she'd made it up the stairs, to her room, to her bed, where she slipped under the covers and let herself cry.

Thirty-eight

Jake took three steps after her and stopped. She was already to the porch, then inside the house in a matter of seconds.

He forked his fingers through his hair, clutching fistfuls until his scalp tightened. He'd been confused until she'd looked at him, until he'd seen the look in her eyes. And then he knew.

She was afraid.

Afraid because he made her feel things, things she hadn't felt with Stephen or probably anyone else, because this was real love. Not some tepid, watered-down version.

But Meridith wanted tepid. She wanted safe.

His scalp burning, he lowered his hands. Something nudged his leg. Piper stared up at him, and Jake set a hand on her head, absently rubbed her ear.

He wondered what part of Meridith's childhood had left her afraid of something as natural and necessary as love. Was it her mother's mental illness? T. J.'s leaving her?

If she'd only open up to him, maybe he could help her sort it out. He was a patient man. He'd wait her out, love her until she realized he was safe.

But she was unwilling to try. Wanted to run as far and fast as she could from what he offered. What was he supposed to do? He couldn't make her try, force her to shed her fears. If only he could make her see what she was missing.

But he was running out of time. He was nearly finished with the house, had two weeks, tops, if she didn't kick him out first. And soon after that she was leaving the island.

And she still didn't know who he was.

Jake kicked the ground, sending a spray of sand into the air, then started down the beach steps. He had to get away from here, breathe some fresh air, think. Piper barked as she jogged along the property line, keeping pace with him.

Why did Meridith have to be so stubborn? Why couldn't she just give him a chance? He knew they'd be amazing together. She'd opened her heart to the kids, admirably so. It couldn't have been easy accepting her father's other children, but she'd done it.

Why couldn't she open her heart to him? Jake retrieved a shell and hurled it into the ocean. He needed to throw about a hundred more before he even began to work off the excess steam.

Piper barked and whined, having reached the property's edge. He'd take off her collar and bring her along, but the dog was afraid to leave the yard.

Piper barked louder, almost squealing. Jake stopped, then walked toward the dog. He slugged through the thick sand, up the grassy incline.

Piper wagged her tail at his approach.

All right, Piper.

He leaned down, released Piper's collar, and tossed it on the lawn. Backing away, he called her.

She stared back, wagging her tail.

"Come on, Piper!" He called again over the wind, patting his leg.

She danced around, her paws at the edge of the property. She let loose a sharp bark.

Jake retreated farther, down the incline to the sand. "Come on, girl!"

Piper whined, then sat, wiggling restlessly in the grass. The wind ruffled her fur.

"Piper, let's go!" Stupid dog. Didn't she know she was free? Jake glared at her.

Piper lifted her nose to the air, then lowered her head, nose to the ground. She looked up at Jake soulfully.

Jake marched toward her, up the slope, through the sea oats. He gathered Piper in his arms, a tense bundle of fur, carried her down the hill, and deposited her on the sand.

He walked away. "Come on!" A dozen steps later he turned. She was huddled in a circle, unmoving.

"What is wrong with you?" He gestured down the shoreline. "You have the whole beach, the whole world! You're free!"

And yet she cowered in the sand, afraid to move.

Jake glared at the dog, catching his breath. Why wouldn't she move? If she'd only try, she'd see it was safe.

Piper was frozen in place, her head down, her front legs half bent. Her ears lay flat, and her tail curled protectively around her body.

Just try.

But Jake could see that wasn't going to happen. She was locked in place, helpless to move.

Jake settled his hands on his hips, staring at her. She looked pitiful cowering on the beach. A tremor passed through her body.

As quickly as the anger rose, it drained away. Jake gave a hard sigh, then walked back.

Piper lifted her eyes, watching his approach, her brows lifting, though her nose nearly touched the sand.

Jake sank beside her on the sand. He wanted to help her, wanted to fix the problem, but there was nothing he could do, was there?

Piper timidly sniffed his shirt, darted a glance at Jake. A moment later she rested her head on his leg and gave a deep sigh.

Jake set his hand on her side. "I know, girl. Believe me, I know."

Thirty-nine

Meridith curled her fist and rapped on the door. Her eyes ached from lack of sleep. She was stifling a yawn when the door opened.

"Meridith! What a lovely surprise!" Rita's wide smile and big hug were just what the doctor ordered.

"Sorry to drop in on you."

"Nonsense." Rita held up her rubber-gloved hands. "You've saved me from the dishes. Come in."

The home smelled of lilacs and coffee, and when Rita offered a cup of the brew, Meridith accepted. She'd been in such a hurry to escape the house she hadn't made a pot.

Meridith sat at the kitchen table. The weekend had been miserable. She'd pasted on a smile for the guests, went through the motions with the children, and tried not to wonder where Jake went when he disappeared.

She should ask him to leave. But the fireplace was half dismantled, and a new leak had sprung up on the kitchen ceiling below the children's bathroom.

Rita set a steaming mug at her fingertips and sat across from her. Light streamed through the patio doors, but Meridith wished the sun would go away.

She lifted the mug and inhaled before taking a sip. The liquid warmed her throat, and she prayed the caffeine would lift her spirits.

"Honey, what's going on? You were quiet as a mouse at church yesterday, and you look so tired. Are the kids giving you fits, or are you missing Stephen?"

Meridith shook her head. "The kids are fine. It's not Stephen either."

Rita laid her soft hand on Meridith's arm. "Then what is it? I'm worried about you."

Meridith ran her finger along the mug's fat rim. "It's—" The rest of the words clogged her throat. There were too many words, too many problems. "I don't know where to start."

"What happened to frazzle you so?"

She *was* frazzled. It was so unlike her. "Jake kissed me. Or I kissed him, I'm not sure." She looked up at her friend, sheepishly.

The frown lines on Rita's forehead dissolved, and her lips lifted at the corners. "I see."

"No, you don't. This is not a good thing."

"Because of Stephen . . ."

"*No* . . . Why does everyone think this is about Stephen?" As soon as the words were out, Meridith sighed. "Of course everyone thinks it's about Stephen. If I were normal, this *would* be about Stephen—oh, what is wrong with me?" Meridith palmed her forehead.

"It's okay. Talk to me."

Maybe Rita could give her perspective. Meridith opened her mouth, and the story of her childhood spilled like a glass of milk onto the table. From her parents' arguments to her dad leaving to her mother's bipolar disorder.

"Eva mentioned the mental illness once," Rita said. "Talk about an unstable childhood."

"That's it exactly. There was no order, no control. I feel like my childhood happened to me, and I was helpless. I never knew what to expect. One day she'd be nearly suicidal and the next she'd be frantically energetic and so touchy I had to walk on eggshells."

"You practically raised yourself. No wonder you're so competent."

"And then when I was twelve I found out the disease was hereditary. I spent my teenage years fearing I'd wind up like her."

"But you didn't."

Meridith traced the threads on the quilted placemat, her thoughts returning to Jake. "I escaped the disease. But I feel so broken inside, Rita. And I think I've fallen in love with Jake, but he makes me feel . . ." She wished she could describe it. "The way he makes me feel terrifies me."

"Why?"

"It feels, on some level, the same as when I was a child."

"Like things are happening that you can't control?"

"*Yes.*"

"Honey," Rita said gently. "That's just love. And life. There's very little we control. That's why having God as our foundation is so important. He's unshakable."

"But with Stephen it was different."

"Why?"

Meridith sighed. "I don't even miss him, exactly. I miss the security and steadiness of our relationship." She forced herself to vocalize the thought that had circled her head for a month. "Maybe I didn't love him."

"Maybe he was just comfortable. Less scary than real love, huh?"

Meridith buried her face in her palm. "I'm an idiot."

Rita touched her wrist. "You're human. At least you ended the relationship before any real harm was done. That was a blessing from God, you know?"

"But how am I going to find real love if I'm afraid of how it makes me feel? I don't want to spend my life alone." Rita made having a family and a healthy marriage look so easy. "How do *you* do it?"

Rita tucked her shiny hair behind her ears. "One day at a time. It's not always been easy, and I know what you mean when you say love is scary." She sipped her coffee. "Lee is actually my second husband. I married young, and my first husband cheated on me and left within a year."

"I didn't know."

"When Lee came along, I was pretty cautious. But then I found the Lord and learned to make Him my foundation. Just knowing He'll never leave me, never betray me, is enough, you know? If everything around me fails, I have that."

Meridith had heard many similar comments since she'd come to the island. Things she'd never heard in her St. Louis church. She didn't have what Rita had. God wasn't the foundation of her life; He was more like a historical figure she admired.

"I mean," Rita went on. "I trust Lee, love him to death . . . but I know he's fallible, just as I am. Christ is the only one who loves me perfectly, and that's enough for me to hold on to, enough to hold me steady."

Meridith wanted that too. She was only beginning to see how much God loved her. She wanted that love to be her foundation so that everything else held steady.

"He loves us so much. Look at how He's blessed you with those kids. Your dad left them to *you*, Meridith. He knew leaving you was wrong, and I know he felt ashamed. Eva didn't say much about it, but enough to make me aware that T. J. regretted the void he'd left you with. Thank God we have a heavenly Father who can fill all our voids."

I want that, God. I want what Rita has—a real relationship with You. I want You to fill all my voids. She remembered what the pastor said every Sunday about repentance. *I'm sorry for all the wrong I've done, for the way it's stood between You and me.*

"What's wrong?" Rita's nose wrinkled, the freckles gathering. "I've only confused you, haven't I?"

Meridith smiled for the first time that morning. "Actually, things are very right. You've helped me see some things—the difference between religion and faith, I think."

Rita smiled. "Oh, wow. Really? All that blathering made sense?"

"It did to me. Thank you."

"My pleasure, honey."

"Now if I can just get a handle on this Jake thing."

"Well, I don't how to tell you this, but sometimes the thing you're most afraid of is the thing you need most."

Meridith pedaled toward Brant Point. The afternoon heat had burnt off the morning chill hours ago, and her legs ached from pedaling. But she wasn't ready to go home. She still had so much thinking to do before she faced Jake.

When she reached the lighthouse, she dismounted and set the kickstand. The lighthouse stood like a solid sentinel guarding the harbor. It had withstood the tests of time and storms. As if some of that fortitude might rub off, she lowered herself at the structure's base among the boulders, bracing her back against the weathered white shingles.

A few cumulus clouds had gathered, and one slid in front of the sun, darkening the landscape.

All the things she'd experienced since coming to the island had culminated in a kind of spiritual understanding that clarified things. Trusting wasn't easy for her, and trusting God would be a daily challenge, but she saw now it was what she'd been missing. A crucial piece of the puzzle had slid into place.

But what did she do with these feelings for Jake? *Sometimes the thing you're most afraid of is the thing you need most.* Rita's words had haunted her all morning.

How could she fear the very thing she needed? And how could she surrender to something so terrifying?

One day at a time. Her friend's words had a way of surfacing at the most annoying times.

Would the fear ever leave? Maybe if she came to trust Jake and found him reliable. Maybe if she saw that the unsettled feeling he triggered could lead to something good. The kiss had been good; she couldn't deny that. Very good.

The clouds shifted, and Meridith squinted against the glare on the water. *God, I don't know what to do. Show me the way and give me the courage to do what I should.*

The wind blew across the sound, fanning her face with a cool breath. Could she face her fear and let her love for Jake bloom? What about their future? She had no doubt he'd be a great father for the children, but she was selling the house. Was he willing to leave Nantucket?

One day at a time. Maybe it wasn't such bad advice. Despite what she'd learned in childhood, change could be good, right? If she could just let loose and let it happen. The thought sent a tremor of fear through her.

She'd learned early to hold on tightly, to control her surroundings, her feelings. But control didn't buy safety. She couldn't even control her feelings, much less anything else. Control was a false foundation that crumbled and left her vulnerable.

She didn't need to control. She needed to let go and trust God, and it was hard. But He was her new foundation. She pictured it beneath her, solid and unwavering. It would be okay.

Meridith checked her watch and saw it was nearing time for the children's return. She stood, dusting the sand from her jeans, then hopped back on her bike and pedaled toward the house.

Forty

Meridith stayed busy all week waxing the wood floors and finishing the scrapbooks in her spare time. The Goldmans had returned their signed papers with a down payment, and the sale was a done deal. The closing was in thirty days.

She should've been relieved. Not only was the house sold, but it was going to a nice couple who appreciated its history. Instead, though, she felt only trepidation about telling the children. About leaving Jake. She found herself praying a lot, feeling lost, and praying anyway. She'd have to tell them soon. Next week, before the end of school, so they could say good-bye to their friends and have almost a month to adjust to the idea.

She'd expected Jake to pressure her, but he'd surprised her. He was nothing more than friendly, and she wasn't sure what to make of it. Sometimes she caught him staring with longing in his eyes, but as soon as she caught his eye, he looked away. If not for those moments, she might've thought she had imagined the kiss and his declaration of love.

On Wednesday as she was making dinner, she saw movement on the beach. She set the casserole on the stovetop to cool and walked to the window. Jake was out there. She could only see him from the shoulder up because of the grassy slope. He bent over, disappeared, then stood.

The wind tousled his hair, and he shook it from his face. He was talking to someone, she could see his lips moving, but she saw no one else. Strange.

"I'm done," Ben said, entering the kitchen. "What are you looking at?"

"Nothing," she said, but Ben was already beside her.

"He still working with Piper?"

"Working with her?"

Ben shrugged. "Trying to get her to walk on the beach, you know. Can I watch TV now?"

"Dinner's ready. Can you call Max and Noelle?" Meridith slid on the oven mitts and grabbed the casserole.

"Max! Noelle!"

Meridith gave Ben a look. "I meant go get them."

"Oh." Ben shrugged and lopped off toward the dining room.

Ten minutes later they were at the table, the kids scarfing down dinner and complaining about school.

"There's only a week and half more," Meridith said.

"A week and half too much," Max said.

"I hate school." Ben blew on a bite of the casserole before shoving it in his mouth.

"Hard part's over," Jake said. "Man up."

"I'm only seven!"

Meridith smothered a grin.

"And I'm not a man," Noelle said.

"Duly noted," Jake said.

Outside the window, Piper barked.

"Probably has a squirrel treed again," Max said. "You'd think they'd figure out that Piper won't leave the yard and build their nests next door."

"Not for long," Ben said. "Jake's helping her."

"Good luck with that." Max scooped another helping of corn.

"Just needs a little coaxing is all," Jake said.

Max shrugged. "I think you're wasting your time. Dad tried that already, and she wouldn't budge."

"She's too afraid," Ben said.

Meridith's eyes darted to Jake's face, just a quick look.

But Jake was looking back, and the quick look stretched into long seconds. "I'm a patient man." His brown eyes warmed under her gaze.

The double meaning kick-started Meridith's heart. She couldn't drag her eyes away until she felt warmth climbing her cheeks.

Meridith finished Ben's scrapbook on Saturday morning, but she waited until the guests were out to dinner before she tucked the albums in separate boxes and called the children to Noelle's room. She was pleased with the results and thought the children would be too.

Noelle clicked offline and rolled back from the desk. "What's up?"

Max and Ben entered the room and flopped on Noelle's unmade bed.

"What's that?" Ben asked.

Meridith settled beside them and set the boxes on the floor. "I put something together for each of you . . ." Now that the moment had arrived, she second-guessed herself. What if the albums only made them sad? What if the memories deepened their pain, reminded them of all they were missing?

"What is it?" Max's feet dangled from the bed, the strings of his tennis shoes flopping as he swung his feet.

"Well . . . I think I'll just show you, okay?" She handed the first box to Noelle, the second to Max. "This one's yours," she said to Ben.

They lifted the lids, and Noelle was the first to see the album. The cover featured a photo of her standing between her mom and dad. They were gazing at her like she hung the moon while she smiled shyly at the camera.

Noelle ran her fingers across the photo. "A photo album."

Max pulled his from the box and began flipping slowly through it. "Cool."

"We each have our own?" Ben asked quietly.

"Yes." Meridith watched them, her heart in her throat, as they flipped the pages reverently. "I found the photos tucked away and thought you might like to have them in an album."

Noelle paused over a photo. "Remember going fishing at Hummock Pond?" she asked Max. "Mom took this right before you fell in."

"Here's one when we got Piper," Ben said. "She fitted in my arms."

Max flipped through his quietly, stopping at each page to study the photos. He tugged the bill of his dad's ball cap.

Noelle wiped her eyes, but the curtain of her hair screened her face.

"Now if I ever start forgetting what they looked like," Ben said, "I can just open my special album."

"That's a wonderful idea." Meridith put her arm around his bony shoulders. She still wasn't the most outwardly affectionate person, but it was getting easier.

They continued flipping through their albums, showing each other their photos and reminiscing aloud about vacations and holidays.

Meridith listened, enjoying the privilege of sharing their special moments.

When Max reached the end, he closed his album and set it behind him on the bed. "Thanks, Meridith."

Ben hugged his album against his chest. "Yeah, thanks. I love it."

Piper barked outside, and Max went to the window.

Ben popped off the bed and started toward the door. "I'm putting mine in my room."

A moment later Noelle flung herself into Meridith's arms. Meridith embraced her, ran her hand down the silky length of her hair.

Something bubbled up inside she'd never felt before, a mixture of relief and pride and love. She had a sense, finally, that things would be okay, even with Noelle. That when the storms hit, they'd work through them.

When Noelle pulled away, she ducked her head, but not before Meridith saw her wet cheeks. Meridith gently wiped away the trail of tears.

"Hey, look at Piper!" Max called, oblivious to the tender moment. Noelle approached the window, wiping the rest of her tears, sniffling.

Meridith followed, stood behind the children, peeking between them. Jake was on his haunches on the beach. A few feet away, Piper stood, one paw poised in the air. Jake patted his knees, said something.

Piper set the paw in the sand, took a step. Jake clapped his hands, then held them out, coaxing.

Piper, crouched, took one more tentative step.

"She's doing it," Noelle said.

Max unlocked the window, and the wood frame squawked as he raised the sash.

Jake's words carried faintly on the wind. "Come on! That's it, girl, a little farther."

Piper took another step, then another. Jake gathered her in his arms. "Good girl!"

Max pressed his face close to the screen. "You did it!" he shouted. Jake and Piper looked toward him, and Jake gave a thumbs-up.

"I'm going down," Max said.

"Me too."

Five seconds later she heard them clomping down the back stairs. Meridith edged closer to the window and watched Jake ruffling Piper's fur, watched the dog's back half wagging.

Then Jake was looking toward the window, toward her, a satisfied grin stretching his mouth, and she couldn't stop the one that spread across her own face.

Forty-one

"Can we take Piper for a walk on the beach?" Max was out of breath from his jog back to the house. "Jake said we had to ask."

"Put her on a leash, and stay out of the water."

The screen door slapped behind him.

"Don't go past the point!"

"Okay," Max called over his shoulder.

The kids had been out there for an hour and had Piper darting around, kicking up sand in their game of tag. *What do you know, Jake did it.*

Meridith dried her hands, started the dishwasher, then turned to look out the window where Ben, near the waterline, was already strapping a leash onto Piper. And they were off.

She'd known, had known since she'd met Jake's eyes from the window upstairs, that God was going to work this out. She didn't know how, only that He was. She felt it down to her bones. Still, she was afraid.

She watched Piper dragging Ben down the beach and wished for that kind of bravery. If only she could shed her fears so easily. Maybe she needed a few sessions with Jake.

She took a deep breath and slipped through the door into the mild evening. It was that time between daylight and nightfall when the sunset cast a golden glow over the world. She took the porch steps and worked her way down the flagstones.

When she reached the beach steps, she saw Jake seated in the sand, elbows planted on raised knees. He stared into the darkening ocean, apparently lost in thought.

Meridith took the steps and shuffled across the sand, well marked now with footprints and paw prints. The kids were two yards down, still walking. She turned her attention back to the broad shoulders, the hair waving like a black flag under the ocean breeze.

Biting her lip, she moved forward. "This seat taken?"

Jake turned, straightened, then his face relaxed. Almost a smile. "Saved it for you."

She lowered herself in the sand, not too close, and gathered her knees inside the circle of her arms. The kids had stopped a few houses down and were throwing driftwood into the water. Piper pulled on the leash, barking.

"She wants in the water now," Meridith said. "Apparently land is no longer enough."

Jake said nothing, but she felt his eyes on her as surely as she could feel the breeze caress her skin.

Piper turned in a circle, chasing her tail, then barked up at Max, who threw the wood.

Meridith turned a smile on Jake and got stuck there in the center of his eyes. She remembered the first time she'd seen him and thought him arrogant. Now when she looked in his eyes she saw confidence. Very appealing.

He was studying her face. "Something's different," he said finally.

"Me?"

"You."

She shrugged and looked away. "I got some things squared away. Spiritual things." She wondered how she'd changed outwardly. She only knew how she felt. More at peace, more loved. The rest, she just had to trust God for.

Jake didn't respond. He was looking out at the water again, and she realized this wasn't going the way she'd expected. He wasn't pressuring her, even asking her . . . maybe he didn't want her anymore. Maybe time had given him perspective. Maybe he was regretting what he'd said.

The thought shook her confidence. She was fearful that he loved her, then fearful that he didn't. *Make up your mind, Meridith. Which do you want?*

No question there.

But she didn't know what to say. Maybe she should start at the beginning. She took a deep breath, letting the fresh air expand her lungs, and started.

"You know my dad left when I was young. But I never told you that my mother had bipolar disease. You know what that is?"

"Yeah."

"Things were pretty crazy around my house. I never knew what to expect. Her moods swung erratically from severe depression to mania. I never knew which mom I'd get when I walked in the door after school, or even if she'd be there. Bills didn't get paid, collectors called. She was either not there mentally or so there it was frightening."

"I'm sorry."

"I learned to cope. However, some of the coping skills turned out to be the unhealthy variety." She smiled at him, then looked away quickly before she lost her nerve. "I learned to live by structure so I know what to expect. I control everything around me to maintain some level of stability. I put up walls to keep people from hurting me. Walls I've never taken down, not for anyone."

"If you're trying to scare me away, it's not working." His words started an ache behind her eyes. Was that what she was trying to do? Even now? Scare him away? Self-sabotage?

He curled a finger under her chin and turned her toward him.

His eyes said so much. That all those things, all her faults didn't matter. That he loved her enough to walk beside her as she worked through them. That he saw beyond her flaws to the woman she was deep inside. That he wasn't going to let go so easily.

"I don't know how this is going to turn out," she whispered.

"Life is uncertain."

"I might make things difficult. There's a part of me that, no matter how much I want your love, I want to run from it at the same time."

"Say that again."

She swallowed around the knot in her throat. "I want to run from it."

"Other part."

She rewound her words. "How much I want your love?"

His lips relaxed, curled slightly upward. "That's the part."

The ache behind her eyes turned into a sharp sting, and he blurred in front of her. "I do want your love, but I'm afraid—"

"Stop saying that."

A tear rolled down Meridith's face, and she brushed it away.

"If you guard your emotions, you'll miss out on the best things of life—joy, excitement . . . love. Fear is just an opportunity to be courageous."

"But what if I'm not courageous?" She bit her quivering lip.

"God will give you courage."

Would He?

Jake's gaze dropped to her lips, an invitation if she ever saw one. Her previous thoughts faded in the wake of his offer. She leaned forward, and he lowered his head, brushing his lips across hers. He tasted of sea and sunshine.

Jake cupped her jaw and deepened the kiss. She leaned into him, wove her fingers into his hair, loving the feel of it between her fingers, surrendering herself to his kiss.

Jake kept reliving the moment, unable to sleep with the delicious taste of love and triumph in his mouth. He wanted to fold Meridith into his arms and never let go.

God will give you courage. His words to Meridith ricocheted back, piercing him. He was the one who needed courage. He had to tell her who he was. Would it change her feelings? Would her trust dissolve when she found out? He prayed it wouldn't. He'd felt so guilty when she'd told him about the bipolar, and she'd looked so vulnerable on the beach. He'd wanted to gather her into his arms and keep her safe, not break her heart.

But he didn't want to think about that now. He only wanted to remember how Meridith had felt in his arms. Jake pushed the other thought deep into the shadows of his mind. He'd tell her tomorrow. Surely he could have this one night to savor their newfound love.

Forty-two

Finally, Meridith said good-bye to the Middleton family, and they exited the house, pulling their luggage toward the waiting cab. Her other guests had checked out that morning, and as the afternoon wore on, she'd begun to wonder if the Middletons had decided to stay another night.

She wanted to give the sale documents one final read before she took a copy to the attorney, but decided to put soup on for dinner first. After stowing the Middletons' check in the drawer, she went to the kitchen. Out back Max and Ben were trying to teach Piper to roll over and didn't seem to be having any success.

Meridith pulled the vegetable soup from the fridge, set it on a burner, and turned up the heat. After collecting the legal document, she took it to the check-in desk and read it over. Everything looked to be in order.

"Something's boiling over!" Noelle called from the kitchen.

Rats, the soup. "Will you turn it down?" Meridith called while hurrying to the kitchen to prevent a mess.

Noelle had pulled the pot from the burner.

"Thanks." The spill averted, Meridith took the salad from the fridge.

"Noelle, can you set the table, please?"

"Sure."

So nice to have a spirit of cooperation around the house.

"Glass or paper?" Noelle stood in front of the open cupboard.

Meridith surveyed the sink she'd emptied and cleaned less than an hour before. The buffet breakfast had dirtied most of their glassware, and the dishwasher cycle wasn't finished. "Let's go paper."

"Yay, it's my turn for dishes."

Meridith set the soup back on the burner, and as she stirred, she heard the front door open. She smiled. Jake was home. Since last night on the beach, she couldn't seem to get enough of him, and judging by his glimpses over breakfast, the feeling was mutual.

She hadn't told the children about them yet, and he seemed to be on the same page. Meridith didn't know if she was trying to protect them or wanting to keep their relationship private awhile.

They'd have to tell them soon. It was too hard hiding it, restraining herself. Her thoughts flashed back to earlier this morning, when he'd pulled her into the darkness of the back staircase and kissed her socks off. Even now her heart fluttered like butterfly wings.

Meridith turned up the heat and gave the soup another stir. The fragrant herbs wafted upward. She heard Jake greeting Noelle, heard a bag rattle as he set it on the island, felt his breath on her neck.

"Hello, beautiful."

"Shhhh."

He kissed her neck, then turned to empty the contents of his bag just in time for Noelle's entry.

Meridith unwrapped the salad. "Did they have everything you need?" she asked Jake.

He caught her eye. "Almost," he said, winking.

Meridith's gaze swung to Noelle, but she was busy pulling silver-ware from the drawer.

She shot Jake a look as the phone pealed. The extension was missing from its base.

"Noelle, would you mind grabbing the other phone?"

The silver clattered as the girl set it down. "Turn down the heat, set the table, answer the phone . . ." she grumbled playfully.

As soon as Noelle left the room, Jake pulled Meridith close. "You just wanted to be alone with me."

She thought of denying it, but then she looked into his eyes. Oh, who was she kidding?

He brushed his lips across hers. Heaven.

She heard Noelle's muted answer from the other room. "Summer Place, may I help you?"

Jake deepened the kiss and Meridith slid her arms around his waist.

"Hi, Rita," Noelle continued. "Yeah, she's here. Just a minute."

Meridith forced herself to push Jake away. "Naughty boy," she whispered.

She dragged her eyes from his and retrieved the salad dressing, trying to gather her wits before Noelle entered.

"It's Rita," Noelle said.

Meridith took the phone. "Hey, Rita." She watched Jake return to his hardware goodies.

"Hey, Meridith. Sorry to call at dinnertime, but this is important."

"What is it?"

Jake looked up at her tone.

"I ran into Dee Whittier in town awhile ago."

"Who?"

"She owns a sporting shop and is on the chamber of commerce with me. She's also Max and Ben's soccer coach."

"Okay . . ."

"Well, she called and told me she saw the kids' uncle in town this afternoon."

"What?" Meridith caught Jake's eye, then flickered a look toward Noelle.

"She recognized him because he goes to the boys' games sometimes and, well, according to her he's a total stud, and she's single, so . . . you haven't heard from him yet?"

"No."

"I thought you'd want to know."

"Yes, I—thanks, Rita. Forewarned is forearmed, right?"

A scream pierced the line. "Brandon, leave your sister alone!" Rita yelled. "Listen, I gotta run."

"Thanks for calling," Meridith said absently.

"What's wrong?" Jake asked.

He would be coming soon. Surely it wouldn't take long for him to discover his sister had passed away. She felt a moment's pity at the thought, then remembered he'd gone over three months without checking in.

"You okay?" Jake asked again.

Noelle entered the room and grabbed a stack of napkins from the island drawer.

"Noelle, your uncle hasn't called or e-mailed, has he?"

Noelle's hand froze, a stack of napkins clutched in her fist. Her lips parted. Her eyes darted to Jake, then back to Meridith. "Why?"

"Rita said someone named Dee saw him in town today."

Noelle closed the drawer slowly. "Oh. Uh . . . no."

Meridith turned to the soup. Thick broth bubbles popped and

spewed. She turned down the heat again and stirred. "Well, I guess he's back. You'll be seeing him soon." She tried to inject enthusiasm in her voice, tried to be happy for the children. A piece of familiarity, a renewed bond, a living reminder of their mother. It would be good for them.

And yet.

What if he wanted them once he found out what had happened to Eva and T. J.? What if he fought her for them and won? Her stomach bottomed out. She loved the children now. They were her siblings. Her family.

She remembered coming to the island with every intention of handing them over like unwanted baggage. What she'd once wanted most was now a potential reality. Only now she didn't want it at all.

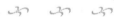

Dinner was a silent affair. Jake did all he could to keep the conversation casual, but it wasn't easy when he knew what was coming. The kids, obviously apprehensive, alternated between staring at their plates and shooting him panicked glances.

Watching Meridith was even harder. She wore a brave smile, trying to convince the kids she was happy they'd see their uncle soon. Her fake smile fooled no one, least of all him.

He recognized fear when he saw it. It settled in the furrow of her brows, crouched in the shadows of her eyes. She felt threatened by the uncle—by *him*. He had to tell her after dinner. Couldn't stand to see her suffer any more.

Maybe she'd be relieved. He wasn't set to take the kids from her anymore. He wanted all of them together, and he'd move to Timbuktu if he had to, to be with them.

Jake lifted a spoonful of soup and slid it into his mouth, swallowing, not tasting. He just had to tell her the truth, then everything would be okay. And maybe if he repeated it to himself enough he'd believe it.

The phone rang, and Meridith froze. Her eyes swung to Jake's, and then she gave him a trembling smile. "I'll get that." She set her napkin on the table and went to the kitchen, breaking her own rule of voice mail during mealtime.

With Meridith's back turned, the kids shot him looks of panic. *Do something!*

He held out his hands, palms down. *Relax, I've got it covered.*

"Summer Place." Meridith's voice filtered in. There was a pause while she listened, then, "No, I'm sorry we're booked for the Fourth of July."

He heard her offering another date, then ending the phone call. She smiled when she entered the room.

"A customer," she said, her relief palpable.

Dinner dragged on as the kids pushed their food around their plates. Jake wanted to spoon-feed them and rush them off so he could talk to Meridith.

When she finally took her empty plate to the kitchen, the kids followed, trashing the paper plates and bowls and dropping their silver in the sink. He gestured them toward the living room, then approached Meridith in the kitchen.

"Can we talk?" he asked. "The porch?"

She opened the dishwasher. "Be right out. Just let me wash the silverware first."

It was on the tip of his tongue to say it was Noelle's turn, but then she'd be in the kitchen, and they'd have no privacy.

"All right." He had no idea how Meridith would react. Jake stepped onto the porch, wishing evening had fallen, wishing for the cover of darkness. He crossed the porch, unable to settle his anxious mind, and by the time he turned to pace back, Meridith was slipping through the door, walking into his arms.

Forty-three

Meridith stepped into Jake's embrace and drew a deep breath, letting the familiar smell of him calm her. It was going to be okay. It was. Surely Uncle Jay wouldn't want custody, not with his vagrant lifestyle. But despite her attempts at self-comfort, her fears surfaced.

"What if he wants them?" she said. "What if he fights for them and wins?" She buried her face in the softness of his T-shirt, tightened her arms around his waist.

"Meridith—"

"Shhhh. I just want to stay like this a few minutes." In the security of his embrace, the strength of his arms wrapped protectively around her. She inhaled deeply, closing her eyes.

At the moment she didn't care if the children walked out and found them together. She was in love with him and didn't care who knew it.

Had she even told him? She pulled in another breath and whispered the words. "I love you, Jake."

"What?" His voice rumbled through his chest into her ears.

She pulled back and looked into his bewildered eyes. "I've been fighting it a long time, and I just wanted you to know."

Something flickered in his eyes. "Oh, Meridith—"

A scream pierced the air, shattering their privacy.

It was clearly Noelle, though she'd never heard that sound from the girl.

"What in the world." Meridith darted toward the door. *Please, not another broken bone.*

She raced through the kitchen, through the dining room, into the living room, Jake on her heels.

Noelle stood by the check-in desk, her face set, her cheeks red. Fire spit from her eyes.

"What? What's wrong?" Meridith surveyed Max and Ben, standing by the fireplace, staring at her, apparently unharmed.

"You're selling Summer Place!"

Noelle clutched a fistful of papers. The sale documents. She'd left them out. Meridith felt the foundation shift under her.

"Don't try and deny it. I'm not an imbecile, I can read!"

Okay, okay. Deep breaths. Meridith held out her hand. "I was going to tell you this week, Noelle. I was going to tell you all."

"Liar!" Her frantic eyes swung to Ben and Max. "She's selling it to the Goldmans, it's all right here!"

"Yes, that's true, but calm down. We can talk about this. I've done a lot of thinking, and there's no way we can afford to stay here. We can't afford the mortgage, Noelle. But you'll love St. Louis, I promise."

"St. Louis! I'm not moving! *We're* not moving, are we?" Noelle went to stand with her brothers. Three against one.

Max and Ben eyed her, confusion ebbing out as the tide of anger rose.

"We can't afford to stay here, honey."

"Don't *call* me that. You were just going to sell our home and take us away and not even give Uncle Jay a chance!"

"I know you're upset, but I was going to tell you this week, Noelle. Boys, I—we *can't* stay. I wish we could. But you'll like St. Louis once we get settled there—"

"What about Uncle Jay?" Max asked, crossing his arms.

"Yeah, what about Uncle Jay?" Ben's chin quivered.

She'd forgotten Jake was there until he touched her shoulder. "Meridith—"

"You said you'd give him a chance!" Noelle screamed. Tears leaked from her eyes. "You've been planning this all along and lying to us! You're a liar!"

She hated that word. Meridith tamped down her own anger. "I didn't lie, Noelle. I just hadn't told you yet."

"You were never planning to give Uncle Jay a chance! You were planning to sell our home and take us away from day one."

"No, I wasn't—"

"Uncle Jay would never take us away, he'd never sell Summer Place, and he'd never *lie* to us like you have!"

"Well, your Uncle Jay wasn't here to make those decisions, and if he'd be such a wonderful guardian, why isn't he here now?"

"He *is* here!" Noelle's eyes went past Meridith's shoulders. "He's been here all along, right beside us, and we want him to be our guardian, not you!"

The words sank in slowly. Noelle's eyes, darting toward Jake. His hand tightening on her shoulder. The boys staring wide-eyed at him.

He's been here all along, right beside us.

"Meridith, I—"

Meridith jerked away from him. *Think.* She needed to think.

Scenes from the past three months raced through her mind.

Jake arriving on her doorstep.

The low bid.

Jake carrying Ben to his truck.

Jake teaching her to dance.

"Meridith."

Jake asking to stay here.

Her chiding him for being alone with Noelle. Hysteria bubbled in her throat. His *niece*.

Jake saving her from Sean.

The day of the parade.

The kiss in the dark. His declaration of love. She choked back a laugh. Her *own* declaration of love.

"Meridith—" He set his hand on her shoulder.

"Don't talk to me." She pushed his hand off, backed away.

It made sense now, all of it. The way the kids had bonded to him so quickly. They'd been keeping a secret from her. Jake, the children. Everyone in the house knew but her. She felt like such a fool!

But . . . the tender moments between her and Jake, his words . . . Was it just a show, some horrible pretense to get access to the kids, to get custody of the kids? She'd let herself trust him, let herself love him—*told him she loved him*—and it was all . . .

"Get out."

He held out his hands, palms down. "Meridith, just let me—"

Meridith put her hands over her ears. "I don't want to hear it!" Her thoughts spun in so many directions, making her dizzy.

Max and Ben were crying. She couldn't process the chaos, didn't want to.

"Get out, Jake. I mean it."

"All right." His hands dropped. "All right." He moved toward the door.

"No!" Ben ran to Jake, wrapped his arms around his leg.

"You're the meanest person ever!" Noelle screamed.

"Let go, Benny." Jake pried his hands off. He set the boy aside. "I'll be back." His gaze flickered to Max, then to Noelle, and back to Meridith.

No, he wouldn't. She was never letting him in her house, in her heart again.

Meridith walked around Jake, opened the front door.

"Don't go, Uncle Jay!" Noelle said.

Jake motioned her to settle down. He paused beside Meridith.

She wouldn't look at him. Couldn't. Could barely contain everything that was building inside. His shoes blurred. She would not cry.

"I'll call you," he whispered.

"Don't bother."

He stood there a second that lasted a lifetime. She held her breath. She would not take one last whiff of his cologne. She wouldn't.

And then he was gone.

She shut the door and turned. Red blotches covered Max's cheeks. Ben was crying. He darted toward the door and pulled at the handle.

Meridith leaned against it. "No, Ben."

Noelle's fists clenched at her sides, her nose flaring.

A sense of déjà vu flashed through her head at the chaos. How had it ended up this way when she'd tried so hard for peace and stability?

She'd let down her guard, that's how. She'd opened her heart, started to trust, began to love. But now she remembered why feeling was such a bad thing.

Love hurt. She'd forgotten how much.

Jake's truck rumbled out of the drive, down the road. Meridith let go of the door.

"I hate you!" Noelle screamed. "I *hate* you!"

But the barrier was in place again, and Meridith hardly felt the jab of anger as she turned and took the stairs.

The road passed in a blur. Jake gripped the steering wheel until his fingers ached.

Meridith. All he could see was her face, her eyes, wild with anger. No, not anger. Noelle had been angry. Meridith had been enraged. Unlike Noelle, her feelings had been tempered with maturity and self-control, but it was all right there in her eyes.

And he deserved every ounce of it. He'd deceived her. Worse than that, he'd instructed the kids to participate in his deception. He was supposed to be the adult here, the role model. He remembered the hero poster Max had made of him and gave a harsh laugh. Some hero he was.

There were so many things he should've done differently, so many things he *would* do differently, if only he had the chance to do them over.

He pounded his steering wheel with his fist. The look in Meridith's eyes haunted him. Beneath the fury he'd seen something that scared him. A deadness. A numbness that said what he feared most: that Meridith had shut down for good, that it was over between them.

Over before it had hardly begun. *I love you, Jake.* A fist closed around his heart. Her words teased him, tortured him. It seemed he'd waited so long to hear them, and now she must wish she'd never said them. Wished he had never shown up on her doorstep.

How could he have hurt the woman he'd come to love so much? And the kids had not helped matters. Noelle pitching her fit, Max and Ben . . . they could've given her the benefit of the doubt. She'd done nothing but look out for them, take care of them.

But that wasn't fair. They were just kids, and Summer Place was their home. The blame belonged squarely in his lap. He swallowed hard, but the lump seemed to have taken up permanent residence.

He wanted to tell her how sorry he was. How wrong he was. How he'd give anything for a second chance. But she needed time. She was too upset for explanations, and no matter how badly he wanted to plead for forgiveness, she wasn't ready to hear it.

Tomorrow, he told himself as he turned toward his old apartment. Tomorrow she'd be ready to listen.

Forty-four

"Oh, honey . . . you look awful." Rita stepped onto her stoop and pulled Meridith into her arms.

Meridith's eyes filled with tears for the hundredth time in three days. There was a perpetual ache behind her eyes, a permanent lump in her throat, a hollow spot deep inside.

She drew a shuddery breath.

"It's going to be okay." Rita rubbed her back.

Meridith nodded, sniffling, but she didn't see how.

"Come inside and have a seat at the table. I'll pour you a nice big mug of coffee, and we'll sort this out."

Meridith took a seat at the table and folded her arms across the quilted placemat. She was so tired, she wanted to lay her head down and fall asleep. At night her thoughts spun, swirling, pulling her into their vortex. Even when she dozed, her mind still worked in half-sleep mode, and then her alarm went off and she dragged herself through another day.

Rita set a steaming mug in front of her, and Meridith took a sip. "You should hang a shingle outside. *The doctor is IN.*"

Rita's wicker chair creaked as she settled into it. "What's happened since we talked last?"

"Nothing. More of the same. The kids aren't speaking to me. Noelle and Max won't even look at me. Even Ben . . ." The little boy's sad green eyes haunted her, and she blinked against the burn in her eyes. "They hate me."

"They do not. They're just angry and confused."

"It's been three days. What am I supposed to do? I can't afford Summer Place. The business doesn't make enough to support itself, and I can't run it and have another job too. I can't afford even the smallest house on the island. There's hardly any equity and very little in mine back in St. Louis, and I've eaten through most of my savings getting Summer Place back into shape. There's the life insurance benefits, but that money won't be available for months and anyway, that's no long-term solution."

"Sometimes being a parent means making the hard decisions. The kids will adjust to the move. They're angry now, but once you move to St. Louis they'll settle in."

"But what about their uncle?" She still couldn't bring herself to say Jake's name.

Rita sipped her coffee and set the mug down. She cocked her head. "You tell me."

Though her tone was gentle, Meridith knew what she was getting at. "He lied to me, Rita. He got the job under a false identity, and he used that identity to gain access to my home. To my *heart*. I feel like such a fool! How could I have been so stupid?"

"No one thinks you're a fool, honey."

"He came to *live* there, for heaven's sake, right under my nose!"

"Why do you think he did that?"

"I know what you're doing. You're trying to make me feel sorry for him. Well, I won't. Maybe he was trying to look out for the children, or maybe he was trying to steal them from me, but that doesn't excuse his behavior."

"No, you're right, it doesn't. What does he have to say for himself?"

Meridith drew a calming breath, then shrugged. "I don't know. I have no idea what he says or thinks, and everything he's said to me is probably a lie anyway."

"He hasn't called?"

"I don't answer." After picking up the phone twice to find him on the other end, Meridith ordered caller ID. She'd lost count of how many times he'd called.

"How are you going to sort this out when you don't know the truth?"

"The truth is pretty apparent, Rita." She ran her hand over her face. "I'm so tired. I can't sleep, and I keep listening for the children. I'm afraid they'll sneak out while I'm asleep and go to their uncle."

"Have they threatened to run away?"

"Not exactly. But when they do talk, it's only to tell me they want to live with Uncle J, which apparently is *J* for Jake, not J-a-y like I thought." Meridith wiped the corner of her eye. "Maybe I should let them go. But I love them. Isn't that a trip? I came here wanting their uncle to take them, then I went and fell in love with them."

"And him."

Meridith shot a glare at Rita.

"Well, you did, honey. Denial won't change it."

But it wasn't real. Maybe *her* feelings were, but his weren't. He only wanted the children. All this time that she'd thought their uncle was irresponsible and incompetent, he was working a plan to get the kids.

"He used me." Saying the words cut her to the core. "Do you know how that feels? I believed he cared for me; fell for it hook, line, and sinker. How lame can I be?"

Rita set her hand on Meridith's arm. "Maybe he really does love you."

The memories surfaced, unbidden. The feel of his palm cupping her cheek, the sweet taste of his mouth, the sound of her name on his lips.

But just as quickly, caution shut down the thoughts. Love was unsafe. It was unpredictable and cruel. She'd known it when she'd come here, but somehow the magic of the island lured her, made her forget. Jake made her forget.

"If only I'd realized who he was. If I'd known, it would've changed everything."

"Maybe you should hear him out," Rita said.

She shook her head. "No. I'm done with that. Done with Jake, done with love." *Except for the children*, she added silently. They would be her focus. They would have a loving, stable home if it killed her.

ॐ   ॐ   ॐ

Jake darted right. Wyatt followed. Jake plowed through him and put up the shot, scoring his tenth point of the game. The ball swished through the net and into his hands. He gulped in air, threw the ball to his friend.

"Dude," Wyatt said. "This isn't the Final Four."

"Take the ball out."

"Slow down." Wyatt dribbled the ball, panting. "You're killing me."

"Sore loser. Come on." Jake approached, smacked the ball from Wyatt, and drove it in for another basket.

"Congratulations."

Jake shot the ball at Wyatt's chest.

Wyatt caught it. "Why don't you just wear yourself out. Or better yet, when you're ready to face what's really going on, come get me." Wyatt shot the ball back at Jake and walked away.

Jake dragged the back of his hand across his forehead, then dribbled the ball, harder than necessary. He wanted to scream. He wanted to punch somebody.

But not his best friend. "Wait."

Wyatt stopped on the porch, crossed his arms, turned.

Jake dribbled the ball toward the garage, threw it in the ball bin. It clanked against the sides, thudded against the other balls, and settled.

Wyatt was right. He was working out his frustration, but where was that getting him? Nowhere. "I'm losing her, man." The words hurt his body as they left. "It's killing me."

Wyatt walked down the steps, sank onto the bottom one. He rubbed his jaw. "You talked to her?"

"She won't take my calls." He'd even tried calling when the kids were home, hoping they'd answer. "I really blew it, man. How could I have been so stupid?"

"Go over and talk to her face-to-face."

"I tried. Three times. Never home." It wasn't like he couldn't see her if he really wanted. She had to be there at night when the kids were sleeping, had to be there in the morning before they left for school. But it didn't take a genius to know she'd only shut the door in his face. And it didn't help matters to know he deserved it.

"She doesn't want to see me, and can you blame her? She probably thinks everything was a lie, including my feelings for her. And how can I convince her I love her when she believes I'm a liar? She'll think I'm only after the kids."

"You have to talk to her somehow. Leave a message or something."

"This isn't the kind of thing you leave on voice mail."

Wyatt shrugged and pierced him with a look. "It is if that's the only way she'll listen."

Forty-five

Meridith stayed out until the children were due home from school. After leaving Rita's, she took the real estate papers to the attorney's office, picked up Max's allergy prescription, and stopped for groceries.

When the kids returned, she greeted them at the door and got only a mumble from Ben and Max. Then they disappeared to their rooms until it was time to leave for the end-of-year spring concert.

After the show, Meridith praised their choirs on the ride home, telling them how proud she was of them and how darling they looked in their dress clothes, but it was a one-sided conversation that petered out before they hit the main road.

They needed to talk this out, but she was too exhausted tonight to take on one more thing. She glanced at the children in the rearview mirror. And they weren't exactly receptive yet. Maybe after they had a good night's sleep.

When they returned home, the kids took off for the stairs without so much as a good night. She'd given up on tucking them in after knocking futilely on their doors two nights in a row.

Meridith tossed her bag on the check-in desk and kicked off her heels. Nothing was going right. Her life had fallen apart, and she was helpless to fix it.

Summer Place was booking up nicely for the season, though. The Goldmans would have their hands full, but that was what they wanted. She glanced at the unfinished fireplace and reminded herself to let them know it was not usable and, judging from the outrageous quote she'd gotten, wouldn't be anytime soon.

She checked the voice mail, knowing there would be more requests for bookings, and jotted down phone numbers and dates so she could return the calls. The last message stopped her.

"Meri, this is Jake, please don't hang up. I know you don't want to talk to me. That's fine, just listen, 'kay?"

His voice, all deep and . . . Jake-like, stopped her. She pressed the phone closer to her ear.

"I know I only have a minute before this thing cuts me off. Remember when I came to Summer Place that first time? I'd heard about Eva and heard they'd granted custody of the kids to you. I came home to fight you for them, I admit that."

Meridith pressed a fist to her stomach.

"I know I should have told you who I was right then, but when you thought I was there for the work, I started thinking how perfect this was, how I could get to see the kids and maybe—okay, I was trying to find reasons why you weren't the best guardian, but I didn't know you then. Was just trying to do what was best for the kids and—I was wrong. Meridith? I'm sorry you were caught in the crossfire. I'm sorry I hurt you . . ."

There was a long pause. Then a click. The recording followed. "If you'd like to save the message . . ."

Meridith returned the phone to the cradle, staring at the extension as if Jake would materialize from it. Part of her wished he would. Part of her wanted to pick up the phone and replay his message—the treacherous, self-sabotaging part that let her feelings and whims whip her around like a leaf in the wind.

He'd basically confirmed what she already suspected—that he'd come here to take the children from her. And if he'd gone to all that trouble to get them, wanted them that badly, could she trust anything he said? Anything he'd already said?

When the phone rang on Thursday afternoon, Meridith finished folding the fluffy guest towel, set it on the dryer, and went to check the caller ID. It was humbling how a ringing phone could put a tremor in her hands, a waver in her step. Even when Jake wasn't here, he had power over her. Made her feel things. The sooner she got off this island the better.

She reached for the phone. Probably just a reservation request, maybe even Rita or—

The name on the screen stopped her speculation. The phone pealed again, and she set it down, jerking her hand away. It rang two more times. She pictured Jake on the other end, sitting on his bed or pacing his living room. Yes, he'd be pacing. He'd shove one hand in his pocket and his long legs would eat up the distance between the walls while the phone rang in his ear.

The ringing stopped, and the silence was deafening. She stared at the phone. Was he leaving a message? How long should she wait before she checked? Meridith turned and paced the area behind the desk, her flats clicking on the wood floor.

Ridiculous how her breath caught, how her heart fought the confines of her rib cage. He probably wouldn't even leave a message. She drummed her fingers against her legs. How long had it been? Twenty seconds?

And why was she so eager to hear from him? What was wrong with her? Did she enjoy being made a fool of?

She stared at the silent phone. She just needed closure. Hearing his explanations, even if she couldn't guarantee their reliability, would help her put Jake behind her—and from a safe distance. She'd never survive a personal encounter. Didn't trust herself to resist the warmth of his eyes, the crooked grin, the woodsy smell of him.

This was safe. Safe closure. Just what the doctor ordered.

It had been at least a minute, right? She turned on the phone and found a message waiting. She punched in her code and waited.

"Me again, please don't hang up, Meri. Meridith." He sighed into the phone. "I'm sorry I didn't tell you who I was. I was afraid of losing the kids . . . now I'm afraid I've lost you."

There was a pause, and Meridith pressed the phone to her ear, afraid she'd hear the click of him hanging up.

"I miss you, Meri. I love y—"

Meridith jabbed the Delete button, and Jake's voice was gone. She knew her limits.

It was quiet after dinner. The kids had disappeared upstairs once again, and Meridith didn't bother calling Max down to do dishes. After starting the dishwasher, she dried her hands and started up the back stairs.

She couldn't put off the conversation any longer, couldn't stand the silent treatment another day. She couldn't say much more than she'd already said, but maybe now that they'd had time to settle down, they'd see reason. Maybe they'd actually see their own part in this fiasco.

The stairwell was dark, but she felt her way up, using the hand-rail Jake had installed. Her mind flashed back—was it only four days ago?—to the kiss they'd shared in this darkened space. She'd been so happy. How could she have forgotten how quickly things can change?

She reached the top of the steps. Noelle's door was closed, but a thread of light seeped from underneath. The boys' door was open, and the light was off.

Might as well get it over with. She raised her hand to knock.

Noelle's voice carried through the door, and Meridith paused.

"But why?" Noelle whined. A sniffling sounded. "I don't want to!"

Another pause. She must be on the phone—with Jake?

Meridith lowered her hand and leaned closer.

"I hate her!" The sound of a little foot stamping. "All right. Here he is."

"Can we come over?" Max's voice. "We don't want to stay here anymore."

The words were like a punch in the gut.

"That's not fair," Max said.

She wondered what Jake was saying, briefly considered finding the other extension. But it would infuriate the children if they discovered she'd eavesdropped. Anyway, she didn't want to hear Jake's end, didn't want to be hurt anymore.

"No, she doesn't," Max said. ". . . Then why's she making us move?"

Meridith folded her arms across her middle, pressing them against the ache.

"Let me talk to him," Ben whispered loudly.

"But we want you to be our guardian—" Max's voice broke. Now he was crying too. Max sniffled. "Love you too. Okay. Here's Ben."

"Uncle J?"

Meridith held her breath. Ben was the one softest toward her.

"Can we come live with you?"

Meridith's heart cracked in two.

"But I miss you and I don't want to move to St. Louis. Noelle said there's no ocean there or nothing, and Mom and Dad are here. They wouldn't want us to leave them all alone." His voice cracked.

Meridith turned from the door and tiptoed to her room. It was true—you heard nothing good when you eavesdropped. She closed the door quietly behind her.

The children didn't want her. She'd come here because they'd needed her, because she wanted them cared for until their uncle returned.

Well, he'd returned all right. And he was nothing like she'd thought. She was so confused. Maybe she should call Rita. But she was too drained to review it all. Anyway, God knew what she was dealing with, no explanations required.

She fell onto the bed and stared at the white ceiling. "What am I supposed to do?"

She wasn't sure what she expected. A burning bush would've been nice. She'd settle for an audible voice or a vision or anything except the silence that rang through her room.

She thought back to the phone call she'd received in the middle of Delmonico's kitchen, to the shock that her father was gone, that he'd left her custody of his kids. So much had changed, but one thing remained the same: she still wanted what was best for the children. She'd initially thought that was their uncle, then she'd become convinced it was her.

But maybe she was wrong. Maybe Jake was the better guardian for them. The kids thought so. Jake must think so too. He'd gone to great lengths to stay near them. He could keep them here on the island, if not in Summer Place, provide them with stability. That was her goal all along, wasn't it?

She forced the words out. "Are they better off with Jake, God?"

But if that were true, why had she been her father's first choice?

She was glad he'd left them to her. No matter what came of this mess, she was better for having come, for knowing her siblings. Her father had left her the precious gift of his children. Was she now supposed to relinquish them, after she'd grown so attached to them?

But maybe the children weren't the gift after all. Maybe the changes they'd caused in her were the real gift. Her breath stopped on the threshold of her lungs.

That's it, isn't it? The children aren't mine to keep. They were only mine for a season. They belong to their Uncle Jake, and he belongs to them.

The influx of air stretched her lungs, pressed against the hollow spot. Meridith set her fist on her stomach. A knot swelled in her throat, aching and burning. She didn't realize how much she'd come to love the children until just now, when she thought of giving them up, of leaving them, and she wondered how she could bear to lose them when they'd only just become a family.

Forty-six

Jake trudged up the apartment stairs and fumbled in the darkness for his key. When he opened the door, the stale smell of warm air greeted him. He flipped on the air-conditioning and pulled off his work boots.

Wyatt was right, Comfort Heating and Plumbing was busy, and Jake was never more glad for it. He'd worked from sunup until bedtime right through the weekend. It helped keep his mind occupied, kept him from dwelling on where Meridith was, what she was doing, what she was thinking, if she'd listened to his messages. It was enough to drive a man insane.

The message light flashed on his phone, and despite all reason, his hopes bobbed upward like a sunken buoy. He pushed the button and waited for the machine's recording to give way to the caller's voice.

"Hi, this is Meridith." The formal tone of her voice tempered his hope.

"After reflecting on the situation, I believe it's in the children's best interest to grant you guardianship. I've contacted the attorney who handled my father's will, and a hearing at the probate court on Broad Street has been scheduled for this Wednesday at three o'clock to transfer the guardianship and sign the documents."

What?

"Unfortunately, the contracts for Summer Place have been signed, but the proceeds, what little there is, will go to the children. The closing is set for the end of June, so I imagine you'll want to stay here until then. My flight to St. Louis is scheduled for Wednesday after the hearing, so I'll bring the children with me and you can—you can take them from there." She cleared her throat, and the tremor he'd thought he heard in her voice disappeared. "I guess that's all. If you have any questions, they can be directed to the attorney . . ." She left his name and number, then hung up.

Jake played the message again, catching the details this time. She was leaving the kids to him? Leaving them here? He swiped the phone off the table, and it hit the wall with a thump.

This wasn't what he wanted. Yes, he wanted the kids, but not at Meridith's expense; they needed her. *He* needed her. Hadn't she listened to his messages? Didn't she know he loved her? If only he could make her believe it.

How had his resolve to get the kids ended in such disaster? With him losing Meridith, with her losing the kids and going back to her lonely life clear across the country.

Or would it be lonely? Now that the kids were out of the picture, was she planning to reunite with Stephen? That thought set him on a disturbing path that winded and curved its way to an ugly dead end.

Would Meridith go back to that after what they'd shared? It seemed inconceivable.

He had to do something. Something to make Meridith see how sorry he was. To see that he loved her, that they belonged together, all of them.

The phone rang, and Jake retrieved it from behind the TV, surprised it still worked. Maybe it was Meridith. She wouldn't get voice mail this time.

"Hello."

"Uncle J, it's Noelle, guess what?"

He stuffed down the disappointment. "I know, I heard."

"We get to live with you! I'm so happy! I mean, I know we'll still lose Summer Place, but at least we'll be together, and we'll get to stay on the island, that's the important thing."

He thought of Meridith telling the children, how happy they must've been at the news, how hurt Meridith must've felt at their reaction. Didn't the kids have a single heart among them? Didn't they see how much Meridith had done for them, how much she'd sacrificed for them—*was* sacrificing even now to give them what they thought they wanted?

"Uncle J, isn't it great?" Noelle was saying. "We can be together now!"

He tempered his frustration. "I need to talk to you kids. Not over the phone, in person, and someplace we can be alone."

"Why? What's wrong?"

The kids were out of school now, and Meridith kept such a close eye on them. "Where can we meet before Wednesday? What are your plans tomorrow?"

"We're going to Rita's to swim in the afternoon."

"Is Meridith going?"

"She has an appointment with the attorney. That's why we're going to Rita's."

Maybe it would work. "All right. Don't say anything to the boys. I'll try to be there."

"All right . . ." He could hear the shrug in her voice.

Jake retrieved the phone from the floor and set it back on the table, feeling more hopeful than he'd felt in days.

Forty-seven

Meridith knew Wednesday would arrive, but she'd no more than blinked and she was walking into the courtroom with the children in tow. Her eyes scanned the rows of empty seats, the tables up front. Jake wasn't there yet. Instead of calming her, his absence produced more adrenaline.

Over the past weeks she'd become accustomed to his presence, and the recent days had been like withdrawal. Maybe she didn't recognize him for who he was while he'd been with her, but she recognized the changes his presence had brought about. Changes in her.

She went forward and took a seat behind one of the tables, and the children seated themselves behind her. She could hardly look them in the eye. Could hardly bear their excitement.

They'd been quiet. Their anger seemed to have drained away in the wake of her announcement two days prior. That was something. At least, that's what she tried to tell herself as she smoothed her blouse and checked the buttons on her jacket.

She laced her fidgety hands on the wood table, then checked her watch. She was a couple minutes early. Eager to get this over with, and yet . . .

She heard Max behind her, swinging his feet under the bench, his shoestrings tapping against his shoes. An ache swelled inside so great it felt as if it would consume her. She would miss them so much.

"Where's Jake?" Ben whispered.

"Shhhh," Noelle said.

Their voices echoed through the big empty room.

What was she going to do without them? Without Max's dimpled grin, Benny's hugs? She'd even miss Noelle's sassy comebacks. She'd never see them after today. They would go on living separate lives. How could she bear it?

Meridith tightened her clasped fingers. She had to stop thinking about it. Come six o'clock she'd be on a plane bound for home and she could cry her eyes out if she wanted. But for now, she wouldn't think ahead to what awaited her in St. Louis. Or rather, what didn't await her.

With the children out of the picture, Stephen would no doubt come knocking on her door. But as quickly as the thought formed, she dismissed the notion. How could she settle for the backyard when she'd experienced the world?

And yet, how could she embrace the world when it was so big, so scary, so dangerous? *One day at a time, Meridith.* All she needed was a secure foundation, and she had that. Everything else was a bonus.

A door creaked behind her, and she heard the children rustle in their seats. She wouldn't turn. Couldn't look.

God, help me.

Her heart lodged in her throat, a huge throbbing mass. She heard Jake's familiar footsteps echo through the room, getting closer. Would he stop at her table?

The footsteps drew closer, closer, and Meridith thought she'd stop breathing. But then his steps faded and a chair nearby squawked as he settled into it. She tried to tell herself she wasn't disappointed, but that didn't explain the profound emptiness that welled up inside her.

Another door opened, this one at the front of the courtroom. The judge appeared, a bailiff. The black robe swooped over the judge's rotund form. He took a seat, then called the court to order, his jowls shaking.

This was it. It was really happening. It was the right thing for the kids. They were staying here with their uncle where they could visit their parents' graves and keep their friends and have the stability she was unable to provide.

In her peripheral vision, she saw Jake shift in his chair, and she could swear she smelled the familiar woodsy scent of him. She stopped midbreath and waited a few seconds, hoping the air would clear.

Was he looking her way? But why would he? He was getting what he wanted. Meridith had only been a means to an end. She had to pull the plug on these silly feelings. They were unreciprocated. Would she ever get that through her head?

The bailiff was saying something, and Meridith blinked away the thoughts. She had to pay attention, or she was going to make a bigger fool of herself than she already had.

When she was called to the stand, she stood and approached on shaky legs. The bailiff swore her in, then she took a seat on the hard bench. She curled her fingers around the bench's ledge and hung on for dear life.

"Ms. Meridith Ward," the judge began in his gravelly voice. "You are currently the legal guardian of Noelle, Maxwell, and Benjamin Ward?" He eyed her over bifocals.

"Yes, Your Honor."

"And you wish to decline guardianship?"

No! her mind refuted. Where was her courage? She cleared her throat. "Yes, Your Honor."

"As stated in the will of Terrance James Ward, if you decline guardianship of your siblings, the children's uncle, Mr. Jacob Walker, is to be offered guardianship. Is that your intention here today?"

Her eyes flickered toward Jake. He was breathtakingly handsome in a dark suit and tie. His eyes caught hers, deep and shadowed, a look of gravity in them she hadn't seen before. It took all her resolve to tear her gaze away.

"Yes." The word shook, a tiny tremor from the earthquake inside.

"You're declining guardianship of your own free will, under no duress from Mr. Walker or anyone else?"

"Yes, Your Honor."

"Very well, you may take your seat."

Meridith returned to her place behind the table. *Do not look at the children. Do not look at Jake.* She was going to lose it if she did. She tried to swallow the lump in her throat. She was going to bust soon. Breathe. In. Out.

Almost over. It was almost over.

Jake was called to the stand. He stood and walked past, and she realized belatedly that her seat put her directly in front of the witness stand. How was she going to avoid eye contact now?

Her eyes found a scratch on the table, a pale sliver in the honey-stained wood.

The bailiff moved toward Jake. "In the testimony you're about to give, do you solemnly swear or affirm to tell the truth, the whole truth, and nothing but the truth, so help you God?"

"I do." Jake's rich voice rang out loud and clear.

The bailiff retreated.

The scar on the table seemed to stretch longer. Meridith traced the line. The edges of the groove dug into the pad of her finger.

"Mr. Jacob Walker," the judge began. "You're the uncle of the children present here in the courtroom today . . ." Papers shuffled. ". . . Noelle, Maxwell, and Benjamin Ward?"

"Yes, Your Honor."

"These are the children of your sister, Eva Ward, and your brother-in-law, Terrance James Ward, who left custody to Meridith Ward?"

"Yes, sir."

"As you've heard in Ms. Ward's testimony, she is declining guardianship of these children. As per the stipulations in your sister's will, you are to be offered the legal guardianship of the Ward children. Mr. Walker, do you accept the role of guardian for these children and all the responsibilities that accompany that role?"

"No, Your Honor, I don't."

Meridith's eyes darted to Jake. He was staring straight at her. She'd misheard.

The judge cleared his throat. "Mr. Walker, perhaps you misunderstood the question. Do you wish to be guardian of the children?"

"No, Your Honor, I don't," Jake said clearly.

She didn't understand. What was he doing? The children—

"Mr. Walker—"

"Not unless . . ." Jake lowered his voice. "Not unless Meridith Ward agrees to stay." His gaze beat a path to her heart. "In fact, not unless Ms. Ward agrees to marry me. Only then will I agree to *share* guardianship of the kids."

What? Meridith's mind couldn't assimilate the facts. But the love shining from Jake's eyes said more than his words. Her eyes burned.

"As it turns out," Jake continued slowly, staring right into Meridith's eyes, "I'm wildly, madly, and passionately in love with Ms. Ward, and I want us to be a real family."

"Me too!" Benny said loudly.

"Me three," Max called.

"Ditto."

Noelle. Even Noelle. Had they known? She turned and looked at the children. Noelle's eyes were teary. Benny and Max stared back, hope and worry lining their faces.

She turned back to Jake, got caught in his eyes. He blurred in front of her. Her lip trembled, and she bit it still.

The judge cleared his throat. "I see. This is most unusual. Well, I think a recess might be in order. Would you like to take a moment, Ms. Ward?"

He loved her. Jake loved her and wanted to—

Could she find the courage to love, to walk in uncertainty? To risk being hurt? She knew her foundation was stable. Everything else she had to take one day at a time, right?

"Ms. Ward?"

"Uh . . . yes. A recess, please."

The judge and bailiff exited, and Jake stood. She watched all six feet of him close the gap between them. Somewhere behind her, the children were as quiet as fireflies.

Meridith stood, her legs trembling beneath her.

And then Jake was there, standing in front of her, his solemn brown eyes shining. "I'm so sorry, Meri. I was a jerk. I'm sorry I hurt you, sorry for everything."

He took her chin in his hand. "And I do love you," he whispered. "I want you to be my wife. Not for the kids, but because I want you with me every day for the rest of my life."

It was enough. More than enough. She swallowed hard. "I want that too. So much."

Jake drew her close, his lips brushing across hers, the softest of touches. She ran her fingers along his freshly shaven jaw and savored the feel of him, the smell of him, the taste of him.

Feelings could be good. So good. The ones coursing through her at the moment were off the scale. He could stir her up, no doubt. Yet his love had a way of calming her fears, soothing her worries. It seemed illogical that he could do both.

From the edge of consciousness, whispers intruded.

"Are they fiancéd now?"

"Engaged."

"Well, are they?"

"What d'you think, runt?"

Meridith pulled away, her lips curving into a smile that mirrored Jake's.

"Yeah, little man," Jake said, not taking his eyes from Meridith. "We're engaged."

Before he finished speaking, they were swallowed by the children's arms.

"I'm sorry," Noelle whispered in Meridith's ear. "I'm sorry I was so mean and that I lied to you."

"We're all sorry," Max said. "We acted like spoiled brats."

"It's okay." Everything was okay now. More than okay.

"I love you, Meridith," Max said.

"Me too," Ben said.

"I love you guys too." She wouldn't have to leave them. Would get to see them tomorrow and every day afterward.

Even while happiness flooded her soul, a lone thought dampened her spirits. "Summer Place," she said. "After all this, we're going to lose their home."

"Nuh-uh!" Ben said. "Tell her, Uncle J!"

Meridith looked up at Jake's handsome face. "Yeah, tell me, Uncle J."

He smoothed her hair back, tucked it behind her ear. "Talked to Mr. Goldman yesterday and explained everything. If you want to keep Summer Place, they're willing to forfeit the property."

"But they really wanted it."

"Apparently Mrs. Goldman thinks all this is terribly romantic. And I think between the two of us, we could stay afloat. But it's your call."

The joy that bubbled up from inside overflowed in the form of a smile. "As long as we're together. That's what matters."

Noelle whooped, and a group hug followed.

The rapping of the gavel drew them apart.

"I hate to interrupt a good reunion," the judge said, allowing a small grin. "But I have a schedule to keep. Can I assume we have a happy ending here?"

"Yes, Your Honor." Jake wrapped his arm around her waist. "A very happy ending."

"Well, congratulations are in order then. But there's still the matter of immediate guardianship . . . unless you're planning a spontaneous visit downstairs to the Justice of the Peace."

Meridith looked at Jake and found his eyes on hers, his brows lifted. *What do you think?* his eyes asked.

What did she think? She thought life was full of changes and upheaval. She thought that sometimes love could hurt and feelings could be messy, potentially painful. But she also knew Jake was right. That the wonder and joy of the love that filled her now was worth that risk.

Meridith felt her lips curling upward. She nodded.

Jake's grin turned into a full-fledged smile. He turned to the judge. "Downstairs, you said?"

The children whooped and hollered.

The judge tapped his gavel. "All right, all right. Settle down, and let's get this done. You'll need to apply for a marriage license and you'll need a court waiver for the three-day waiting period. Fortunately, I can help with that."

He cleared his throat. "Now, upon the immediate marriage of Mr. Walker and Ms. Ward, I'll grant *shared* custody of the three Ward children, if that's agreeable to you all." He pointed the gavel at Meridith and Jake. "And remember, you're still under oath."

"Yes, Your Honor," Jake said.

"Yes, I accept." Meridith met Jake's gaze and saw the promises reflected there, felt the love she'd longed for all her life.

The judge shuffled his papers. "Fine, fine. I now pronounce you a family. We stand adjourned." He gave a hard tap with the gavel. "Now, go get married."

Dear Friend,

If you're familiar with Nantucket, you'll know that Driftwood Lane is a fictional street. I take special care to get the details right, so I hope you'll grant me artistic license in this one thing.

I hope you've been entertained and inspired by the special love between Meridith and Jake. Meridith learned through her relationship with Jake that her fear was robbing her of life's greatest joys. Maybe you've faced your own fears, whatever they are, and found that doing so will ultimately set you free, just as it did for Meridith.

Writing this letter is bittersweet because it marks the end of my journey to Nantucket with you. I've learned so much about God's love through these four stories and I hope you have too. Going on these adventures would be no fun without you, so thank you, friend, for coming along for the ride. May God bless you and your family with His lavish love.

— In His Grace,
Denise

Reading Group Guide

1. Meridith's father left her the gift and responsibility of his children. Has God ever given you a responsibility that you felt was more than you could handle? What did you do about it?

2. Meridith knew about her siblings before she was asked to be their guardian, but she didn't know them personally until she came to the island. Do you think it's possible to know about God but not know Him personally? Why or why not?

3. Meridith's unstable childhood left her with the need to control everything around her. How does this kind of control give us a false sense of security?

4. Jake had a way of making Meridith feel unsettled. Has God ever made you feel unsettled? Are you afraid to let Him have control over every aspect of your life?

5. Piper was afraid of leaving her yard because doing so in the past had caused her pain. Have you ever had the whole world at your feet and settled for the yard?

6. Jake brought a lot of changes and growth in Meridith before she even knew who he was. Has there ever been a situation where God worked, unrecognized, in your life? How did you come to recognize His handiwork?

7. When Meridith realized Jake could offer the children more stability than she, she gave them up. How does this show her coming full circle in light of her childhood?

8. Driftwood is symbolic in the story. In what ways does it symbolize Meridith or, for that matter, all of us?

Acknowledgments

I am so grateful to the fiction team at Thomas Nelson: Publisher Allen Arnold, Amanda Bostic, Jocelyn Bailey, Kathy Carabajal, Jennifer Deshler, Natalie Hanemann, Chris Long, Ami McConnell, Heather McCulloch, Becky Monds, Ashley Schneider, Katie Bond, Kristen Vasgaard, and Micah Walker. You all work tirelessly to plan, perfect, produce, and place my books on the shelves where readers can find them. Thank you!

My editor, Natalie Hanemann, made this a better story with her insight and encouragement. LB Norton helped me fine-tune the story. My readers, thank you! Thanks also to my agent, Karen Solem, who handles all the messy contract stuff and provides invaluable wisdom.

A certain amount of research is necessary for the telling of any story, and sometimes there's no other way to find answers but to ask someone. Elizabeth M. Brown, a tax collector from Nantucket, was so kind to provide me with details and documents on property taxes. Attorney and fellow author Cara Putman let me pick her brain about the legalities of guardianship. Chad Hunter provided some necessary details for the characterization of Jake.

This story was conceived at Logan's Roadhouse on my fortieth birthday during a brainstorming session with my writing buddies, Colleen Coble and Diann Hunt. Thanks, girls, for the help and the meal!

Lastly, thank you, friend, for coming along this journey with me. I'd love to hear from you! You can visit my Web site at *www.Denise HunterBooks.com* or e-mail me at *Denise@DeniseHunterBooks.com.* I'm also on Twitter (twitter.com/denisehunter) and Facebook if you care to follow me.

She came to Big Sky

in search of answers.

What she found

was something

far more lasting.

A Cowboy's Touch

The first in a new series by best-selling author Denise Hunter.

AVAILABLE APRIL 2011